THE DORADO DECEPTION

THE JACK REILLY ADVENTURES - BOOK 3

BY MATT JAMES

SEVERED PRESS
HOBART TASMANIA

THE DORADO DECEPTION

WWW.SEVEREDPRESS.COM

ISBN: 978-1-922551-79-5

ALSO BY MATT JAMES

THE JACK REILLY ADVENTURES
The Forgotten Fortune
The Roosevelt Conspiracy
The Dorado Deception

STAND-ALONE TITLES
The Dragon
Dark Island
Sub-Zero
Cradle of Death

THE BONES BONEBRAKE ADVENTURES with David Wood
Skin and Bones
Venom
Lost City

THE DANE MADDOCK ADVENTURES with David Wood
Berserk

THE DEAD MOON POST-APOCALYPTIC THRILLERS
Nightmares are Born
Home Sweet Hell
Song of Sorrow
In Memoriam

THE DEAD MOON SHORT STORIES
Nightmare at the Museum
Scared to Death

THE HANK BOYD ADVENTURES
Blood and Sand
Mayan Darkness
Babel Found
Elixir of Life

OTHER STORIES
The Cursed Pharaoh
Broken Glass
Plague

Evolve

PRAISE FOR MATT JAMES

"Matt James is my go-to guy for heart-stopping adventure and bone-chilling suspense!"

—Greig Beck, international bestselling author of BENEATH THE DARK ICE

"If you enjoy globetrotting adventures jampacked with over-the-top action, then you'll love Matt James' work!"

—Nick Thacker, *USA Today* bestselling author of THE ENIGMA STRAIN

"If you're looking for a fast-moving tale with action to spare, give Matt James a try!"

—David Wood, *USA Today* bestselling author of THE DANE MADDOCK ADVENTURES

"Matt James is electrifying!"

—Rick Chesler, international bestselling author of ATLANTIS GOLD

"Matt's novels need a pause button. They do not stop!"

—Lee Murray, award-winning author of INTO THE MIST

"A talented voice in the action-thriller genre!"

—Richard Bard, *Wall Street Journal* bestselling author of BRAINRUSH

"If you like thrills, chills, and nonstop action, then Matt James may just be your next favorite author!"

—John Sneeden, bestselling author of THE SIGNAL

"Matt James has cemented his place among the finest talents!"

—SUSPENSE MAGAZINE

"Matt James has proven that true adventure is found in the fine line between myth and reality. James walks that tightrope with a master's touch."

—J.M. LeDuc, bestselling author of SIN

"Matt James is definitely an author to watch!"

—David McAfee, bestselling author of 33 A.D.

For Nick Thacker

USA Today Bestselling Author of
The Harvey Bennett Thrillers

Thanks for being such a swell guy

THE DORADO DECEPTION

THE JACK REILLY ADVENTURES - BOOK 3

1

Bogotá, Colombia
Present Day

The two men ran for their lives. Their car had flipped behind them a few streets ago. The pair was bleeding from various injuries sustained during the wreck. Hugo was in far better shape than his partner. Matias had a cut above his left eye and several up and down his arms.

"This way," Matias hissed, waving Hugo across the alley.

The smaller man scurried across the backstreet on all fours like a squirrel, banging his head into a metal garbage can. The noise drew the aggravated growl of his friend. He was shushed and pulled along, staying low.

"Why are they after you?" Hugo asked, breathing hard.

"Because of what I know."

Hugo was about to ask what he knew but didn't have a chance. A black van screeched to a halt, coming to a stop at the end of the alley. Hugo and Matias turned and watched as another van blocked off the other end. Hugo tried the nearest door, but it was locked. The restaurant had closed hours ago.

Matias shoved Hugo into the shadow of a dumpster. He procured two large garbage bags from a nearby garbage can and tossed them atop his friend.

"What are you doing?" Hugo asked.

"Saving your life."

"Lorenzo, no. I—"

Matias held up a hand. "They haven't seen you. They are here for me." He pulled his phone out of his pocket and feverously tapped out a message to someone, nodded, and threw the device at the brick building. Hugo felt a piece of the phone slap his skin as it exploded.

He stood, much to the chagrin of Hugo. "I will see you again, my friend."

Before Hugo could beg him to stay, Matias stepped out, tossing his gun away. He raised his hands and turned in a circle, showing that he was, in fact, unarmed.

"Where is your partner?" a man demanded. The speaker was out of sight from Hugo's position.

"Kiss my ass!" Matias shouted, stepping forward. He was blocking Hugo with his own body.

"He wants to see you," a man said.

"Well, you can tell *him* to kiss my ass too."

Hugo grinned. Matias had a way with people sometimes.

The newcomer chuckled. "Tell him yourself."

The cough of a suppressed rifle made Hugo jolt. Matias instantly fell to the cracked asphalt. Hugo spotted a small projectile sticking out of Matias' chest within the beams of the van's headlights. He had been shot, but not by a bullet. Matias had been stunned with a tranquilizer dart. Whoever wanted him, they wanted him alive.

Hugo did as his friend had told him and he stayed put. Once both vans were long gone, Hugo stood on shaky legs. He stepped out and made sure the coast was clear before pulling out his own phone.

Who can I call?

Hugo had more connections than most, but none that could give him answers or the help he required. He brought his foot down on something. Retracting his boot, Hugo saw that it was Matias' ruined phone. He bent and picked it up, watching its screen flash on and off. Even with the screen shattered, he could read the TAC Agent's last message. Hugo knew all about Matias' current employers.

"El Dorado exists."

El Dorado International Airport, Bogotá, Colombia
One Month Later

Flying internationally in the middle of the night made it nearly impossible for Jack Reilly to gauge the time. Now, the sun was almost at its peak. It was noonish by his estimation. He attempted to lift his left arm and check his watch but failed. His overstuffed duffle bags were heavy and awkward. His next destination was just ahead, and with it, the second part of his mission—meet with Hugo Nunez, smuggler extraordinaire. The initial part of Jack's first assignment was now complete. The Tactical Archaeological Command Special Agent had arrived in Bogotá and had done so in one piece.

"Winner, winner," he said, skipping the part about a chicken dinner.

Jack was still getting used to traveling with falsified credentials. His license and passport were phonies, but the people back at TAC headquarters had done their jobs and provided him with the most legitimate-looking fakes he had ever seen. They contained every watermark and hologram that they were supposed to have. Jack felt more like a member of the CIA than that of a preservation organization.

Hugo had been friends with Lorenzo Matias for years and was currently one of the TAC agent's contacts. He had witnessed Matias' abduction up close and was the last person known to have seen him. The two had grown up together, just outside Bogotá, before Matias moved to the United States, went to school, and eventually got into law enforcement. From what Jack knew, Matias had been recruited into TAC much like he had, though Jack doubted Director Raegor had ever shown up at Matias' house unannounced and helped himself to a cup of dark roast coffee.

Locating Matias was Jack's primary mission. He had been kidnapped a few weeks after infiltrating Santiago Aguilar's organization. There were rumblings that the drug lord was looking for something that would change the world. It wasn't a part of his mission, but if Jack were presented with a sliver of additional time, he would burn Aguilar's operation to the ground. It was a classic "two birds, one stone" scenario.

Save the world. Ruin the bad guy's day.

Jack still couldn't believe it. His first assignment with TAC was going to revolve around a missing person's case, which would also include pirates and drug cartels. Jack's briefing via conference call with the legally dead, Solomon Raegor, and his close confidant Edith "Eddy" Marker, had been short and sweet. They had given him all the information they could. Then, they sent him on his merry way, trusting that Jack's military training and survival skills would be enough to keep him alive. He couldn't believe how quickly he had been thrown into the fire. Then again, Raegor warned him that it wouldn't be easy.

"You're serious?" Jack asked the bald African American during the video conference. "I'm going after El Dorado?"

"Yes, Jack, we are very serious."

His hands combed through his hair. "I'm getting my 'feet wet' with El Dorado?"

Raegor smiled. "Yes, you are."

The last correspondence between TAC and the missing agent had been an encrypted message that read, *"El Dorado exists."* Jack had been as stunned as anyone. In fact, he still was. The legendary City of Gold was supposedly just that—a legend. There had never been any concrete proof of its existence. Rumors and outlandish stories swirled around the lost jungle empire, but none of them meshed with one another. The inconsistencies told Jack that there was probably nothing out there. He had read up on it during the entirety of his flight.

Yet, here I am, he thought. He rubbed his wrist. Jack was still getting used to not wearing his bracelets anymore. But it was a part of being a ghost. Wearing them could make him more identifiable. How many white Americans in their late thirties wear Native American beaded jewelry in Colombia?

The answer? None.

He doubted that he would've been sent to South America if there wasn't anything to find. Matias was the mission, but so was figuring out why he believed El Dorado existed, as he stated in his veiled communique.

It was currently 65 degrees Fahrenheit in Bogotá. Jack's leather jacket and jeans should be enough to keep him comfortable for now. He planned on using his "company card" to buy a few things while in town. TAC agents traveled light. They moved around from place to place and rarely brought anything of value with them. If they needed to get out quickly, they could with very little evidence left behind. TAC didn't publicly exist—Jack needed to remember that.

Even now, his luggage contained hardly anything of use. The baggage gave him the appearance of someone traveling with plans of sticking around for a while. He was warned that this operation could take weeks to solve.

A set of double doors slid open to reveal the designated curbside pickup area. He was blasted by the outside temperature but was too focused on the man in front of him to notice the crisp air. The stranger held a piece of cardboard with Jack's name scribbled on it. It was the most pathetic limo service he had ever seen.

Standing at six-foot-two, Jack towered over the local. He easily outweighed the man by forty or fifty pounds too. Still, despite this guy's more diminutive stature, he was thickly built—like an American Pit Bull.

"Hugo Nunez?" Jack asked, setting his bags down.

The man's eyes lit up, and he quickly folded his sign in half. He slipped it beneath his left armpit and stepped forward, reaching out his hand. Jack dropped his bags and clasped it. Instead of being welcomed with open arms, Hugo released his hand and grabbed Jack's belongings.

Voice low, he muttered, "We are being watched."

Well, that didn't take long.

Jack didn't physically react to the warning. If he had, it would've signaled to those surveilling them that they had been found out. That was usually when shit hit the fan. So, Jack stayed calm and smiled and nodded, looking very pleased. He used his peripheral vision to scope out the other cars around them but couldn't see anything of interest. As Hugo loaded his bags into the trunk of his worn Range Rover, Jack nonchalantly slid on a pair of sunglasses, yawned, and stretched. He turned and cracked his lower back.

That's when he saw them.

Two cars back from them was a black van. Its occupants weren't outside greeting anyone like the rest of the cars at the airport. They were, instead, focused on something else—*someone* else.

Jack attempted to open the front passenger side door but was stopped.

"No, get in back!" Hugo hissed, tightlipped. "I'm supposed to be your driver."

Hugo opened the door for Jack and bowed slightly, putting on a show for those around them. Jack felt ridiculous. He had no idea why he was being treated like a VIP, but he needed to trust his contact and follow his lead.

"Um, thanks," Jack said, sliding into the running vehicle.

"You're welcome, sir," Hugo replied quite loudly.

Hugo hurried around the rear of the car and climbed into the driver's side. He sat and slammed his door, quickly opening the center console. Jack was surprised to see the man produce a loaded Glock 19 pistol, two reserve magazines, and a shoulder holster.

"Here," he said, "take these."

Jack didn't argue. He slid out of his jacket and looped the holster around both of his shoulders. He quickly gave the handgun a look-see and found it to be in good condition. The magazines looked to be in perfect working order, as well. He replaced his jacket and asked the one question that needed answering.

"What the hell is going on?"

"They," Hugo said, pulling the car out, "are the reason you are here."

Jack's face must've emoted what he felt. Confusion.

"The last time Lorenzo Matias was seen—by me, no less—he was unconscious and being loaded into a van exactly like that." Hugo pointed a thumb over his shoulder.

"Oh, shit," Jack said, turning around.

"Yes, my friend. 'Oh shit,' indeed."

Jack grinned. "Your English is good."

Hugo shrugged. "I deal with a lot of Americans..."

Really? Jack let the comment go. He wasn't here for that.

"How's your Spanish?" Hugo asked.

Jack wiggled his hand back and forth. "I know the basics."

"Good enough."

Surprisingly, Hugo didn't take off like a bat out of hell. He adhered to the speed limits of the busy airport roads and patiently waited his turn to exit. Then, he carefully merged on El Dorado Avenue, staying in the slower moving, outside lane. Jack was about to suggest that they get going, but Hugo explained his motives.

"They don't know that I know," he said. "They've been following me for some time now but have had no reason to go any further." Jack spied a smile form on his face. "Besides, I have some less-than-polite friends that they'll have to answer to if they harm me."

While some people moved drugs, and even people, through Colombia's loose borders, Hugo Nunez was in the business of dealing in everything else. His wares included clothing, animals, medical supplies, electronics, and even weapons. But never narcotics or human beings. Jack didn't know why Hugo still owned a conscience, but he did, and Jack respected the man for it.

The reason he had yet to be shut down was that he had buyers in powerful places. A few of them were said to be hiding within the country's government, though Jack doubted anything could be pinned on them. Civil unrest had caused revolutionary types to step up. They weren't quite as brazen as the Congo region's militias in Africa, but they were nearing that point. Not every "state" within the South American country was led by a corrupt governor, but many were, and mainly in the smaller, rural areas where the media was less involved.

Jack nervously watched the van pull up right behind them. But Hugo didn't seem to mind it. His confidence in the situation, while reassuring, also felt incredibly foolish. If Jack were the man in control, he would've floored the pedal and attempted to lose them.

"So," Hugo said, eying Jack in his overhead mirror, "you must be hungry?"

"Hungry?" he asked.

"Yes, hungry. You know, 'food?'"

"Uh, sure, food." Lunch was the last thing Jack wanted right now. But what could he do? He was at the mercy of his driver. "Yeah, I could eat."

Hugo smiled wide. "Very good. I know a place on the edge of town. We can relax and enjoy ourselves."

The van fell back but was still following them.

Maybe they're just escorting us out of the city? Jack hoped that was the case.

Hugo flicked on his turn signal and passed a heavy-duty hydraulic crane truck. It came complete with a thick boom arm and everything. Its bright yellow paint job made it stick out like a sore thumb. It was a beast-of-a-vehicle and must've been a hell of a lot of fun to operate.

A wrecking ball would be too.

The highway rose off the ground, bypassing a few busy-looking intersections. Jack guessed they were maybe thirty feet off the ground now—and rising.

"Where are we headed?" he asked, imagining himself swinging a giant stone sphere into the side of a condemned building.

"*Abuelita's.*"

The answer caught Jack off guard. "We're going to your grandma's house?"

Hugo laughed loudly, snorting twice. "No, my friend, you are mistaken. Abuelita's is a local spot. Fabulous food! I conduct some of my business there."

"How's the coffee?" Jack asked, yawning.

"Terrible, but it will still get you feeling right."

He shrugged. "Good enough for me."

"Alright, we'll be there in..."

Jack zoned out, noticing something terrible to his left.

"Aw, shit."

The Range Rover's roof detonated inward, revealing the crane truck's hook. It landed with a bang directly between Jack's spread legs, embedding itself in the floor. He had just gotten his lower half out of the way in the nick of time. Jack snuck a look to his left and saw the impossible. Someone was sitting behind the controls of the mobile construction crane. The operator pulled back on a lever, and shockingly, the Range Rover lifted off the ground while still in motion.

"Holy crap!" Jack shouted, reaching for his pistol.

Hugo was screaming at the top of his lungs somewhere on the other side of the crane hook. His cries, along with the shrieking metal of the SUV's ceiling, were difficult to distinguish from one another. Their constant bouncing caused Jack to fumble around with his gun and he did the only thing he could—he held on for dear life.

The hook slipped and nearly dropped them back down to the highway, which gave Jack an idea. He waited for the rocking SUV to settle a little and dove into his jacket. He swiftly drew his Glock and aimed it at the crane operator. He squeezed off four successive shots. The close-quarters gunfire assaulted his ears, and unfortunately, none of the 9mm rounds struck home. All they did was shatter the rear driver's side passenger window and ping off the steel frame of the crane operator's cab. The other guy ducked down, his chest pressing up against one of the control levers. The Range Rover, in turn, swung around to Jack's left. They swooped over the still pursuing van, just barely missing its roof by inches.

Jack was tossed around the rear seat like a ragdoll in a clothes dryer. There wasn't a part of him that hadn't struck something rigid and unmoving. The back of his head spiderwebbed the other passenger window, and he thought he felt blood.

No time for that, he thought, readying himself. He was only going to get one more chance.

Jack waited for the crane operator to regain command of the controls. When he did, he swung them around again. This time, Jack was more prepared.

The Range Rover was back in its original spot—off to the right of the crane truck. Jack sat up, gripping his pistol tight in both of his hands. He lifted the gun and pumped two more projectiles into the crane's cab. One of the two bullets struck the operator in the chest. The energy snapped the man's upper body backward. He quickly rebounded off his seat and fell forward, slumping directly atop the instrument panel. Gratefully, the SUV, and Jack and Hugo, were slowly returned to the street, but they were also rotated back around to the rear of the yellow crane truck.

The Range Rover's driver's side tires clipped the pursuing van and rocked it hard enough to cause it to flip onto its side in an explosion of sparks. The collision almost knocked Jack and Hugo free too. If it had, it would've been a miserable experience. They would've ended up in the same boat. Jack cringed as a fast-moving semi smashed into the roof of the immobile van, flattening it like a tin can.

They continued around to the left side of the crane truck and went weightless as they were dropped. Jack heard the engine come to life, and when they hit, they fishtailed. But once the spinning tires found purchase, they sped off and zigged and zagged through traffic.

Over the rush of air and car horns, Jack shouted, "I guess you aren't so untouchable after all, huh?"

Hugo growled and gripped the steering wheel hard. "No thanks to you and your friends." He retorted. "You Americans... You bring your problems with you wherever you go." Jack didn't know about that, but he was going to let Hugo have his little victory. The two men didn't speak again until they were *safely* outside of downtown Bogotá. Jack chuckled softly when Hugo pulled them into the parking lot of a beat-up strip mall. There were only a couple of businesses still in operation from the looks of it. One of them was—

"Abuelita's?" Jack asked, flabbergasted that Hugo would still stop for lunch after what they had just survived. If anything, they should've gone underground for a few days. Regardless of what they did, Jack needed to contact Raegor back at HQ and report what had happened. It couldn't have been a coincidence that he had been targeted only minutes after arriving.

The TAC mole? Jack wasn't sure, but someone was definitely feeding the bad guys information. Raegor was rightfully paranoid. If someone was working against TAC, then Jack needed to confirm it. He might even have to kill the person. His first suspect was Lorenzo Matias. He had disappeared without a trace, and only Hugo knew what had happened. It was one of the first questions Jack was going to ask the smuggler.

What happened that night?

Then, there was Hugo himself. Did he give up Matias? Like Raegor had said, only a few people inside TAC knew where the agent had been and what he'd been investigating. The only other person that knew anything was Hugo.

"What?" The local's reaction brought Jack's attention back to the here and now. Hugo shrugged and opened his door. "All this adventure has made me even hungrier."

With nothing else to do and nothing else to go on, and now without a guide, Jack followed Hugo out of the decimated Range Rover. Luckily, it wasn't a newer one. Still, a vehicle of this make and model was a valuable asset to have in a place such as Colombia. The powerful engine and durable design were perfect for off-road expeditions.

“Sorry about the car,” Jack said, placing a gentle hand on Hugo’s shoulder. He would give the local the benefit of the doubt. Jack and Matias’ lives weren’t the only ones hanging in the balance if things stayed ugly.

Hugo patted Jack’s hand and looked up at him. “It’s okay,” he winked, “I have two more just like it.”

2

Like a specter, a boy of no more than fourteen magically appeared. It wasn't until Jack noticed the dinging bell that he realized the kid had come from inside Abuelita's. Without a second thought, Hugo handed the youth his keys and rambled off something in Spanish. Jack understood enough of the language to get around town but nowhere near enough to hold an intelligible conversation. Hugo, it seemed, spoke the language at lightspeed.

He waved Jack forward. "Come. Now we eat."

"And the kid with your car?"

"Oh, don't mind, Juan." Hugo smiled. "He's going to ditch it someplace where it will draw the interest of some unscrupulous people."

"You're going to get it stolen?" Jack scratched his head and followed Hugo inside. "Won't the police inevitably trace it back to you either way?"

Hugo belched out a laugh. "No, my friend, things do not work like that down here. Besides," his smile morphed into a mischievous grin, "the owner of that particular vehicle *died* six years ago." Hugo gave the word 'died' finger quotes.

So, Jack thought, impressed, *Hugo forged the registration. Smart man.*

Abuelita's was set up much like a diner back home. The quaint dining room held eight tables—all of which were empty. At the back of the space was a counter complete with a pastry case and register. It was a simple place, and it smelled glorious.

Jack sniffed the air. It wafted with the scent of greasy meats and burnt coffee. Some of his rising anxiety subsided as they sat at the centermost table. Without speaking up, a tiny, haggard old woman shuffled out from the kitchen entrance. She wore a plain dress and sported a filthy, well-used apron.

"Abuelita?" Jack asked, thumbing over to the elder.

Hugo nodded and let loose another round of lightning-fast Spanish. Abuelita didn't flinch, nor did she pay any attention to the American. As Hugo had said earlier, he routinely did business here. The matriarch would've been used to strangers walking in and sitting with Hugo.

She's probably on his payroll, Jack deduced. It made sense. The area was struggling, and a place like this should've closed years ago, like everything else around it. Yet, here it was, still in operation even though it was empty save for Jack and the smuggler.

"So," Jack said, sitting back folding his arms, "Matias."

"What about him?"

"Tell me what happened the night he vanished."

Hugo didn't look excited to talk about it, but he nodded.

"Lorenzo called me and asked me to meet him. He said it was urgent, but he didn't want to speak of it over the phone."

"Why not?" Jack asked.

"He said he was being monitored."

Jack's eyes opened wider. "Really? By whom?"

Hugo shrugged. "Who else?"

"Aguilar?"

"Yes, Aguilar. Lorenzo seemed on edge—more than usual. There was more to the story than what he told me. He sounded shook—spooked—like he had seen the boogeyman."

"How was he before?"

Hugo laughed and pounded his chest once with his fist. "Like me! *Fuerte*! Strong! I've known him for many, many years and have never seen him so frightened."

"And you think it was Aguilar who scared him?"

"I do."

They were interrupted for a moment by Abuelita. She brought out their food. Jack was expecting to see something extravagant. Instead, all he saw was two cups of black coffee and two ordinary-looking breakfast burritos.

"*Gracias*," Jack said, thanking her.

As she had done before, she paid Jack no attention and shuffled off back into the kitchen. Even though the food looked *blah*, Jack couldn't argue with the aroma. It also didn't hurt that he was now starving. His sleep schedule was currently a mess, which meant that his eating habits were off-kilter too.

He went for the coffee first, hoping it would do its thing quickly. Sipping it slowly, he recognized that it was incredibly smooth and roasty—very little bitterness at all. It was delicious! Hugo nearly gagged as he took his sip. It was plain to see that he and Jack didn't enjoy the same styles.

Nearly halfway through what he knew would be multiple refills, Jack continued with their conversation. "Tell me about Aguilar."

Hugo dropped his fork. If he was uncomfortable talking about Matias, now, he was downright petrified. Something awful had happened to Hugo. And it was easy to see that Aguilar had been somehow responsible.

"Santiago Aguilar murdered my sister."

And there it is.

Jack sat back while Hugo explained.

Two decades earlier, Valentina Nunez began dating a young man named Santiago, much to the chagrin of her parents and her older brother, Hugo. Aguilar's family was wealthy, and he showed Valentina a life she had always dreamt of experiencing. They traveled abroad and went to lavish parties. They met some very influential people—both honorable and not so honorable. Aguilar's personal life hadn't been as in control as he had publicly displayed. He habitually abused drugs, primarily cocaine. Valentina developed an interest in the former. As the months passed, she became a shell of her once beautiful self. By the time she turned nineteen, she had run off with Aguilar for good and never returned to the Nunez household. Some years later, the news of her death came via phone call. Police said that she died of a drug overdose and had been seen wandering the streets before she had collapsed.

But Hugo knew what had really happened.

"Aguilar and Valentina were together the night she died—I know it! He dumped her body to keep himself from being implemented. He threw her away like she was trash!"

Jack wasn't going to get into an argument about whether or not he thought that Aguilar had been accountable for Valentina's death. He had to have been undeniably partly at fault, though. Ultimately, Hugo's baby sister had been the one to blame. She made her own choices.

And she paid for it with her life.

"I'm sorry for your loss." Jack raised his mug. "To Valentina."

Hugo wiped his nose and clinked Jack's cup. "Thank you, my friend. You remind me of Lorenzo." He smiled. "Valentina would have liked you both, I think."

They both drained their coffees and slammed their mugs down. Abuelita answered the call and came rushing forward with a refill. And once again, she didn't even look at Jack.

"What's with her?" Jack asked, needing to know.

"Abuelita?"

"Yeah, she hasn't given me the time of day since I stepped foot in here."

Hugo understood. "Oh, yes. Well, Abuelita doesn't care for Americans."

"Why's that?"

Hugo cracked a smile. "You're lousy tippers."

Both men laughed. It was refreshing. But Jack still had a mission to complete.

"Look, Hugo, I know it's a touchy subject, but I need to know more about Aguilar."

Hugo nodded and took a deep breath. He shoveled a forkful of his burrito into his mouth and spoke. "Yes, of course. We still have a job to do, right?"

"We do," Jack replied, smiling. Hugo owned an admirable resolve.

"The reason Lorenzo called me was that Aguilar had found something—something so big that it was going to change history."

"El Dorado," Jack said.

"Yes—well, no. Lorenzo warned me that Aguilar had found a map, not the City of Gold itself."

"A map?" Alarms went off in Jack's head. *Warning! Warning! Warning! Pertinent information is forthcoming!* "What kind of map?"

Hugo leaned forward and grinned. "The kind that leads to treasure." He held up a hand, halting any follow-up questions. "Come. Let us continue this discussion in my office."

"Your office?"

Hugo looked confused. "A businessman requires an office, yes?"

Jack stood, but not before draining his refill. The caffeine was already taking effect. Whatever concoction Abuelita had cooked up was like a less bitter blonde roast with the energizing load of a Cuban formula. Jack was buzzing—his brain firing on all cylinders. They passed through the kitchen, heading to the door to a supply closest. Hugo didn't try to open it. Instead, he produced a keyring and unlocked it.

I swear, Jack thought, *if this guy's 'office' is nothing more than a dirty mop room...*

The door swung open. Inside was a dirty mop room, cleaning supplies and all. Jack sighed but was intrigued when Hugo ushered him inside. "Quickly, away from prying eyes."

"But there's no one else here. Who could possibly see—"

He was yanked inside by his shirt. Hugo shut the door behind them, casting the pair in darkness. An audible click announced that the lock had been re-engaged from the other side. *Abuelita...* Oddly, a faint humming noise picked up all around him, and the ground dropped out from beneath them. Jack expected to fall, but the descension immediately righted itself, and both he and Hugo went for a ride.

What the hell?

Jack figured that they traveled three stories before stopping. First off, the floor to the mop room was, in actuality, an elevator. The lift settled three feet off the ground, and Jack and Hugo had to jump down to get off. Then, Hugo walked over to the nearest wall and pressed a large red button. With a hiss of hydraulics and a hum of machinery, the false floor rose into the ceiling. The lifting apparatus was like an oversized scissor lift. The engineering was impressive.

"If you're curious, no, it's not of my doing."

Jack turned and looked at the local. "Who built it?"

"No idea. This place was cleared out years ago. I heard about it and moved in." He grinned. "Then, I bought out the neighboring businesses and expanded my operation."

"I can see that."

The basement beneath Abuelita's was much too big. If he guessed, it extended beneath the other businesses attached to the strip mall. The concrete walls had been knocked down to allow the expansion. Jack could see the different colors of each room from where he stood.

He and Hugo weren't alone either. Six other people were hard at work. Two were organizing sections of weapons, while the other four were offloading what must have been a new delivery. A hole at the rear of the main room gave Jack a look at how things were brought in.

"I have tunnels all over the place," Hugo explained. "We rotate our loading docks to keep anyone interested off our scent and bring in whatever we need."

The munitions were what caught Jack's eye. A large portion of them looked old and worn. A crate of AK-47 assault rifles and even a few Rocket Propelled Grenades. The latter concerned Jack.

"RPGs, really?"

Hugo coughed and found something else to look at. "They're for a...rainy day."

Jack rolled his eyes. "You really are a pirate, aren't you?"

Hugo didn't think that was funny. "No, I am a revolutionary."

Jack crossed his arms and leaned against a crate. "If it walks like a duck and quacks like a duck..."

"I steal from those who don't deserve it, like Aguilar. Then, I help those who do."

"You know, you're right. You aren't a pirate." Jack laughed. "You're Robin Hood!"

Hugo couldn't hold back his smile. "And you can be my Little John. Together, we can—"

"Thanks," Jack interrupted, holding up a hand, "but I have my own crap to deal with."

"Fair enough," Hugo replied, motioning Jack to follow him.

He was led to a small, crudely built cubicle in the far right-hand corner of the storehouse. The walls were as tall as Jack, missing the ceiling by four feet. Still, it offered the two men a relatively private place to continue their conversation. As they spoke, Jack's eyes bounced around the storehouse, studying everything he saw. He took in the room's inventory and what he would need for the next leg of his journey—whatever it was.

"So," Jack said, sitting, "you said something about a map."

Hugo plopped down behind a small desk and procured a bottle of God-knows-what from a shelf behind him. Hugo gave Jack a smaller pour than him, winking as he handed Jack the glass. The liquid was clear and smelled of anise.

"*Aguardiente*?" Jack asked.

Hugo smiled. "Yes, very good, my friend."

Jack took a sip. It burned like hell. The proof had to have been off-the-charts.

Aguardiente, or *schnapps*, was a traditional drink in both Central and South America. Local moonshiners were known for producing incredibly potent variations of the beverage.

This must be one of them.

Jack wrinkled his nose at the fumes—not the fragrance. It smelled lovely but was way too strong for Jack to enjoy without ice. If anything, he needed some ice to water it down. Hugo casually sipped it, watching Jack intently as he did. It was apparent that he wanted to watch Jack squirm a little before they 'talked shop.' Getting it over with, Jack tossed the entire thing back and locked his jaw. His reaction to the schnapps was minimal, garnering a nod of approval from Hugo. But Jack couldn't hold it back forever. He coughed, and his eyes watered.

That also made Hugo happy.

"Not for you?" he asked.

Jack shook his head. “Not for my car either.”

Hugo leaned forward. His eyes were serious. “What do you know about Diego de Ordaz?”

“The Spanish explorer?” Jack shrugged. “Just what the history books say. He was the first outsider to come across the El Dorado legend, right?”

“In the early 16th century, correct. Years earlier, Ordaz was also involved in Cortés’ conquest of the Aztecs in Mexico.” Hugo leaned back and laced his fingers behind his head. “Aguilar’s map is said to have been drawn by Ordaz himself.”

That perked up Jack. He sat straighter. “Really?”

“Yes, but...”

Jack’s shoulders dropped. “*But,* what?”

“We don’t have a copy.”

Oh, right...

“Matias?” Jack asked. “Did he take a picture of it?”

Hugo shrugged. “I don’t know. If he did, he destroyed his phone before he could show me.”

Both men looked and felt defeated. The only evidence they had of El Dorado was a map that a long-dead Conquistador might have drawn. It was an iffy lead. However, it was still a lead. It was better than anything else they had to go on. Jack couldn’t be sure of it, but he needed to trust Aguilar knew what he was doing. The guy believed the map to be genuine, spending what must’ve been millions of dollars on it, and who knew how much more over the last three years to advance his search. If that was the case, then Jack also needed to believe it was real.

“We need that map,” Jack said.

“Yes, but how?”

Jack was quickly developing a plan, but so far, it was batshit crazy. He stood and looked through the plexiglass windows of the cubicle. He formed a mental checklist of what he’d need and was happy to see that much of it was present.

Jack glanced over his shoulder and grinned at Hugo. “We’re going to steal it.”

3

Eastern Colombia

The jungle surrounding the excavation was dense and mostly unnavigable. Danger lurked around every corner, threatening to leap out and make you its next meal. The chief predator in the area was the powerful and stealthy jaguar. But there were also creatures within the rainforest that ran on two legs and wielded assault rifles. It was those hunters that Jorge Gonzalez was running from now.

Aguilar's captives—and that's what Jorge was, a prisoner—rarely ever escaped. If they did, they were never heard from again, one way or another. Jorge had no idea how many had made it to safety—if any at all. He also had no idea where he was or where he was going. He had been moved to the dig site a couple of months ago. Jorge didn't know where he was. Aguilar's men had forced a hood onto his head before manhandling him aboard a boat.

At the moment, whatever light he had was being produced solely by the moon. He had fallen several times, tripping over tree roots and rolling his ankle on a loose stone. He stopped to catch his breath and looked behind him, waiting for movement. Besides the sway of tree limbs and the shaking of shrubbery, there was none. It was as if the entire jungle had gone to bed.

Which means they are close, he thought.

His pursuers, two of the excavation's guards—well-paid mercenaries—were skilled in guerilla warfare and were, no doubt, closing in on him. Aguilar's men knew the area well. It was all the more reason for Jorge to get moving again. But his strength had departed long ago. Aguilar purposely kept his detainees, especially those that openly defied him, in poor condition. Jorge was malnourished and overworked. He was exhausted even before his perilous journey back to civilization began.

By his estimation, Jorge was still miles away from the nearest village. That was, of course, based on whether or not he was traveling in the correct direction. Jorge had trusted his gut and beelined for the trees to the west of the site. Now, he had no idea what direction he was headed. Either way, it would take Jorge a few days to reach the small community he sought in his condition. If he found something to eat and stayed far enough ahead of Aguilar's men, Jorge was confident that he could make it. Still, he prayed like mad.

"God, please let me see my family again," he whispered, limbs shaking.

He shook his head hard and blinked. The thing he needed more than food was rest.

"Not yet," he said, looking up. A droplet of rain struck his face. Then, another.

Typically, being caught in a storm while out in the wilds of Colombia was a bad thing. But Jorge took it as a sign from the Almighty that he was watching over him. The incoming downpour would act as a veil and cover his tracks.

Jorge placed his trembling hand atop a fallen log and carefully vaulted over it. As he cleared the rotten tree trunk, something stung him in the side. He tried to arrest his fall but quickly discovered that there was no ground beneath his feet. Jorge fell a short distance before clumsily crashing to the jungle floor a heartbeat later. Nearly lost in it all was the crash of thunder echoing around him.

Jorge rolled for twenty feet before flopping to the earth face down. In agony, he turned over and sat up and looked down at his torso. Jorge couldn't see a thing. He felt it, though. Viscous, warm liquid enveloped his hand. He put two and two together. The singular thunderclap wasn't natural. It was the concussive report of gunfire.

Jorge Gonzalez had been shot.

Unable to get to his feet, he stayed on his rear and scootched through the thick foliage, and found what he hoped would be a decent hiding spot. Settling in, he poked at the wound and found that it was closer to his side than his stomach. That was the good news. The bad news was that it would still be a death sentence unless he could stem the blood flow.

He silently leaned back on his elbows and listened. The area was silent once more. Nothing around him moved. So, he would follow suit and wait it out as long as he could. He, once more, prayed, asking God to have the hunters bypass his location. Maybe, if he were fortunate, they would give up and return to the dig site.

Jorge attempted to adjust himself but stopped. Lightning lit up the sky above him. Within it, he spotted an anomaly on the ground beside him. The irregularity wasn't naturally formed. The lump in the jungle floor was a body.

In the flash of a second lightning strike, Jorge realized what had happened to the dead man. Like him, he must have attempted an escape from Aguilar's custody. And like Jorge, this man had been shot—but in the head. And he wasn't the only one. Multiple corpses, in every state of decomposition, encompassed Jorge. Some were much fresher than others. A few looked to have been dead for quite some time.

He had stumbled upon a mass grave!

At first, Jorge had thought the inbound storm was a blessing from God. Now, it was clear that it was, in fact, a premonition of his departure from this world. Evil existed in the Colombian rainforest, and it wasn't the Devil.

It was Santiago Aguilar.

A tree branch broke somewhere overhead. Jorge's pursuers were near. Maybe if he stayed still long enough, they would think he was one of the dead. If not, then he would be.

Hugo's Storehouse
Bogotá, Colombia

Hugo leapt to his feet and paced back and forth in his quaint office. "Steal from Aguilar? That's a terrible idea!"

Jack shrugged. "I never said it was a good one."

"No, Jack, you don't understand."

The TAC agent held out his hands. "Enlighten me."

Hugo paused mid-stride and placed his closed fists on his desk. The prospects of facing Aguilar didn't sit well with him, which didn't surprise Jack in the least. Still, if they wanted that map, then they would have to get close to the man—close enough to steal one of the most valuable assets he owned.

"Aguilar's compound is located in a remote area in the southeastern part of the country. It is guarded on all sides by heavily armed mercenaries and treacherous terrain."

Jack shrugged. "Nothing I can't handle."

Hugo looked surprised with Jack's bravado.

"Trust me." Jack smiled. "I have a familiarity with people like Aguilar."

"How so?"

Jack needed to be careful with what he told the smuggler. Giving away too much information could come back to haunt him.

"I worked in the business of counterterrorism for the better part of my adult life." Moving quickly while doing it quietly was his specialty.

Hugo's eyes went wide, and thankfully, he didn't push Jack for more details.

"None of what I've told you is what truly concerns me," Hugo explained. "It's the people that operate his facility." His eyes bore holes into Jack. "They don't do so willingly."

Oh shit, Jack thought. He knew what Hugo meant, but he still needed to ask.

"Slaves?"

"To a degree, yes." He calmed down enough to sit, letting out a long breath as he did. "Most of his captives are people who were stupid enough to cross him. Others are those that simply owe him money. He works them to exhaustion and kills those that cannot carry on. The perimeter is said to be impenetrable. Is this going to be an issue for you?"

"No, because I'm not going alone." Jack leaned forward. "You're coming with me."

"Absolutely not! I've already gotten myself involved more than I should."

"What about avenging Valentina?"

Hugo opened his mouth to speak, but nothing came out. He snapped his mouth shut and, once again, pushed away from his desk. He reached for the door but was stopped.

"We have to take this monster down, Hugo."

"Why?" Hugo stared through the plexiglass. "You have no—how do you say—skin in this game." He turned and faced Jack. "Why put yourself in that kind of danger if you don't have to?"

It was a good question. Why should Jack do such a thing? The answer was pretty simple, though.

"Because it's the right thing to do."

Hugo bit his lip and thought it over. His internal struggle was plain to see. He wanted nothing more than to put Aguilar in the ground for his part in Valentina's death.

"Look," Jack said, standing, "we need that map. If Aguilar gets a hold of what we think is out there, then it's game over. He will have an infinite amount of finances in his back pocket. Plus, do you really want a man like him to be known as the discoverer of something so important to your country's history?"

Hugo stared into Jack's eyes. "No, of course not." He sighed. "If we're going to do this, then we need to be certain of what we are doing. And we're going to need some help."

Jack's eyebrows raised. "Reinforcements—who?"

"You, uh, might not like the answer to that question."

Jack didn't take his eyes off the smuggler. He waited for an explanation.

"I know a pair of brothers that will gladly assist us, but they are not as...honorable...as I am."

"What's that supposed to mean?"

"Unlike me, Miguel and Manuel Arroyo are, indeed, pirates." His brow deepened. "Real scoundrels. But they also don't care for Aguilar."

At least we have a common enemy.

"Okay, well, if that's what we have to work with, then, let's do it!" He slapped Hugo on the shoulder. "Sounds like a load of fun!"

"Yes," Hugo nervously replied, "lots of good times ahead for us..." He turned and opened the door. "Take whatever gear you need. I'll make sure my men treat you right and make all the necessary arrangements."

Hugo shouted a flurry of Spanish to the men. Each one of them called or waved back to him, acknowledging his instructions. At least, Jack thought they were instructions.

I really gotta learn some more Spanish. The only foreign language he was fluent in was Arabic, which was a result of the amount of time he had spent in the region when he had been in the military.

"Can we trust the Arroyos?" Jack asked, following close behind.

"More or less," Hugo replied. "They are businessmen. As long as they get paid, they probably won't try to kill us."

"That's not comforting."

Hugo stopped and faced him. "That's more than most will give you. I know men and women that will happily help you and then turn around and slit your throat as soon as you pay them. Others will flat-out kill you and rob you on the spot."

"And the Arroyo boys won't?"

"They haven't tried to kill me yet."

"Again, not super comforting."

Hugo shrugged and headed off. "Welcome to the Colombian underworld, Jack Reilly. 'Comfortable' doesn't exist here."

Jack sighed and thought back to the big yellow crane truck. "Yeah, I've noticed."

"Are you referring to the incident on the highway?" Hugo chuckled. "That, my friend, was nothing compared to the things that I've seen."

What's he talking about?

Jack knew it didn't matter. Hugo's past experiences meant nothing right now. What concerned him the most was whether or not Hugo could follow through with what he said. At the very least, the Arroyo brothers would supply Jack with a big enough of a distraction to get him in and out of Aguilar's compound with the map—Hugo too. He'd need the man's deep knowledge of the area, as well as a second set of eyes, especially those that understood Spanish better than him.

The first thing Jack inspected was a pair of Night Vision Goggles. Unfortunately, the devices weren't operational. They each had intricate pieces missing, or they were damaged. Having the equipment would've significantly increased their chances of success. It looked as if they would be going about it the old-fashioned way. Luckily, Jack had keen eyesight. He saw better in the dark than most people. This ability had helped him quite a few times while back with Delta and, more recently, as a member of the Yellowstone National Parks Services.

His Glock 19 would be a perfect companion, but he would also need something that packed a heavier punch. Hugo must've sensed as much, and he led Jack over to the crates of assault rifles.

"Feels like home, yes?" Hugo asked, pointing to the half-dozen Colt M4A1 carbines. The select-fire assault rifles owned full-auto capabilities and were still a staple within the United States military. They had also been sold to various governments worldwide through the Foreign Military Sales (FMS) program. Unfortunately, unless it was properly monitored, the FMS program opened opportunities for shadowy funny business too.

Just like this, Jack thought. But he wasn't here to shut Hugo's distribution down. In fact, without it, he would've been screwed.

Jack hefted the imposing rifle and checked it over like it was nothing—because it was. He had used this exact model hundreds of times in the past. It was one of the most durable weapons on the planet and could be outfitted with all sorts of neat gadgets. This particular weapon was fitted with a CQBR. The shortened, 10.3-inch barrel was perfect for clearing rooms and moving around in tight spaces. *Like a tangly jungle.* It offered its operator the penetrating power of a rifle cartridge but was packed inside a firearm closer to the size of a submachine gun.

"M4A1 with a Close Quarters Battle Receiver," Jack announced.

"Yes, it is," Hugo replied. "You like it?"

Jack shouldered the weapon and gazed down its sights. "I do."

"Then, it's yours!"

Jack slung it over his shoulder and continued his unlawful shopping spree. Hugo gave him anything he wanted—without question. Jack didn't try to acquire an RPG, though. He doubted Hugo would give him a rocket launcher—not that he wanted one. They were huge and hard to maneuver, especially where they were going.

He was also handed a KA-BAR fighting knife. Its blade was seven-inches-long and made of carbon steel. Then, Jack was supplied with all the ammunition he could carry. Hugo nodded his approval and then disappeared back into his office. Under the scrutiny of the smuggler's peers, Jack cataloged his gear for a second time and was taken off guard when two of the locals approached him.

The shorter of the two spoke in broken English. "You kill Aguilar?"

Jack shrugged. "If it comes to it, yes."

The two men glanced back and forth at one another. One of them stepped forward and placed a hand on Jack's shoulder. Jack thought about going for his pistol but didn't. There was no malice in either of the locals' eyes.

The man squeezed Jack's shoulder hard. "You *kill* Aguilar."

"Uh..."

Jack understood. It wasn't a question. They weren't asking him if he was here to kill the drug lord. They were making sure that he was going to do it. They wanted the man dead as much as Hugo did. Jack figured that they each had lost someone dear to the man's heinous operation—just as Hugo had. Technically, Jack wasn't here to kill anyone, but he didn't know what else to say.

He nervously laughed and ran his hand through his hair. "I'll see what I can do."

4

Miguel and Manuel Arroyo were two of the toughest, grittiest people Hugo had ever met. They came from a small, crime-riddled town on the Colombia-Venezuela border and had been brought up in the business they currently excelled in. But unlike the more honorable Hugo Nunez, the Arroyo brothers happily distributed drugs. The one thing the Nunez and Arroyo organizations did agree on was that the buying and selling of human beings was off-limits. Not all criminals stooped to that kind of low.

But Aguilar did, Hugo thought. He didn't do it often, but the man had been known to traffic people in the past if the money was right. He was, indeed, a despicable individual.

The phone rang eight times before someone finally picked up. The Arroyos had Hugo's number, just as he had theirs. They knew it was him that was calling now. After their last dispute, he was surprised that they answered at all.

Hugo operated the southern part of Bogotá. The Arroyos ran goods in the northern half. Occasionally, one of their "mules" would cross into the other's territory. One of Hugo's men had done just that two weeks ago. So far, he had yet to hear of any impending consequences.

"Hugo Nunez," Miguel said. "You've got a lot of nerve to be calling me after what you've done."

Hugo swallowed. *Here we go.*

"Ah, Miguel, hello!" Hugo replied, pushing past the veiled threat. He tried to sound as cheerful as possible but was too anxious to do so. Deep down, the Arroyos scared him. "Is your brother there? I have a lucrative business proposition for you both."

Two seconds later, Hugo heard the click of another phone connecting. And per the usual, Manuel didn't announce his presence. The second man hardly ever said a word at all. The two brothers had a pretty straightforward relationship. Miguel was the businessman, and Manuel was the enforcer. Plus, Manuel had broken his jaw in a fight when he had been a young man and had since developed a quirky speech impediment. He was unable to open his mouth all the way, causing him to mispronounce several words. One man even went as far as to joke about him sounding like a drunken Spanish Elvis Presley.

That man was now dead.

Pedro was an idiot, Hugo thought, shaking his head. Prodding Manuel was like poking at a hungry shark. Typically, it was an ill-advised move.

"We're listening." Ever the businessman, Miguel never turned his back on a potential payment, even if it came from his main competition.

"How would you like a shot at shutting down Santiago Aguilar for good?"

The other man chuckled. "In your dreams, Hugo. Aguilar is the very definition of the word 'untouchable.'"

Hugo grinned. He glanced behind him, gazing through one of the plexiglass windows of his office—to Jack. The operative was rifling through some additional gear. "I thought so too...until now."

"Oh yeah?" Miguel asked. "Tell me then, what has changed?"

"There's an American agent here with a crazy plan—a plan that might just work."

"American, huh?" Miguel grumbled. "Why should we trust him?"

"Call it a hunch," Hugo replied, sitting at his desk. Jack had since moved on to inspecting belts and holsters.

Miguel openly laughed. "Your hunches tend to injure people!"

Hugo pulled his phone away from his ear and snarled at it. He offered the two men a shot at taking down *the* big fish, and they had the gall to insult him.

"What if I told you there was something else waiting for us at the end of this rainbow."

"And what would that be?" Miguel asked. His tone was back to normal.

Hugo leaned forward and visualized the Arroyos sitting in front of him. "El Dorado."

Both Miguel and Manuel lost it. They loudly guffawed for what felt like minutes. Hugo let them, too. He calmly took a deep breath. Even though he was on somewhat friendly terms with the two, they could end their truce and become a dangerous enemy overnight—but so could Hugo.

"You have got to be kidding!" Miguel yelled, sighing hard.

"No," Hugo replied, "I am not, and Aguilar has the proof."

That little tidbit shut the man up. Miguel cleared his throat. "Proof, you say?"

Hugo quickly recounted everything that had happened to him and Matias—then the incident on the highway with Jack. He also told them everything he knew about the map. He didn't need to go over his personal stake in the mission. It was known to everyone in the underworld what had happened to his sister.

"Yes, proof. My sources say that Aguilar has a map that Diego de Ordaz himself drew."

Miguel softly laughed again. "Oh, Hugo, you and your schemes. Let's be honest. They haven't always panned out."

"This isn't the same!" Hugo shouted, leaping to his feet. "Why do you think Aguilar has mobilized his people into the jungle and spent so much money? You must've noticed that?"

Miguel was silent. His lack of retort told Hugo that he had, indeed, noticed the change in Aguilar's *business philosophy*.

"If we're to go along with this," Miguel said, "what will you need from us?"

Hugo smiled. He had them. Now, all he had to do was stroke their ego a little and reel them in.

"We go in as a small team—just the four of us. No one knows more about the El Dorado legend than you." That was true. Miguel was a nut on the subject. He had been studying the City of Gold's mythos for years. "And between Manuel and my new friend, Jack, well, let's just say that I'd hate to get in their way."

Hugo didn't know a lot about the American, but he did know that he could handle himself. He was obviously ex-military—most likely Special Forces based on his "counterterrorism" remark. The fact that Matias' people had hired him also told Hugo that he was smart, and that he respected history. TAC didn't just bring in anyone. From what Matias had told Hugo, the Tactical Archaeological Command only employed a few dozen agents at a time. The organization moved fast, and they did so with small numbers.

"What kind of deal are you offering?" Miguel asked.

"That's easy. It's just the four of us on this one. We split it down the middle." He grinned. Here was his hook, line, and sinker. "Technically, you two would be getting fifty percent."

"Yes, congratulations, you can do simple math," Miguel jabbed. But his tone wasn't as direct as it usually was. Hugo could tell, based on the distance in the man's voice, that he was thinking long and hard about the offer.

"Come on, Miguel—Manuel, this is what people like us have been dreaming about our entire lives. El Dorado! Plus, Lord knows what kind of increases we could all see with a monster like Santiago Aguilar out of the picture."

Hugo had just appealed to the men's hearts as well as their pocketbooks.

Voices mumbled off the line. The Arroyos were conversing with themselves.

"Okay, Hugo, you have a deal. We get this map of yours, take down Aguilar, and split the findings evenly, correct?"

Hugo looked up and found Jack staring at him from outside his office. He gave the American an enthusiastic thumbs up.

"Yes, you get half of *everything* we find."

Hugo quieted and waited. The offer was too good to pass up. If they succeeded, the Arroyos were about to become ridiculously wealthy.

After a long silence, Miguel gave him their answer. "Okay, Hugo, we'll bite. What do you need from us?"

The Aguilar Compound
Puerto Esperanza, Colombia

On the edge of the small town of Puerto Esperanza sat an unimpressive razor-wire-enclosed property. The complex strategically sat up against the intersection of three waterways; Río Guayabero, Río Ariari, and Río Guaviare. Aguilar Enterprises moved everything under the sun and had passed every government inspection it had received with flying colors. To the public, it was a beacon of good business practices and well-oiled leadership. But to those that worked within its flat, white walls, it was something else entirely.

Aguilar could send his ships in several different directions from his docks depending on his client's location. He could also use Calle 65, the main road in the area, if need be. The highway nearly ran all the way back to Bogotá. The combination of road and tributaries gave Aguilar instant access to half of Colombia. He also had people that specialized in getting his wares to the United States. Aguilar even owned a private helipad. Yes, he had everything covered. His *donations* to the local inspectors and judges had, quite literally, paid off. He was untouchable in every sense of the word.

Aguilar closed his hand around the set of bloodied brass knuckles and drove his fist into the insolent man's temple. Typically, someone of his influence and power wouldn't need to do the dirty work. But Aguilar enjoyed it. It allowed him to show his men how serious he was about his business. Plus, it let him blow off some steam.

The security guard dropped, but he didn't fall. He was suspended by his wrists, held up by twin pullies in the middle of the factory floor where everyone could see him. Aguilar's subordinate had been responsible for allowing a worker to run free. That man, Jorge Gonzalez, had been in Aguilar's custody for months. If he got back to real civilization and alerted the authorities—those Aguilar had yet to pay off—as to what he was up to, then his entire operation would be at risk.

On his knees, the guard moaned in pain, half-conscious to what was happening to him. His failure was something that needed to be seen. The others, both his loyal men and those here unwillingly, needed to understand what would happen to them if they failed.

Aguilar brought his right hand up and picked away a clump of hair and scalp. He had done a number on Ricardo, one of his most faithful men. Mercifully, Aguilar paused his assault and turned around, seeing what he had hoped. All eyes were on him. Everyone on the factory floor was watching his ferocity. He was not a man to be trifled with. Ricardo's otherwise exemplary track record was the only reason he wasn't dead. He would live, and he would learn.

Slipping the soiled brass knuckles off his fingers, Aguilar dropped them to the concrete floor with a clatter and stepped away from the scene. His white tank top and expensive slacks were ruined, but he didn't care. Aguilar could afford all the clothing he required.

"He's one of my best!" Aguilar shouted, pointing back to the near-dead man. "Imagine what I'll do to a lesser individual if you disobey me." He reached out his other hand and was immediately given a towel to wipe off his hands and face.

"Sir," the *towel boy* said.

"What?"

"I have news."

Aguilar pushed his glasses higher on his nose and faced his assistant, Cesar. "What kind of news?"

"Hugo Nunez."

Aguilar growled. "Nunez? What about him?"

Cesar shrank away from his boss. He, like all of his closest allies, knew the angst Aguilar felt toward Hugo Nunez.

"He escaped our latest attempt with the help of the inbound American."

Aguilar paused mid-wipe. "The American? So, our contact was right? Is he still with Nunez?"

"I believe so."

"This is unpleasant. Do we know who this American is?"

Cesar shook his head. "No, sir."

Aguilar's eyes darkened. "Maybe you should find out."

"Y—yes, sir," Cesar stuttered, quickly dialing his cellphone. The number's owner would know what to do.

Aguilar smiled. "While we wait, send in our distinguished volunteers to have a chat with Hugo and this American."

Cesar stopped dialing and looked up at his superior. "Sir?" His face flushed. The 'volunteers' terrified Cesar, as well as most of the people within the compound. Their medical treatments were a recent addition to Aguilar's business portfolio. They no longer manufactured just mind-altering narcotics. His scientists, most of whom were banned from practicing in the United States, had also moved into a more specialized form of drug production, experimenting with a handful of rare, hazardous plant toxins and animal venoms. Aguilar had been inspired by a novel that pertained to the Norse berserker warriors.

"You heard me." Aguilar stepped away. "I want to see them in action. I want to see if our tests have paid off."

Aguilar returned to his second-floor office and stripped down to his boxers. He discarded his soiled clothes in a nearby wastebasket and stretched, catching his reflection in a full-length mirror on the far wall. His mop of black hair was beginning to gray around his temples, but he didn't mind. Aguilar thought it made him look more distinguished. He pushed his glasses back up his nose and eyed the right-hand wall. Marching over to it, he placed his left palm on a seemingly nondescript area and pushed. With a soft click, the false partition recessed and slid away, revealing a hidden compartment.

Aguilar kept his personal belongings here. Some of them had never been seen by anyone else. He stepped inside the eight-by-eight space and drew back the line of hanging clothes on the far wall. He grinned. Imbedded into the rear wall of the private alcove was a safe. Aguilar pressed his right thumb up against a small glass square and waited. The fingerprint scanner correctly identified him, and the lock disengaged.

The only object within the safe was his precious map. He had purchased it from a man who was known to *acquire* relics from all around the globe. The map had pointed Aguilar to an unexplored area to the east of a small town called Calamar. The site had been quickly cleared, and its contents confirmed.

The tomb of Diego de Ordaz.

The significance of the find meant nothing unless you knew that Ordaz was supposed to have died in Venezuela—not Colombia. It was clear what had taken place.

"You faked your death to pursue your prize undisturbed."

Aguilar didn't care how the explorer had done it. All that mattered was that he *did* do it. It made perfect sense. Once Ordaz was reported dead, he would have the freedom to continue his search for the City of Gold without his superiors back in Spain watching his every move. It had become *his* expedition, just like how it was now Aguilar's.

He smiled. His eyes opened wide with mania. "I am Ordaz reborn." He closed his eyes and took a deep breath. "El Dorado will be mine."

5

Outside Abuelita's
Bogotá, Colombia

The sun was setting by the time Miguel and Manuel Arroyo arrived. Jack and Hugo met the two men out back in a dark alleyway. Neither of them held visible weaponry. Jack wasn't going to take any chances and met the Arroyos unarmed. He still carried his Glock beneath his jacket. As did Hugo. The cool weather made the jackets appropriate to wear. If it were warmer, they would've had to figure out something else. Nothing screamed "I have a gun!" than wearing a jacket in the summer months.

The Arroyos weren't so shy. As they climbed out of their truck, Jack saw their armaments. They boldly carried pistols out in the open with no regard as to whom might see. The brothers carried themselves confidently. And they were huge.

"They grow 'em big down here, huh?" Jack asked, nudging his partner.

Hugo gave him a look that shut Jack up. Cracking jokes around the Arroyos was, seemingly, forbidden. However, Jack couldn't help himself. He would need to fix the two men's uptightness—and do so immediately.

In the aura of their headlights, the two thickly built men stopped, pausing ten feet in front of Jack and Hugo.

"Jack Reilly," Hugo said, starting the introductions, "this is Miguel and Manuel Arroyo."

The man to Jack's left, Miguel, was well put together. His white dress shirt was neatly ironed, its long sleeves rolled up to his forearms. His slacks looked expensive, as did his shoes. Jack could just make out a series of swirling tattoos on the man's forearms. They disappeared beneath his cuffs.

His brother had similar ink on his arms. Manuel dressed down in comparison to his brother. He wore a simple black tank top. His exposed arms and shoulders were covered in a series of colorful, artistic patterns—his chest too. Unlike his twin's, Manuel's pants and boots were built for combat.

Miguel's sidearm was holstered much like Jack's—dangling inside of a shoulder holster setup. Manuel's was strapped to his right thigh, and even in low light, Jack could see that it was a big boy—a .50 caliber Desert Eagle.

Right, Jack thought, recalling what Hugo had said about them. *Miguel is the businessman, and Manuel is the muscle.*

Both men were cleanly shaved from the top of their heads down to their chins. It was going to be impossible to tell them apart if they changed into similar garbs.

"So," Miguel replied, "you are the American that Hugo has told us about."

Jack's eyes flicked back and forth between the Arroyos. He didn't trust them a bit, but he had no choice but to go along with Hugo's plan.

He shrugged. "That all depends on what he's said."

"He says you have a crazy plan that will make us rich."

Jack shot his *friend* a look but relented. "El Dorado."

Neither of the brothers reacted. But Jack did.

He glanced at Hugo while thumbing over to the newcomers. "Does anything surprise these guys?"

"No, Mr. Reilly," Miguel replied, "nothing does. We, like many people, have been attempting to locate El Dorado for years."

"To no avail, I suspect."

"You are correct. Every clue we've found has been met with a dead end." Miguel motioned to Hugo. "But Hugo tells me of a map that we're set to acquire."

Jack nodded. "From Santiago Aguilar."

That got a reaction out of the twins. They stood tall, and their faces hardened even more—if that were even possible. Like Hugo, these men didn't care for the drug lord either. But Jack suspected that it was for more of a business reason versus personal for these two. Hugo didn't care about the money. He wanted to see Aguilar put out of business and, if possible, put in a coffin.

"So," Jack said, "are we in agreement?"

Miguel turned and received a nod from his silent brother. He returned his gaze to Jack. "We are."

"Okay, then." Jack relaxed a little. "Let's get to work."

Hugo's Storehouse

The four men gathered down below in Hugo's office and went over the plan Jack had laid out. Infiltrating the perimeter fence surrounding Aguilar's compound was going to be the easiest part of the operation. After that, they would need to split up into two teams.

"Hugo and I will go after the map while you two set the charges."

"No," Miguel said, "I don't trust that you'll wait for us."

Jack rubbed his face hard. They weren't going to make this easy.

"Fine," Jack said, eyeing Miguel. "You and I will find the map." Hugo was about to protest the change but was quieted by Jack's raised hand. "Hugo and Manuel will tear the place a new one." He patted Hugo on the shoulder, then looked for approval from the Arroyos. "Okay?" They each gave him a quick nod.

"Right... Once we have the map, we meet here—a mile to the south of our access point—where we've left our transportation."

"My brother's truck."

Jack's attention turned from Miguel to his stoic counterpart. Manuel's demeanor reminded Jack of Bull back home in Cody, Wyoming, though Bull wasn't a criminal with a mean streak. Bull allowed others, like Jack, to do the talking.

"Okay, Hugo, you're up."

"All right, as far as the compound goes..."

"We know it well," Miguel said.

Jack eyed Miguel. "You do?"

The man shrugged. "We've dealt with him in the past and have seen his operation a handful of times." The statement shook Miguel's confidence. Whatever business he'd done with Aguilar, it didn't sit well with the man. Jack was about to ask what he had seen but decided that it wasn't necessary.

"Oh, well, that changes things," Jack said. "I figured we were going in blind."

"No," Miguel said, "we should be able to get you in and out without an issue."

Hugo shrugged.

"Fine. Miguel and Manuel will lead the way."

It made sense, but Jack still didn't like the adjustment. He hated changing things on the fly, especially when the people he relied on were inherently unreliable. There was no 'honor among thieves' in the real world. If the twins wanted to screw Jack and Hugo, they could do so without remorse. In fact, Jack suspected it was bound to happen the closer they got to their prize.

"Hugo!" a voice called. All four men turned and peered through the plexiglass windows of the corner office. Happily, Hugo translated everything the man said.

"We have visitors," Hugo relayed. "Three cars just pulled up to the front door."

Th foursome looked at one another, but it was evident that none of them were responsible for the newest arrivals. Still, Jack needed to ask.

He turned to Miguel. "They with you?"

The local shook his head. "No. These aren't our men."

Hugo rushed out of his office and headed back toward the elevator. Jack and the Arroyos followed closely. All four men gathered around a pair of monitors displaying various camera angles showing the outside of Abuelita's. Three large SUVs were parked out front. Two men emerged from each vehicle. All were dressed in black military-grade fatigues, and they held rifles.

"Come," Hugo said, stepping onto the platform. "We must repel them. I can't lose my business."

Jack stepped forward, but the Arroyos didn't.

"You aren't coming?" he asked.

Miguel shook his head. "This isn't our fight."

Jack rolled his eyes and mumbled, "Definitely no honor among thieves." He rubbed his forehead with both his palms. "Whatever, man. Just meet us out back with our stuff and get ready to burn rubber."

Without another word, Miguel and Manuel grabbed the team's gear and disappeared through the rear tunnel. Jack had no idea where they would pop out.

One of Hugo's men handed Jack the M4A1 rifle he had picked out and then stepped back. Jack nodded his thanks. Hugo depressed a button and sent them chugging upward. They disappeared into the darkness, emerging from the mop room once the lift had settled into place. Moving slowly, Jack waited and listened. All was quiet on the other side. Hugo unlocked the door, and they slunk into the kitchen in silence, finding it abandoned. It seemed as if Abuelita had disappeared when trouble arrived.

Smart woman.

Hugo reached for a wall-mounted metal rectangle and flipped open a lid. Jack recognized that it was a breaker box. The local quickly threw all of the switches, casting him and Jack, and the parking lot, into darkness.

Between the late hour and the lack of artificial light, Jack could barely see a thing. He stayed calm and allowed his vision to adjust. His better-then-average night vision took over. He shouldered his rifle and followed Hugo through the central corridor back into the restaurant's main room. Seeing movement outside, they both ducked behind the front counter and peered over it like a pair of cautious meercats.

"No!" Hugo hissed, nearly standing up.

Jack held the man down and looked, seeing what he had. Abuelita didn't get away as Jack had initially thought. She was outside with the six gunmen. One of them held a pistol to the back of her head. The headlights of the three vehicles backlit the seven individuals. The illumination made it hard for Jack to tell them apart. *There you are.* The only silhouette that would need saving was the short, slouched one.

"Throw down your weapons!"

Hugo translated the order for Jack.

"No chance," Jack muttered, happy that the other five men had yet to point their rifles their way. So far, the only one that had made a threatening movement was the man holding a gun on the old woman.

"But we must," Hugo said. "If something should happen to Abuelita..."

He was right. They needed to do whatever they could to keep Abuelita alive.

"Okay!" Jack shouted, hoping they understood him. "We're coming out!"

He nodded at Hugo. They stood together—but they didn't drop their weapons. They held onto them but kept them aimed at the floor. The pair witnessed the lead man pull a tubular object out of his pocket. At first, Jack thought it was a sound suppressor. Oddly, the guy flicked its cap off and plunged the exposed end into his own neck. Jack figured that a jab to the captive's neck would be deadly, but since the man thrust the object into his own neck, it must be something else. The reaction was nearly instantaneous. The gunman howled into the air like a beast and pulled the trigger.

Abuelita's head snapped forward, and she fell to the parking lot.

Hugo shouted, lifted his sidearm, and shot the stranger in the chest. Jack watched the bullet impact his flesh. None of the men were wearing protective body armor. Jack was taken aback when the shooter didn't flinch, let alone drop next to the dead woman. Instead, he inspected the wound and began to cackle wildly. The other five men pulled out tubes and injected themselves in their necks.

Their reactions were identical to the lead gunman. They all roared into the air like a pack of feral animals. Bullets tore into the restaurant's main room, sending Jack and Hugo to the floor in a shower of broken glass. They regrouped and leaned against the decimated front counter.

"Well," Jack shouted, "I guess Aguilar isn't into just cocaine!"

Hugo didn't respond. Jack wasn't sure the smuggler had even heard him. His hands were over his ears, and tears ran down his face. Jack didn't understand the relationship between Hugo and Abuelita, but it was apparent that the matriarch had meant something to him.

As for Aguilar's men...

It seemed as though they had been given some kind of experimental drug cocktail. The results were that it made its user mentally unstable. But it also made them feel no pain.

"Super-soldiers?" Jack asked himself. "That's unexpected." Numerous governments had attempted to create a Captain America-like serum. This must be Aguilar's variation, as it were. Jack couldn't fathom what a man like him had cooked up.

Popping up to one knee, Jack pulled the trigger of his full-auto rifle and pumped six rounds into the first man he lined up. All six projectiles traced a line upward, finding their marks. The last of them penetrated the gunman's skull and dropped him in his place.

Jack ducked back down next to Hugo. *Well, that's promising.*

"Aim for their heads!" Jack shouted.

Hugo shook his head. He couldn't hear Jack over the next wave of gunfire. Jack switched gears and tapped himself in the forehead. The message, thankfully, was conveyed. They launched to their feet and opened up with their weapons. Multiple bullets hit their mark, but most sailed harmlessly past their intended targets. Half of the headlights were extinguished in the process. The dimmer lighting gave Jack an idea. He refocused his attention on the SUVs, and, one by one, he squelched all the artificial light. The parking lot fell into complete darkness.

"Stay here," Jack whispered, silently laying his rifle on the floor.

Jack didn't draw his Glock. He went for his knife, instead. He slid out from behind the counter, staying close to the ground. He used the low light to his advantage and serpentined his way to the front door. It opened to the sound of a bell, freezing Jack in place. A single set of footfalls stepped inside. Either they were coming in one at a time, or the team leader had sent the others around back to make sure no one escaped that way.

Ducking under a table, Jack spied the lower half of a man twenty feet away. He kept his breathing under control and waited for the opportune moment. It came seconds later. The newcomer continued forward, toward the counter. He passed right next to Jack. Jack duckwalked up behind him and slashed at the back of his left knee. The blade sliced through the tendon, causing the man to stumble. Jack leapt out of his low stance and drove the man headfirst into the broken glass case.

Hugo scrambled away from his hiding spot and disappeared back into the kitchen area. Jack didn't know what he was up to, and he didn't have time to contemplate it. He spun and flicked his wrist, aiming for the origin of another noise. Jack's blade struck the next gunman in the base of the throat. Across the room, he decided that stealth was now out of the question. He drew his sidearm and shot the gagging man in the forehead.

Jack hurried to the shattered front windows and surveyed the parking lot. The three SUVs were still present, but not all the men were. A few must have gone around the back. With a moment to spare, Jack inspected the dead. He procured a small tactical flashlight from a pocket and flicked it on, kneeling next to the guy he had shot in the head and was shocked by what he saw.

This man's face was sunken in, and he had heavy bags under his eyes. If Jack had to guess, he was a long-term drug addict. Aguilar was employing drug users as his super soldiers. It all made sense, in a way. He guaranteed the people their fix while also getting the shock troops he desired.

The sounds of gunfire and stomping feet predated the arrival of Hugo. He came bursting back into the dining room and tumbled up and over the counter, falling hard. Jack met him halfway and helped the smuggler to his feet. Hugo was bleeding from a wound beneath his hairline.

"You okay?" Jack asked.

Hugo nodded his head. "Yes, but they will get through at any moment."

Jack sprinted around the counter and collected his rifle, checking it over. A boom announced the successful intrusion of Aguilar's men. Jack backed away, tightly shouldering his carbine. But he didn't fire. Hugo grabbed his jacket and pulled him toward the front door before he could.

"What are you doing?" Jack asked.

"I have a plan."

"You do?" Jack asked, shocked by what Hugo was holding. "Is that a detonator?"

The local nodded. "A man like me requires contingency plans."

"Like decimating your business?"

Hugo shook his head. "No, just the strip mall. My operation will live on with or without Abuelita's."

Jack could see that it pained Hugo to say that. Both men looked outside and saw the old woman's body lying face down. If her death stung Jack as bad as it did, then Hugo must've been a mess on the inside.

Jack nodded and continued outside. He and Hugo hid behind the nearest SUV and waited for their pursuers to appear. When they did, Hugo lifted his hand and depressed a circular red button.

Nothing happened.

Jack stepped out and applied pressure to his rifle's trigger. He met its wall but didn't finish the movement. The fireball erupted before him, engulfing Abuelita's and the three gunmen inside. The shockwave tossed Jack against the front of the SUV, bouncing him off it.

He climbed to his feet and placed his hands on his knees, breathing heavily. "Is this a normal night for you?"

Hugo shook his head. "No, not at all."

"So, why now?" Jack was struggling to connect the dots. He was here for Matias and El Dorado. So far, the attacks against him had also been aimed at Hugo. The two men were linked in some way.

The smuggler scratched his head and shrugged. "What can I say? I'm a popular guy!"

Jack stood and recalled what had happened to them on the highway. They had been attacked almost as soon as he had landed in Bogotá. If this was all about Hugo and his local operation, then Jack imagined that they would've made an attempt on his life before Jack had gotten involved. *Dammit,* he thought. Someone knew who he was and why he was here. The prospect of a spy within TAC was becoming more and more plausible.

Unless he was forced to talk?

Jack knew it wasn't just Hugo that Aguilar was after. If Aguilar had wanted to kill Hugo, he would've already done it.

Jack was his primary target.

"Sorry, buddy," Jack said, patting Hugo on the shoulder, "but I don't think it's you they're after."

Hugo placed a hand on his chest. He gasped. "I'm hurt that you would say such a thing."

Jack grinned. "Better hurt than dead."

Hugo thought about it for a moment. But he agreed. "Quite true."

"There's a mole in my organization, and they are trying to stop me from discovering the truth."

A noise originating from the fire startled both men. They watched on in horror as an unidentifiable burned man limped out of the raging inferno. Neither of them raised their weapons to finish him off. They were too stunned to move.

But the Arroyos weren't.

A large four-door truck came screeching into view. It zoomed past Jack and Hugo and bowled into the burnt gunman with a bone-shattering impact, tossing him right back into the conflagration. Manuel backed the truck away from the fiery building, stopping it next to the frozen pair. The passenger side window lowered.

"Come," Miguel said, looking around, "we must leave before the police arrive."

6

Outside Bogotá, Colombia

Jack had no idea where they were going. At least he had the rest of his gear and had a chance to make a wardrobe change. Instead of his t-shirt and jacket, Jack now sported a black, long-sleeve thermal. They all did. The color would help them blend in with their surroundings. Sleeves were a necessity in the rainforest, even in extreme heat and humidity. They aided against swarms of mosquitos—something they were bound to run into, eventually.

Quite literally, Jack thought, shuddering at a memory. He'd been in a Mexican jungle once before, and it had been bad. Bugs everywhere. Too many to count.

He felt a little uncomfortable with his pistol being exposed like it was, freely hanging beneath his armpit for all the world to see. But everyone else carried their weapons in the same manner. And as the landscape transformed and became greener and less urban, it was abundantly clear that there would be no authority figures to tell them to carry them any other way.

Or anyone at all, Jack thought. The land had quickly gone from a bustling metropolis to nothing at all in minutes.

"Where are we going?" he asked.

Miguel answered him. "A small town called Puerto Esperanza."

"'Puerto?' It's on the water?"

Miguel nodded. "Most settlements are once you get outside of the major cities. Around here, the roads aren't as reliable as the rivers."

"How far is it?"

Miguel shrugged. "One hundred and sixty miles away, give or take."

Jack groaned. It was going to be a *long* ride. Luckily, he didn't have to pee.

The sun had just set. They were set to arrive in the middle of the night. It would be the perfect time to enact a plan such as theirs. Reaching into his pocket, Jack decided that now was as good a time as any to update his people back home. His company phone held no stored numbers. He was forced to memorize the important ones. At least there were only a few.

"What are you doing?" Hugo asked.

"Calling HQ. I need to check-in and let them know what's going on."

The line rang once. The person on the other end was straightforward and to the point. It was nice to hear the man's voice. It was still hard for Jack to grasp that his current boss was, technically, dead.

"This is Raegor. What do you have, Jack?"

Jack opened his mouth to reply but couldn't come up with anything on the spot.

The silence was noticeable. "Jack?" Raegor asked. "You there?"

"Sorry, yes, I'm here. I'm just not sure where to begin."

"That bad?"

Jack peered out his window, not that he could see much of anything. The world around him had been consumed by night. Rural Colombia had not been given the gift of artificial illumination. There was mostly jungle and narrow dirt roads now. Jack couldn't see where any of the latter led. There were also rivers and streams—dozens of them—sprinkled in between.

"Yeah. It's pretty bad."

Jack recounted everything that had happened since he landed at El Dorado International. Raegor stayed quiet and allowed Jack to finish. He never once interrupted him or verbally scoffed at the ridiculousness of the things Jack was describing. Jack suspected that this wasn't the strangest report Raegor had ever been given.

"We're on the road now."

"Where are you headed?" Raegor asked.

"Some place called Puerto Esperanza. Aguilar has his operation set up on the water. It's a perfect location, now that I think about it. He can send his goods up and downriver with minimal interruption."

"I don't like this."

Jack chuckled softly. "That makes two of us."

Raegor grumbled. "I was afraid this would happen."

"Afraid of what?"

"Of you being dragged into local conflict. That's not your job, Jack. You are there for Matias and El Dorado. Fighting the war on drugs isn't TAC business."

"With all due respect, we have to do this if we're going to locate El Dorado."

"TAC isn't the DEA, Jack."

"I know, but we need the map, and it just so happens to be in the possession of a drug lord." Jack was frustrated. "Look, you sent me here because of my past experiences. *This* is how we're getting this done. Without the map, the mission and possibly Matias' life are both over."

Raegor grumbled again. "Are you telling me how to run TAC?"

"Not at all." Jack gritted his teeth. "But I *am* telling you how I'm going to run *my* operation. I'll call you back after I've found the City of Gold. Jack out."

He hung up his phone and nearly threw it out the window. He probably would've if the tinted glass partition had been down. Jack was angry that he wasn't being trusted to get the job done. He hated bureaucratic micromanagement, especially when it was included in field ops.

Calm down, Jack. He had a good point.

TAC wasn't in the business of fighting drug cartels. But, in this case, there happened to be a man like Aguilar in the way. Jack now saw that Raegor was just trying to be a good boss. He was worried for Jack's life.

"You okay?"

Jack rubbed his temples and nodded. "Yeah, Hugo. Everything is peachy."

"Trouble back home?" Miguel asked mockingly.

Jack stopped massaging his head and glared at him. "Please, don't make me shoot you."

Manuel took his foot off the gas. He had, seemingly, left his sense of humor back in his tank top.

"Easy, Manuel," Hugo said. "We're all friends here," he glanced at Jack, "right?"

Jack looked back and forth between the muscular twins. "Yeah, sure. We're all BFFs."

Miguel muttered something in Spanish, and Manuel picked back up on the speed. The interior of the truck fell into a long silence—which was precisely what Jack needed. They zoomed by a smudged sign that read, "*Something, something* 65." He couldn't make out the words that proceeded the highway number. The road, 65, stayed smooth and navigable. Manuel kept them moving at a steady pace, hardly ever having to stop. Occasionally, out of the blue, there would be a flashing signal, but even then, Manuel didn't stop. Nor did he slow. They were the only ones out here.

A grim sense of dread washed over Jack. If the Arroyos, or even Hugo, decided to turn on him, there would be no finding his body. He doubted Hugo would do such a thing, but Miguel and Manuel absolutely could. Jack reflexively tightened his shoulder holster, getting the attention of his partner.

Hugo gave him a silent, concerned look.

Jack shook it off and went about looking over his rifle again. Busy work, any kind at all, would make the time go by faster. He avoided napping. Jack didn't want to be coffee-less and groggy when he needed to be at his best. Even as capable as his cohorts seemed to be, Jack knew they would fail miserably without him focused and on point.

Before he knew it, they had nearly arrived.

"Over there," Miguel said, pointing to the southwest.

Jack leaned around Hugo and looked through his window. There, across a sizeable river, was a sea of lights and rectangular buildings. Aguilar's operation stuck out like a sore thumb. The man didn't fear being found out because the authorities already knew what he did.

Manuel guided them over a modern concrete bridge. Jack was half-expecting to see a dilapidated mess of wood and rope. The reinforced engineering was in excellent condition—better than the road. It rose to over forty feet in height, allowing vessels to easily pass beneath it.

When the bridge made landfall on the southern side of the waterway, it darted east, away from their target. Jack was about to voice his displeasure but kept quiet and waited. Patience was key in situations like this. A minute or two later, Manuel hung a left and got off the highway. The local road remained paved for a couple hundred feet. Then, it turned to compacted dirt. It was smooth, which meant it was well-traveled. They passed a restaurant complete with a sizeable dock. Even at this late hour, Jack noticed that it was still open for business. He couldn't see the water from where he sat, but he figured that there were a few boats tied off, waiting for their heavily intoxicated captains to emerge and stagger aboard.

The road wrapped under 65 and headed back toward Aguilar's facility. It wound back and forth, snaking through the wilds, but it stayed on target, for the most part. Jack gripped his rifle tighter as they pulled off onto a nondescript path. Manuel gently eased his truck in the grass and parked. The foursome opened their doors and were greeted by the cool air. The temperature was lower than Jack had figured it would be. It was still humid, nevertheless. This was his least favorite atmosphere to be in.

Rainforests were unbearable at times. You were constantly wet and would quickly smell like bad cheese and dirty feet.

When he was back in Delta, he had a teammate named Brett O'Brien. The man's initials perfectly described his *mission stench*. In settings like this, Brett's "B.O." had been legendary. It's not like Jack could talk, though, as his wasn't much better. B.O. had been a good soldier and was someone that Jack had stayed in touch with. Now, B.O was retired, like Jack, and had moved down to Key Largo, Florida. Jack had attempted to call the guy after he himself had left the service but was unsuccessful. Brett, it seemed, had disappeared a few months earlier.

They were immediately attacked by bugs. A mosquito swarm quickly descended upon them. Hugo produced a bottle of something that smelled like wet earth. Whatever the concoction was, it appeared to work. Hugo passed it to Jack, who doused himself in it. The Arroyos did too. The repellant didn't keep all the pests away, however.

Better than nothing.

"Okay," Jack said, shouldering his rifle, "where to?"

Miguel pointed down the road. "The entrance is five hundred yards up the path. It sits on the southern end of the property and is, as you'd expect, heavily guarded."

Jack shook his head. "We can't go charging up the road and expect them not to see us." He faced the tree line. "Can we go this way?"

Hugo scratched his head. "Possibly, but it will slow us down."

"Hugo's right," Miguel agreed.

Jack shrugged. "We don't have a choice. We'll get mowed down if we don't."

The others relented, and they filed in behind Jack. He didn't know the area at all—but he knew the jungle. Though he had spent the vast majority of his service time in the deserts of the Middle East, Jack had also logged several hours in the rainforests of Central and South America, as well as a few hotspots in Africa. He knew what to expect in terms of Mother Nature and military tactics. His time in Yellowstone had helped as well.

Before they even made it a hundred yards into the dense trees, Jack was soaked with sweat. The moisture clung to every part of his body. The sweat building up around his eyes concerned him—mostly because he would be unable to wipe it off without using his filthy hands. Even his shirt sleeves were already unusable. The natural world was a filthy, nasty place.

Wonderful... Just wonderful.

He shook his head and blinked away the salty liquid. If his vision became compromised, he would be screwed.

One after the other, they crunched through the rough terrain. They followed the road but stayed fifty feet into the trees. At the very least, they wouldn't get turned around and lost. At the worst, they would be exhausted from the grueling trek.

"How much further?" Jack asked, glancing over his shoulder.

"Not too far," Miguel replied. "A few more minutes, tops."

They reached the southeastern corner of the property line 159 seconds later. When they did, Jack's jaw dropped. Dozens of armed men were scattered as far as the eye could see—which was pretty damn far. The lights within the chain-link fencing were bright and plentiful. They illuminated a handful of rectangular, outlier buildings, but nothing, human or not, was within fifty yards of the dark perimeter fence. And there, at the center of everything, was the big, cube-shaped kahuna.

That's gotta be Aguilar's factory.

Sneaking in and out wasn't going to be as easy as Jack had thought.

Manuel silently rummaged through his pack, producing a pair of folded bolt cutters. Without pause, he got to work on the blockade. Jack looked up and saw why. Like a high-security prison, the peak of the twelve-foot-tall barrier was topped with nasty-looking razor wire. Touch it, and you bled. Jack, unfortunately, had a run-in with something similar over a decade ago.

A trio of armed guards sauntered past them. Each of them carried identical AK-47 assault rifles and sidearms holstered on their hips. That's where the similarities ended. Their clothing, body armor, and chest rigs were of their own choosing, it seemed. The guards looked more like a group of private contractors than anything else. It didn't matter where the men came from, though. The militia within the compound was of a larger scale than Jack had anticipated.

Hello, Mr. Monkeywrench? Welcome to my plan! Why don't you get comfy and stay for a while?

"That's a lot of firepower," he said, voice low.

"Yes," Miguel added, "it seems that Aguilar has added to his security force since the last time we were here. Still, it shouldn't change anything."

"The hell it doesn't!" Jack argued. "We didn't come here to engage in open combat. We don't have an army!" He motioned to the compound. "Aguilar does." Miguel opened his mouth, but Jack cut him off. "If we get into a firefight, we die."

"So," Hugo said, looking worried, "are we going through with this, or not?"

Jack bit his lip and answered. "Yes, we are." He eyed Miguel. "You ready to find that map?"

Miguel's bravado had vanished. In its place was an understandably nervous human—Jack was too. But he nodded. Hugo and Manuel did too.

The silent Arroyo sibling snipped the last piece of chain-link fencing and carefully laid the three-by-three section on the ground. Without looking back, Jack and Miguel entered and headed off. The local led the way, shotgun at the ready. As they moved, they kept to the shadows the best they could.

They stopped and ducked behind a stack of crates. Miguel was about to continue, but Jack stopped him and forced him back into the darkness. A pair of crunching boots announced the arrival of two guards, and they were right on the other side of the pair's hiding spot. The newcomers would have to be dealt with before Jack and Miguel could continue their trek across the heavily fortified facility.

Here we go.

7

Santiago Aguilar's Compound

Hugo and Manuel darted to the left as soon as they entered Aguilar's property. Just being there made Hugo's skin crawl. He was so close to his revenge, but Hugo was also terrified of what might happen if he and the others were captured. Unlike the Arroyos, Hugo preferred not to get his hands dirty. He wasn't a violent man at all. Until the conflict back at Abuelita's, Hugo had never killed anyone in his life. He hoped he would never have to do it again.

It took them a few minutes, but he and Manuel made it to the southwest corner of the fence line. Both men went about setting charges. The explosion wouldn't kill anyone, more than likely, and the blast wasn't designed to do so. It was meant to distract the security detail within the complex. Hopefully, the thoughts of an open attack would send a significant number of them away from the central factory.

That was their primary target.

"Okay, we're good."

Manuel nodded and pointed north toward the water.

Hugo nodded. "Yes, now the dock, and if possible, we—" They were forced to the ground by a beam of light. Fortunately, it swept past them without stopping. Their black attire had done its job. Both men got to one knee. "As I was saying... If possible, we hit the boats too."

Manuel grinned. The thought of blowing shit up made the big man happy. Typically, Hugo didn't enjoy this kind of thing, but he couldn't hold back his own smile. Anything he could do to ruin Aguilar's day was okay in his book. Staying close to the fencing, Hugo and Manuel set off to the north, nearly running full-bore into a lone man relieving himself. He was dressed similarly, wearing all black.

Mercenary!

Hugo fumbled with his weapon, but Manuel didn't. Swiftly, the silent giant unsheathed a wicked-looking blade. He slowed and came right up behind the unsuspecting guard. Not wasting any time, Manuel covered the smaller man's mouth and slit his throat. He held his hand in place until the very end, dropping the deceased where he had stood. The deep shadows and dark clothing would keep the body from being seen. Manuel knelt and cleaned his blade on the guard's pant leg.

Hugo didn't comment on Manuel's methods. He just waved him on and continued to the north. Luckily for Hugo's stomach, and his nerves, they didn't encounter anyone else until they arrived at the portage. Like the southern and western property lines, the water was also surrounded with fencing topped with razor wire. *Except around the* docks, he thought. But unlike the perimeter, the entrance to the docks was well lit. They would be out in the open.

Hugo put a pair of small binoculars to his eyes and took in the scenery.

The entrance was still a few hundred yards away, and it was guarded by two men with assault rifles and walkie-talkies. If they failed to eliminate these men before they were spotted, they would be in a lot of trouble. Not only were they armed, but they would be able to call for backup.

Manuel must've sensed Hugo's rising anxiety because he, once more, produced his foldable bolt cutters and went about clipping the chain-link fence. Hugo protected his rear and watched for anything out of the ordinary. The factory stood out like a beacon. Jack and Miguel were somewhere on the other side, doing whatever they could to infiltrate it. Hugo was happy he was here with Manuel and not Jack. He wasn't sure he could enter the place where the cocaine that killed his sister was being manufactured.

Come on, Jack. Do it for Valentina. But it wasn't just the Nunez family that had suffered at the hands of Santiago Aguilar. There were thousands of others just like them that would like nothing more than to watch this place crumble to the ground.

Do it for all of us.

Jack and Miguel knelt atop the stack of crates. The pair was fifteen feet above the motionless gunmen. These two appeared to be friends, or they at least knew each other well enough to talk soccer and women. They spoke English too. One of them had a thick Russian accent. The other man was Latin. People from all over the world worked for other people all over the world in every industry, so it didn't shock Jack to find that someone was so far from his home country.

Especially mercenaries, he thought.

Typically, their kind avoided "working at home." You had a better chance of being recognized if you did. Killing people for money was generally frowned upon. Instead, they traveled wherever the cash was most bountiful. In this instance, a man from Russia had accepted a contract from an employer in South America.

Jack was lined up with the Rusky, and he prayed to God that the guy wasn't a former Spetsnaz. Russian Special Forces soldiers were no joke. They were some of the deadliest people on the planet, just like Jack's old unit, Delta.

Slowly drawing his knife, Jack flipped it around into an underhanded grip and got his boots beneath him. He rolled onto the balls of his feet, finishing in an athletic catcher's squat. He looked at Miguel, nodding to the man. The local silently replied with a curt tip of his chin, and they stood in unison. Jack counted to three with the fingers of his left hand and then dropped from the sky like a bomb. He timed the attack perfectly and landed on the Russian's back just as he swung his knife hand around and jammed the blade tip into the unsuspecting man's chest. The force of Jack's brief freefall was enough to drive the gunman to the ground.

The Russian landed atop the knife, burying it deep. The earth drowned out any noise he made. Jack grabbed a handful of the man's greasy hair and shoved his face into the dirt.

Miguel had not timed his assault as well as Jack. He was just as successful, though. Miguel growled and plunged his blade into the small of the Latin gunman's back four times until he moved to the throat. Jack looked away from the gruesome scene and surveyed their surroundings. No one had seen their arrival, and he wanted to keep it that way.

"Come on," he whispered, grabbing the Russian by the ankles.

He and Miguel dragged their targets around to the rear of the crates and laid them down in the shadows created by lights on the other side. Jack knew the bodies would, eventually, be discovered. They needed to be long gone by then. Peering around the crates for a second time, Jack waited for a trio of guards to pass fifty feet further ahead. The centrally located factory was still a way off. He estimated the distance at around five football fields.

Five hundred yards... Great.

"Where is Aguilar's office?" Jack asked, slinking back behind the crates.

"Inside the factory. It overlooks the floor and the docks to the north."

Which means it's highly visible to everyone else.

"Any way inside besides the front door?"

Miguel shrugged. "I think there is access into the building from the roof."

"You *think*?"

"Why would I know? It never occurred to me that I might have to enter from there."

Jack rolled his eyes and leaned out and looked over the factory again. In actuality, the structure was composed of several buildings. Each was a little different than the other in size and shape. Jack proposed that, over the years, Aguilar had built additions onto his original factory as the need to increase production arose. The architecture looked slightly pyramidal but designed by a strung-out abstract artist.

Probably multiple builders, Jack thought. It would account for the variety of styles he was looking at.

"You ever play *Q*bert*?" Jack asked, glancing over his shoulder.

Miguel looked at Jack like he was crazy. He was, but Jack also had an idea on how to gain access to the roof. Like Q*bert, he and Miguel would hop from cube to cube—in this case, building to building—to reach the peak of Aguilar's factory. Wall-mounted lights hung from various points of the hodgepodge factory. The irregularity of its shape created some favorable shadows—but none of them were close to his and Miguel's current position.

With the way clear, Jack moved, staying low and keeping his head on a swivel. The ground transformed from dirt and grass to concrete. It forced him to slow and walk heel to toe. Still, he kept his pace fast, weaving through a mass of crates and heavy machinery.

Jack stepped out from between a pair of backhoe excavators and was quickly yanked back into cover by Miguel. Two guards had just rounded the corner of a small, squat building. Jack had been looking the other way when he had made his move. He nodded his thanks to Miguel and waited for them to pass.

"Toilet," his partner whispered. Jack followed Miguel's outstretched hand. He was pointing at the same structure the guards had just emerged from. But Jack's attention wasn't on the concrete outhouse. He was focused on the thirty feet of scaffolding and cables running from its roof to the factory. There was some sort of construction going on. Jack produced a pair of small binoculars and put them up to his eyes. Aguilar's people were installing an additional spotlight atop the concrete outhouse. The scaffolding gave the electricians access to the light while also allowing them to reach its power source. Jack could barely see a rectangular metal box on the roof of the nearest factory building.

"Dammit," he muttered, looking around. There were too many guards wandering about for them to make it there unseen. The scaffolding was the only real option. If they mounted the outhouse, they could cross the rest of the compound.

This is a terrible idea, he thought, looking around.

Shuffling forward, Jack's foot struck a loose stone. He glanced down and smiled. Bending down, Jack collected a trio of the baseball-sized rocks, pocketing two of them. Miguel eyed him, looking ready to go. Jack winked and wound up. He hurled one of the stones as far as he could. When it landed, it drew the attention of the guard closest to their position. The man turned and cautiously stepped away to investigate the disturbance. In doing so, it gave Jack and Miguel the opportunity they needed.

They ran for the restroom. Jack slid to a stop and laid his back against the concrete wall, quickly cupping his hands together. Miguel stepped into the makeshift stirrup and scurried up Jack's body and onto the structure's roof. The local immediately laid on his stomach and reached a hand down.

Jack leapt into the air and clasped it on the first attempt.

Like his brother, Miguel was strong. He effortlessly accepted Jack's weight, pulling him high enough for Jack to get a grip on the building's ledge. Once he did, Jack lifted his right leg and finished the climb himself while Miguel kept watch.

"Go, go!" he whispered, pushing Miguel forward.

Jack threw another of the rocks. He didn't wait to see if the guard took the bait again. If he didn't, Jack would know based on the gunfire. The scaffolding gave them instant access to the rooftops, but the path was uncovered, making them vulnerable.

Jack nearly fell when they reached the roof of the first outlier building. He had lost his balance when the last plank had shifted beneath his weight. Miguel caught his arm, and the two men stooped down and caught their breath.

"I can't believe that worked," Miguel said.

"Same here." From a kneeling position, Jack gauged their path. "Where to?"

Miguel tilted his head back and stood, staying low. "We go up. Follow me."

As they went from building to building, they scaled the four of them as they had done at the concrete outhouse. Jack and Miguel took turns helping each other up. Then, whoever was on top would give the other one a boost. It was a display of teamwork that impressed Jack. Miguel was supposed to be a ruthless criminal.

"You aren't what I thought you'd be," Jack said.

"What do you mean?"

Jack needed to choose his words carefully. "You play well with others."

Miguel chuckled. "Hugo telling his stories again?"

What's that supposed to mean?

Jack was honest about what he had heard. "He said that you and your brother were far more willing to get your hands dirty than he was."

Miguel smiled widely. "Quite true. I'd be shocked if he said anything remotely positive about us and our fallout."

Jack stopped. "Fallout?"

"Yes, you see, we used to work for him some years back."

"You did?"

Miguel nodded and clasped his hands together. "Manuel and I wanted to expand the operation, but Hugo got comfortable with the small-time. We wanted to move to the northern end of Bogotá, where the business would be more bountiful. Hugo didn't."

Jack knew why. After everything Hugo had told him about his family, it was clear as to why Hugo had refused to leave the southern half of Bogotá.

"So he could keep tabs on Aguilar..."

Miguel hoisted Jack up to the next rooftop but didn't immediately take the American's hand. "What do you mean?"

Jack looked around before explaining.

"Hugo has been waiting years to exact his revenge against Aguilar—for Valentina's death. If he moved further away from the man, it would be harder to do so."

Miguel's face faltered. It was plain to see that he and his brother had thought it had been something personal against them. Jack could see the man putting it together in his head. When he did, he clasped Jack's hand and climbed. Once they were both atop the next building, Miguel patted Jack on the shoulder.

"Then we will help him. Valentina deserved better."

"You knew her?"

He nodded. "Yes, she was a vision, even towards the end. She would come around and beg Hugo for money. She said it was for rent and groceries, or what have you, but we all knew it was to pay for her next fix." Miguel laughed, but it wasn't out of humor for the situation. He was reacting to the ridiculousness of it. "Even after Aguilar cut her off, she was still his pawn."

Jack stood tall. "We need to bury this guy."

Miguel gazed out over the lit compound. The light didn't reach this high. The pair relaxed, feeling the cool breeze whip by, confident that they wouldn't be seen. They were five stories up and could easily see the dock and a duo of boats. All three would be on Hugo and Manuel's list.

Jack turned. There was still one more structure to scale. The main building's rooftop was straight ahead of them. Hopefully, their access point was there and unguarded. He doubted it would be. Aguilar's ground force should've been able to repel anyone who tried to force their way inside.

Jack grinned. *Right, should've...*

The river water was refreshing. Hugo and Manuel stuck to the shallows, carefully wading through the chest-high depths. The dock stuck out sixty feet, giving them ample options to plant their charges. All they would have to do was decimate a few of the supports, not all of them. The weight of the heavy wooden jetty should do the rest and tear itself apart.

In theory.

Hugo hoped that would be the case. He wanted to see it drop into Rio Guaviare with gusto. And he wanted to laugh and cheer when it happened.

The pair made it to the first, thick post and got to work. They froze when a set of boots pounded overhead. One of the guards was making his rounds. He didn't stop, though. Hugo doubted these guys were doing what they were supposed to do. Nothing ever happened out here. The monotony of guarding a dock at night must've been frustrating and incredibly dull. The attitude of the men here would've been that of resentment.

Manuel's hands flew over the plastic explosives. Hugo could've done it too, but not as speedily as his counterpart. He was better suited as the bag man on this mission.

"Do this much?" Hugo jokingly asked.

Manuel didn't reply, nor did he ever have to ask for supplies. Hugo handed him what he needed as soon as he was ready for it. Surprisingly, the two men made a good team. He had rarely ever worked one on one with Manuel in the past.

Finishing in record time, they moved laterally to the next support post.

They were presently ten feet from the rapidly rising shoreline. If they stopped here and blew the dock, Hugo doubted it would be enough to obliterate it. They needed to take out at least one more pair of supports. Unfortunately, it meant they were going to have to go for a swim. Hugo didn't mind. His bag was waterproof, and it floated. Its contents were dry and would stay that way until they fell into the river.

Along with the dock.

It wasn't easy, but Hugo and Manuel kicked to the next set of posts. They were forced to hold onto it lest they get swept away. Either that or they had to frog kick nonstop to stay in place. Manuel's right hand moved slowly—methodically even. His left hand was latched onto the post, as was Hugo's. He held the buoyant bag in place, allowing Manuel to dig through it with relative ease.

It took them much longer to set these last two charges, and by the time they were done with the task, they were also exhausted physically. Both men breathed hard. Neither man was trained to do something like this. The water took a toll on them. It was ironic. The calming presence of a river was the thing that worked to sap the strength of two hardened men.

They doggy-paddled over to the next dock and did it all over again. By now, they were both ready to let the water sweep them away.

"Now the boats," Hugo whispered.

Manuel nodded, exhaustion present on his emotionless face.

They swam out further. The freshness of the water was beginning to bite. It no longer felt pleasant. Now, it felt like a chilling nuisance. But they pushed on and swam out to the starboard hull of the nearest watercraft, freezing in place when the guard returned.

His light swung their way, driving the pair underwater. The only thing left on the tributary's surface was the black bag. Hopefully, it wouldn't be noticed. After ten seconds, the light still didn't waver. Hugo hadn't taken a deep enough breath to hold it for much longer. Just as his lungs began to burn, the flashlight's beam lifted away from the river and moved on. Hugo and Manuel slowly popped up and took a few lungfuls of much-needed oxygen. They nodded to one another and returned their attention to the boat's hull.

Manuel slapped a brick of plastic explosive onto the vessel's hull a foot above the waterline.

"Will this work?" Hugo asked, unsure if the detonation would be strong enough to pierce the metal hull.

Manuel gave Hugo a confident smirk and slapped a second brick on.

Hugo returned his smile with one of his own. He checked his watch and saw that they were running behind. The plan included setting more charges on the outskirts of the main building. Hugo began to doubt they'd get it done given their current pace. The pair still had one more boat to rig. Then, they would have to make it back to the fence line and re-enter the compound—all without being detected. If they didn't time their moves with Jack and Miguel's, one of the two teams would be discovered and most likely killed.

Hugo couldn't let that happen. If Miguel died, there was little doubt that Manuel would take his wrath out on him. And if he and Manuel died, Jack would be done for. Hugo peered up to the topmost roof but couldn't see a thing. It was too far away and much too dark. The lack of gunfire gave Hugo hope that they had successfully made it inside. Once they found what they were looking for, the fireworks would begin.

8

The air vent was tight enough to make Jack and Miguel skulk along in a single file line. It was also constricting to the point of forcing them to leave their heavier-hitting weapons behind on the roof. Now, they were only armed with their sidearms and a knife, respectively.

Before Miguel offered, Jack climbed in first and wiggled forward on his elbows. He also used the tips of his boots to propel him along. Neither man knew where the hell they were going, so Jack just kept moving until he found what he wanted. Their entry point wasn't all that far from Aguilar's office. Jack and Miguel had stumbled upon a stroke of luck.

"Shit," Jack mouthed.

Aguilar was currently inside his office—and he was screaming at someone.

Jack watched the entire thing from directly above the man's desk. He could just barely make out a figure standing along the northern wall of the room. If Miguel's intel was correct, then the drug lord must have been looking out his window—toward the dock.

"The map is a dead-end!" he shouted, pounding his fist on the glass. "So is the excavation!"

Dammit, Jack thought, leaning in closer. *A dead-end?*

"I don't care what our agreement was," Aguilar continued. "I've spent millions on nothing!" He paused his tirade and listened. So did Jack, but the TAC agent couldn't hear what the caller was saying from here.

"No, not a chance," Aguilar said.

The person on the other end of the call spoke again. Whatever he or she said, it pissed off the drug lord.

"Oh yeah? Well, you can tell Suarez to go to hell!"

Instead of simply ending the call, Aguilar ended his cell phone's life and hurled it across the room. Jack heard it hit a wall somewhere out of sight. Aguilar was seething—brimming with fury. From what Jack had just overheard, the map led to nowhere significant. It bummed-out Jack, but he kept his chin up. He wasn't Aguilar or whoever was helping him.

Jack figured that Aguilar had hired an expert to dig up his lost city. The drug lord was a lot of things, but an archaeologist wasn't one of them. It was evident that the man didn't have the patience for the work. Jack barely did either.

He awkwardly peered over his shoulder at Miguel and mouthed the name, “Suarez?”

Miguel shrugged. Whoever the other man was, he was an enigma to the northside smuggler. It either meant that the caller didn't operate in the Arroyo family's circle, or perhaps, he did, but in a different part of the world. Jack put his money on the United States, or possibly even Mexico. Regardless, Jack now knew who had supplied the map to Aguilar.

He made a mental note to look into Suarez at a later date.

Jack took a deep breath and prepared for the long haul. Aguilar didn't look like he was about to leave any time soon. He walked over to his desk, giving Jack his first look at the man.

He was well-built and weighed about the same as Jack—around 200 pounds or so. His hair was combed neatly straight back and was graying at his temples. Jack placed his age somewhere in his mid-forties. Aguilar wore glasses and had a thick, five o'clock shadow.

Sitting down, he reached forward and picked up a rectangular box from his desktop. He set it down in front of him and opened the lid. Jack spied a handful of cigars. Cubans made a lot of sense, but they could've also been that of a local variety. Aguilar opened a drawer to his right and procured a matchbox. He opened it and struck a matchstick against its side, instantly igniting one of them. Even from inside the air vent, Jack could tell that the smokes were of the highest quality. The smell was incredible. Now and again, Jack would enjoy a cigar—along with a good scotch.

Standing to his feet, Aguilar moved to his left. Jack lost sight of him but quickly reacquired the man after he shifted his weight to the right. Jack could barely see Aguilar. He watched the man walk up to an empty wall, and oddly, he placed his hand—his right thumb—against it. Jack grinned as the partition silently slid back and opened. Beyond was something Jack couldn't see, no matter how hard he tried.

“Dang,” he whispered.

Even though he didn't see what was inside of Aguilar's secret walk-in closet, Jack knew it had to be the map.

What else could it be?

The phone on Aguilar's desk began to ring. He waltzed over and answered it, puffing on his cigar the entire time. He didn't say a word except when he explained that his cell phone's battery had died. Jack almost laughed. The battery was, most definitely, dead—right after the device had detonated against the wall. Aguilar hung up the desk phone and spun on a dime. He exited the room in a hurry, but not before sealing the closet.

"Of course you did," Jack whispered. It would've been convenient if Aguilar had left it open for Jack's prying eyes.

Jack waited a full minute before making his move. He carefully applied enough pressure on the inside of the air vent's grill, removing it with ease. Gripping it tightly, he wiggled it back into the duct and laid it down further ahead. The desk was too far to drop in headfirst, so Jack had to bypass the opening until his legs slipped through awkwardly. Then, he backpedaled and slithered out of the hole. His boots found nothing but air. Looking through his feet, he saw that he was still another eighteen inches above the desktop.

Biting his lip, Jack released his hold on the ceiling vent and dropped, crouching as he landed. He hardly made a sound. The feat caused a smile to form on his face. Pleased with his efforts, he looked up and waved Miguel forward. Jack dismounted the desk and rushed to the office door, throwing the deadbolt. Worst case, Aguilar would think he accidentally locked himself out. Best case, he wouldn't come back at all.

Jack turned his attention to the left-hand wall, but not before peering through the southern window. It gave him a view of a very busy factory floor. He had no idea what was going on down there. It's not like Jack had a lot of experience with the drug manufacturing side of things. Miguel would know, but he didn't bother to ask him.

Hmmm. Jack thought, examining the wall. Then, he saw it. There, in the center of it, was a nondescript fingerprint scanner. It was the same color as the wall. Without Aguilar's fingerprint, they weren't getting their prize.

Jack perked up some, getting an idea. He spun and speed-walked to Aguilar's desk. Searching the drawers, Jack found what he needed.

"Scotch tape?" Miguel asked, confused.

Jack grinned. "Watch this."

He carefully picked up Aguilar's cigar box and angled it up toward the overhead lights. It took him a second, but he ultimately spotted what he was looking for. Jack set down the box and drew out a six-inch piece of tape. Methodically, he hovered it over the container's lid before finally pressing it down. After rubbing it a few times, he peeled the tape off and held it up to the light, proudly whistling at his handy work.

"Gotcha."

"Nice work," Miguel said, impressed. He stepped aside to let Jack and his newly pilfered fingerprint through.

Moving quickly, Jack pressed the lifted print onto the scanner pad and waited. It took a moment, but it worked, and something within the wall clicked. To their amazement, the wall recessed six inches and then split down the middle. It opened with hardly a sound and revealed their prize.

"The map," Miguel said, stepping forward. His eyes were wide, borderline manic.

Jack didn't budge, however. The sight was something he dreaded.

The map was beautiful, but it was wholly unobtainable. It was mounted to the secret vault-like room wall, behind a thick sheet of what he assumed was ballistics glass. Aguilar was treating it as if it was the Mona Lisa!

Miguel reached for the artifact.

"No!" Jack hissed. "Don't touch it."

Miguel stopped and looked over his shoulder, but he didn't lower his hand. Jack finally stepped up next to him and explained his fears.

"We can't remove it. This is Aguilar's Holy Grail, right? He probably has an alarm attached to it—a pressure plate of some kind. If we even breathe on it, it'll go off."

Miguel didn't look happy. "Are you sure?"

Jack shook his head. "No, but we need to act as if I'm right."

"This is ridiculous!" Miguel drew his pistol and raised it in a foolhardy attempt to smash the bulletproof glass.

"Don't!" Jack caught his arm. "He can't know what we're up to."

The two men were at a stalemate physically, pushing hard against one another.

"Even if we get the map..." Jack said, straining, "what happens if I'm right?" Miguel's facial expression changed a bit. He was thinking it over. Jack continued. "Do you want to get into an all-out war against that?" He released his left hand and pointed toward the window overlooking the factory floor.

Miguel grunted and lowered his weapon, holstering it hard. He knew if they were met in open combat that their team would be dead in seconds.

"Fine," Miguel muttered. "What do we do now?"

Jack slid his phone from his pocket and snapped a few pictures, leaning in close. The map depicted a river, probably the Amazon, if Jack had to guess. Several tributaries were branching off the snake-like waterway, as well as small drawings of step pyramids.

Ruins? Jack deduced, unsure.

The bottom right corner of the map was in poor condition, as were the words scrawled into it. As Jack figured, they were in Spanish. The state of the find was such that the last few words were smudged and illegible. It was also a piece of something much bigger. The entire thing had been torn out of what must've been a large naval chart.

"Come on," Jack said, motioning to the ceiling. "We'll take a closer look once we're long gone from here."

Miguel looked as if he was about to argue, but he didn't get the chance. A series of booms and fireballs somewhere out of view drove the pair toward the window facing the dock. Nothing. Then, the anchorage, as well as a couple of large boats, detonated. Hugo and Manuel were starting their half of the plan.

"Son of a bitch—they went early!"

The room shook as another—closer—charge detonated.

Jack turned and dashed for the air vent. Miguel climbed atop it first and leapt into the air, catching the edge. He quickly hurried back into the opening and disappeared. headlong, but stopped and pivoted to the vault to close it before mounting the desk. Then, he followed Miguel's escape pattern, but paused to back himself up over the entrance and resealed it before disappearing.

He shuffled along as fast as he could, emerging from the vent on the other side as the building rumbled for a second time. Jack fell to the rough rooftop, scraping his knee through his jeans. He ignored the annoyance and collected his rifle, stepping over to the ledge. The dock was a mess, just as they had planned. So were the boats. If anything, the damage would slow down Aguilar's distribution. Maybe they would even bring the man some unwanted attention. An explosion and fire that size wouldn't go unnoticed.

The northwestern edge of the facility was on fire and smoking too. So was the northeastern corner. If Hugo and Manuel were able to set all their charges, then the factory's southern half was next.

"We need to hurry," Jack said, pulling Miguel along.

The two men's descent went much faster than their climb had. Instead of helping one another reach the next level, all they had to do was sit and hop down to the next rooftop. In minutes, they had made it back to the scaffolding of the lowest building leading to the outhouse. They were halfway across when a third detonation collapsed it. Jack and Miguel dropped into the mangled pile of metal and wood and were somehow spared from significant injury.

They made a run for it. Neither man drew their weapons. They sprinted to their original entry point, paying the chaos around them no nevermind. People frantically moved about but were too focused on the fires and explosions to notice that Jack and Miguel didn't belong among their ranks. Hugo and Manuel's "distraction" had paid off big time. Not only did it allow Jack and Miguel safe passage, but it also decimated Aguilar's operation.

When Jack and Miguel arrived at the exit, Hugo and Manuel were already there waiting for them.

"Where's the map?" Hugo asked, looking back and forth between them.

Jack rushed past him. "I'll explain later—run!"

They pounded through the jumble of vines, tree limbs, tall grass, and swampy groundwater. Jack didn't have a clue which way they were traveling. Anywhere was better than the compound. Sooner or later, Aguilar would wise up to what had happened and send out a squad of men to take care of whoever was responsible.

All four men were exhausted by the time they emerged from the trees.

They didn't see Manuel's truck.

"Back this way!" Hugo shouted.

Miguel and Manuel were already headed up the road, back toward the compound. They had gone too far before exiting the trees. Jack quickly caught up with the others just as a set of headlights came barreling toward them.

"Hide!" Jack shouted, ducking back into the marshy overgrowth.

Hugo, Miguel, and Manuel followed Jack in. They all knelt and drew their weapons.

"Do *not* engage unless it's unavoidable."

Manuel grunted and pointed at the truck.

"Can it be traced back to you?"

The big guy shook his head.

"We'll leave it if we have to."

Manuel didn't look happy, but he didn't argue either.

A four-door pickup, much like theirs, pulled up and stopped thirty feet up the road. Two men hopped down from the bed, and another two exited from the rear passenger seats. They all had AK-47 rifles at the ready and were slowly creeping up on Manuel's unoccupied automobile.

Fifteen feet later, one of the men gave an order. They stopped and opened fire on the vehicle. Jack and the others hit the dirt and covered their heads while bullets buzzed by their position like angry metal hornets. Luckily, the road was built up higher than the surrounding landscape to prevent flooding. Unless the gunmen angled their weapons down and to the left, they would be safe.

The foursome emptied their magazines into Manuel's truck. Then, they searched the bullet-ridden carcass. Finding nothing of value, they called it in on their walkie-talkies and climbed back aboard their vehicle. Once they were out of sight, Jack, Hugo, Miguel, and Manuel emerged, dripping wet and filthy.

Manuel's shoulders dropped. His truck was a complete loss.

"My condolences," Jack said, staying out of arm's reach. With no transportation, the quartet's mission was up Shit's Creek. "Any ideas?"

Hugo perked up. "The bar—the one back near the bridge."

"What about it?" Jack asked.

"It was open when we went by."

Jack rolled his neck. "You want to steal a car?"

Hugo smiled. "No, not a car." He glanced at Miguel. "Calamar, right?"

Miguel nodded in agreement.

Jack looked back and forth between them. "What's Calamar—besides squid?"

Miguel picked a leaf off his bald head and tossed it aside. "To get there, we'll need a boat."

Aguilar entered his office with caution. His operation was now virtually a complete loss. The docks were gone. So was a portion of the main building's wall. A piece of its roof had collapsed onto the factory floor, blanketing it in debris and water. Fires had broken out almost immediately. They had raged for a few minutes before the indoor sprinkler system had finally gotten them under control.

He faced his beloved facility, seething, gritting his teeth. Aguilar's obsession with El Dorado had clouded his mind. If he had bolstered his security here, this assault could've been avoided. The men he had guarding the excavation would've been enough to keep this from happening.

Who are you? he asked, failing to picture the attackers.

His thoughts returned to the phone call he had earlier. What were the chances that the American had caused all of this? What about Hugo Nunez? Hugo had been a thorn in his side for a long time, but he never would've done anything like this. He didn't have the ability to do so. If the American agent was the one responsible, then he was a person to be wary of—and a man to target.

Happily, Aguilar's office still stood. Even though the map had been a dead end as of yet, it was still invaluable. There was proof it had come from the excavation, but that was all. He and his project leader had yet to find anything else of use. They were currently digging holes all over the place but principally focused on the area directly around the tomb.

The tomb of Diego de Ordaz.

Sadly, the man's coffin had been raided long ago.

Aguilar opened his secret vault and stared in wonder at the map—a piece of Ordaz's navigational chart. It calmed him some, but it was also maddening. He owned proof that Ordaz had faked his death to pursue El Dorado. That alone was groundbreaking. But he couldn't tell anyone about it because a discovery like this would bring competition to the area. Aguilar was confident that he could keep people away from the site, but not forever. Sooner or later, there would be too much attention drawn to him and his activities.

His shoe crunched something hard. Aguilar picked up his foot and examined the object—a small stone. Typically, a pebble wouldn't have caused him such alarm, but Aguilar kept his vault in pristine condition. The stone shouldn't have been there. Someone had accessed his strongroom without his knowledge. The infiltration had to be related to the attack on his compound!

He spun and looked for additional clues, finding one shortly. Aguilar stepped up to his desk and growled. It wasn't much, but it was there.

The drug lord dragged his index finger across the tabletop, mashing his teeth as he did. The digit came away dirty. He looked up but didn't notice anything else suspicious—but the evidence was clear enough. Someone had entered his office and somehow accessed his vault. But, strangely, they didn't take the map. It didn't all make sense—yet. Aguilar picked up his desk phone. There was no dial tone, and with his cell phone destroyed, he had no way of notifying his project leader.

He would, however.

Whatever men Aguilar could spare would be sent to the dig site.

9

Puerto Esperanza, Colombia

Jack was confused. Why did they need a boat instead of a car? The rivers were in heavy use, that much was certain. Still, it made him uncomfortable being left in the dark like he was. Jack needed to trust Miguel. The man had earned it.

The foursome made it to a place called "Restaurante Puerto Esperanza" unscathed. They ducked behind a pair of rusty dumpsters and waited. As Jack expected, they smelled horrific. These, nevertheless, were worse than ordinary. It was as if someone had made a Rocky Mountain oyster milkshake, sat it out in the sun for a week, then drizzled a healthy dose of cat piss on it.

"Oh, God..." he said, gagging. "What the hell, man?"

Hugo sniffed the air and shrugged. "What do you expect? It's not like they have regular garbage pickup around here."

Jack held back his vomit and attempted to focus on something else. The mission was at somewhat of a standstill. He was at the mercy of the three men that he had only just met. So far, they had each proven to be reliable. Still, he needed to remember that they were crime bosses—including Hugo.

Manuel peeked out from behind the dumpsters and waved them on. Jack slinked around the metal container and watched as a pair of restaurant employees flicked their cigarettes away into the river—a river that Jack and the others were now rushing toward. Miguel followed close behind his mute sibling. Hugo and Jack brought up the rear. The TAC agent kept watch, glancing behind the group as they moved, waiting for the truckful of shooters to show themselves again.

"We can't be *that* unlucky, can we?"

"What?" Hugo asked.

Jack just shook his head, kneeling next to the others. They had stopped at the entrance to a rickety-looking dock. At the end of it was a trio of boats. One of them was currently occupied. They needed to subdue the man aboard and steal his POS watercraft. Because when there was a man, there were also keys—and last Jack checked—keys were good. Keys made mechanized thingamajigs go *vroom*. Jack volunteered to take the guy out. He did it mainly because he trusted himself not to kill the person.

"Stay here." Jack duckwalked to the front of the line. "I've got this."

He took off, keeping his footfalls light. When the lapping waves settled, so did he—but he didn't stop. He slowed to a brisk walk, moving heel to toe. The moonlight was just bright enough for him to see. He was also aided by a pair of mismatched lamps mounted on poles at the end of the dock. The lamps contained likewise mismatched bulbs—one a dull white and the other a dim yellow. In seconds, Jack had made it to a boat with a name that contained five words, and all in Spanish.

If Jack's translation was correct, he was pretty sure the watercraft was named after someone's whorish ex-wife...or possibly the name of the next Godzilla movie.

He timed his boarding with the motion of the dipping vessel. The fishing trawler was around thirty feet in length and contained a mess of nets and fishing rods and a single, rotted out wheelhouse. If he had to take a guess, it probably included a torn captain's chair and an instrument panel held together with nothing but duct tape. In the low light, Jack saw a keyring dangling from the person's belt.

It'll have to do.

Reaching up, Jack stumbled over a tackle box but still managed to wrap his arms around the boat owner's neck. The pair fell to the decking with a bang. Even while he choked out the local, Jack could hear the rest of his team pound down the dock to meet him. By the time they found Jack, he was buried beneath the body of an overweight, unconscious woman.

There were very few times Jack was as embarrassed as he was now. He released his grip from the female captain's neck and allowed the Arroyos to drag her off of him and onto dry land, but not before Hugo relieved her of her keys. The brothers dumped her onto the dock and then reboarded.

"Well," Hugo said, holding back a laugh, "that went well." He offered Jack his hand and helped him to his feet.

Jack pointed at the Arroyos. He gritted his teeth, warning them to keep their mouths shut. "Don't even think about it." Before anyone else could say anything, Jack shook loose a net from his foot and untied the boat. They quickly began to float away. Manuel didn't waste any additional time. He sprinted into the centrally located wheelhouse and started the trawler up, guiding it away from shore with little difficultly.

Once they were on their way, Jack, Hugo, and Miguel gathered near the ship's bow under the starry sky. Very little artificial light touched this part of the world. The only illumination was coming from a set of lights mounted atop the wheelhouse. They pointed out in front of the trawler. Manuel was using its yellow aura to guide them along.

Jack crossed his arms and asked the question that had been burning in the back of his skull. "Why do we need a boat?"

"The roads near Calamar have checkpoints that Aguilar controls. The waterways are still, somewhat, free of his reign."

"Military?" Jack asked.

"Yes," Miguel replied. "Our president has become very interested in what Aguilar has found here."

"Wonderful," Jack muttered, rubbing his forehead. Now, not only was he going to have to look out for Aguilar's people, but he was also going to have to be mindful of the Colombian Army.

This just keeps getting better and better.

Hugo nodded. "He's right, Jack. Ever since Aguilar discovered the site, he's taken over much of the town with the help of a general."

Jack walked over to the rail, tested its integrity, and leaned against it. "And you think we can slip in undetected on this rust bucket?" He patted the rail. His hand came away filthy, adding yet another layer of aggravation. Jack wiped it off on his jeans and listened to Miguel explain his plan.

"Boats like this still come in and out of Calamar with regularity. All we have to do is convince the guards at the docks that we—"

"Guards?"

Miguel nodded. "Yes, there will be guards."

"I thought you said the waterways were free of Aguilar's reign?"

"No," Miguel corrected, "I said they were 'somewhat' free."

Jack didn't recall that part of the conversation. He had been focused on the military part of the explanation.

"Right... Go ahead."

"If things haven't changed much, there will be two guards on the docks. One of them will be roaming around, inspecting the incoming boats. Another man will be stationed near the dock's exit onto dry land, checking people in and out as they come and go."

Hugo headed back into the wheelhouse and dug around in the dark for a moment. He was gone for less than a minute, coming back with a piece of folded paper and a grin. He opened it and held it out for Jack and Miguel to see. Jack flicked on a small flashlight and saw what had made his smuggler friend smile.

"Genius," Jack said, holding out his fist. Hugo proudly bumped it.

"Yes," Miguel said, nodding his agreement. "This will work just fine."

It was a work order of sorts for this vessel to transport gear to and from Calamar. Whoever their captain was, she had recently done work for Aguilar. As far as Jack could tell, there wasn't anything of value on board, though they hadn't yet searched the entire thing after *borrowing* it.

"Captain Carolina Lopez," Hugo read, looking over the document.

"What was her cargo?" Jack asked.

Hugo read the manifest to himself first before relaying his findings to Jack and Miguel.

"They called the haul 'collectibles.'"

"Collectibles?" Miguel asked.

Jack's eyes lit up. "From the excavation!" He slapped Miguel hard on the shoulder. "This *is* our way in." He quickly added his plan onto Miguel's. "At some point, Captain Lopez had taken her boat directly to the dig. You guys can pose as her crew."

"Us?" Hugo asked.

"Well," Jack said, winking, "you do look the part."

Hugo didn't understand what he meant.

Jack rolled his eyes and explained it plainly. "I'm a white guy from Wyoming. You're not."

Miguel didn't look so sure. "And what of the captain?" He motioned between him and Hugo. "We are not women."

Jack shrugged. "We'll figure that part out as needed. Maybe they'll recognize the boat and simply wave us through."

"Okay," Miguel said, taking it all in. "We'll go with this. We won't dock in Calamar."

"We won't?" Jack asked.

Miguel shook his head. "No. We bypass the docks altogether and head upriver to the excavation."

"We can do that?"

"Usually, I would say no, but we might be able to convince the security boat that we're merely on route for a pickup."

Ugh... Here we go.

"Security boat?" Jack asked, not liking the sound of it.

"Much like this one, yes. Except it has a machine gun mounted on its bow."

Jack blew out a long breath. This was getting more complicated as the minutes ticked by. He looked around, not sure what he was looking for. Crates of supplies dotted the deck, but nothing within them was going to help unless they were stocked with explosives.

"How far out are we?"

Hugo looked down at his watch. "Still a couple of hours."

The longer travel time didn't bother Jack. If anything, it would give them ample time to prepare and to rest. All four men were visibly tired—except for Manuel. Jack didn't think the guy ever needed to sleep. From his position inside the dark wheelhouse, Manuel was nothing but a shadowy wraith. His stoic presence was calming to a degree, but it was also chilling. Jack had known guys like him back when he had served. They all seemed like nothing more than quiet dudes until, one day, they snapped and went nuts. Jack took comfort in knowing that Manuel had, most likely, snapped a long time ago.

Miguel headed inside the wheelhouse to join his brother. Hugo and Jack searched the rest of the boat for anything useful. They stumbled over a pair of gaffs as they circled around to the stern of the trawler. Jack picked up one of the five-foot-long hooked poles and inspected it. The steel tip was still plenty sharp. It had also begun to rust right where it connected to the long wooden handle. There wasn't much else to see besides a pair of worn tailgate chairs and the previously discovered fishing rods and torn net.

Jack yawned and stretched his back, feeling the lower vertebrae pop and then realign themselves. He needed to get some sleep, even if it was only an hour's worth. He hated the idea of putting his guard down for that long, but he needed to continue to trust in his cohorts. They had proven themselves several times over that they weren't going to stab him in the back—not with something so profitable on the horizon.

He picked up one of the foldable chairs and placed it against the rear wall of the wheelhouse. Hugo took the hint and left him alone. Jack slumped into the chair and leaned his head back against the softly vibrating structure. It, and the gentle bobbing of the trawler, lulled Jack to sleep shortly after he closed his eyes.

10

Outside Calamar, Colombia

Several things awoke Jack from his nap. The vibrations coursing through the wheelhouse, and Jack's skull had stopped. The boat's engine wasn't running. As a result, he quickly picked up on the sound of a second watercraft coming in hot. Then came the shouts. Miguel was yelling for Hugo to do something in Spanish, and before anyone came looking for him, Jack leapt to his feet and rounded the wheelhouse. He nearly collided with Miguel as he came rushing out of the small structure.

Jack was waiting for the local to chastise him for his disappearance, but he didn't. Instead, Miguel shoved Jack into the building and told him to keep his mouth shut and stay out of sight. Jack nodded and entered, keeping his head down. The only other person inside with him was their group's impromptu pilot, Manuel. He glanced at Jack before stepping outside.

A boat ten feet smaller than theirs came barreling toward them. Even from this distance, Jack could see a single man standing on its bow, hands gripping the M2 Browning's spade-shaped handgrip. The .50 caliber machine gun could easily tear through Captain Lopez's trawler as well as everyone aboard it. There was no hiding from that thing if the person manning it decided to act.

"Son of a bitch," Jack said. He ducked lower. Only the top half of his head would be visible. He peeked through a fist-sized hole in the bottom half of the filthy windshield. The bow of their trawler was swiftly illuminated by two large spotlights mounted on the new arrival.

Hugo, Miguel, and even Manuel raised their hands in surrender before the security boat stopped. They knew the deal. These guys were coming in assuming they were up to no good.

Jack smiled when he saw Miguel hold out the old work order. He was shouting at the top of his lungs until the gunboat's pilot throttled down on his craft's engine. When he did, a short, thick man climbed up next to the gunner. His jungle camouflage top was unbuttoned, showing off a sweat-stained white undershirt.

Not to mention an impressive beer belly, Jack decided, dissecting the scene in front of him.

The man in charge, as well as his pilot and gunner, all wore the same military cammies. Indeed, the Colombian Army had sent soldiers down here to aid in Aguilar's search for El Dorado. It wasn't that Jack didn't trust what Miguel had told him. He just needed to see it with his own eyes first.

He quieted his mind and concentrated on the conversation happening outside.

Jack sighed. He didn't understand most of it.

Man, I really need to learn some more Spanish.

So far, Miguel had failed to convince the gunboat's captain to allow them safe passage. Hugo didn't know what he could add, so he decided to keep his mouth shut. Miguel could talk circles around anyone. It was a strength that Hugo had too, but not to Miguel's level. Miguel could be a true con-artist at times. Hugo was just a humble businessman.

Hmmm, Hugo thought. Maybe he could use that to his advantage.

"We'll make you a deal," he said, stepping forward.

The gunboat's captain stopped midsentence, shutting his open mouth. He waited for Hugo to continue. To do that, Hugo needed to come up with a plan on the fly. Luckily, he knew precisely what to offer them. These guys were Colombian Army regulars. It meant that they regularly went through hell and did so without making a lot of money.

Hugo held out his hand. "Give me that," he whispered.

Miguel did as Hugo asked and handed over the false work order.

Let's see how much these guys know.

"This," Hugo announced, "is a contract for us to pick up gold from the excavation." All three soldiers' eyes opened wide. Their reactions confirmed Hugo's suspicion. They weren't privy to what the dig site held. If he chose his next words wisely, they'd buy what Hugo was selling without argument. "If you let us pass, we'll give you each a healthy piece of the haul."

The short, sweaty captain stepped forward. "How much?"

Hugo glanced at Miguel. The Arroyo twin did his best to hold back his smile. He had to feign a cough to do so. Manuel was as silent and unemotional as usual.

Handing the piece of paper back to Miguel, Hugo stood tall. "You each get ten percent."

The captain turned and whispered to his men. After conversing with them, he spun and shook his head. "We want twenty."

"Absolutely not." Hugo laughed boisterously.

Miguel leaned in close. "We're running out of time."

Hugo nodded. He scratched his chin and nodded, pretending to be talking about something else. "I know, but we need to try."

He locked eyes with the sloppy captain. "Fifteen percent each."

"Are you kidding me?" Miguel turned and fake-argued with Hugo about how much he was offering the soldiers. He screamed about how unfair it was that they were paying these men nearly as much as they were about to make. Manuel did his part and growled, squeezing his fists so hard that his knuckles cracked.

Even though it was all an act, Hugo took a step away from the silent twin. He leaned closer to the gunboat and swallowed hard.

"How about thirteen?" He took another step away from Manuel. He looked over at the gunboat's captain. "I would take the deal." Hugo tipped his head toward Manuel. "My friend here, he, uh... Just take the deal, okay?"

Manuel stepped up next to Hugo, causing the smuggler to flinch and shrink away.

The gunner swung the M2 Browning toward Manuel but didn't fire.

"I wouldn't do that," Hugo said, gazing hard at the gunner. "Shooting him will only upset him more." He eyed the captain. "Thirteen percent. Take the deal."

Hugo's right leg bounced nervously. They were so close to freedom, but they needed the security team to go along with their farce. The sloppy captain turned and conversed with his crew. Midway through their conversation, Hugo spotted the pilot lifting and speaking through his radio. His eyes flicked back and forth between the console and Captain Lopez's trawler.

Not good.

Hugo knew the jig was up when the M2 Browning turned away from Manuel and was redirected to him.

"I'm sorry, my friend," the captain said, "but we have our orders. Intruders are to be terminated on sight, and—"

"We are not intruders!" Hugo shouted. "We are here to transport gold for Santiago Aguilar!"

The gunboat captain put his hands on his hips. "We have no such transportation scheduled tonight."

The portly fellow raised his hand and was about to order the gunner to open fire, but he never got the opportunity. The soldier manning the M2 Browning took an expertly placed round to his forehead. Hugo didn't know where the shot had come from. *Jack?* He drew his pistol, but it wasn't necessary. Miguel and Manuel took care of the gunboat's captain and the pilot before he could raise it.

Jack came running out of the wheelhouse, pointing at the drifting gunboat. "Don't let it get away!"

Hugo picked up one of the gaffs and hooked the handrail before it could meander off. Manuel took over and held the craft in place with his brute strength.

"Switch boats!" Jack shouted, leaping aboard the other vessel.

Hugo and Miguel were next. Manuel dropped the gaff after his brother slid in behind the steering wheel. He steadied the gunboat and allowed Manuel to climb aboard without issue. With Miguel in the pilot's chair, Jack, Hugo, and Manuel dumped the bodies overboard.

"Hang on," Jack said, taking position behind the .50 caliber machine gun. "Gotta take care of something first."

He racked the M2 Browning, gripped the dual handgrips hard, and depressed the butterfly trigger. The weapon came to life, and he shredded the fishing trawler. The effect was nearly instantaneous. Captain Lopez's boat listed hard and quickly sank.

Jack stepped away from the machine gun, met with the sour face of Manuel Arroyo. Hugo wasn't sure what was happening. He figured Manuel would've been happy, maybe even enthralled, with Jack's actions. Instead, he looked upset.

Miguel stood up but continued to pilot the gunboat. "Don't worry. He's just jealous of you."

Jack and Hugo's expressions changed from fear to confusion.

Miguel shrugged. "Manuel has never fired one of those before."

Jack grinned and gently patted the giant on the shoulder. "Don't worry, bud. I'm sure you'll get your chance."

From inside the wheelhouse, Jack had witnessed the gunboat's driver pick up his radio. Jack acted quickly, drawing his gun and aiming it through the hole in the windshield. The gunner would be first. It was an impulsive move, but it had to be done, even if there was no guarantee that the gunner would open fire. But as the minutes passed, it became more and more evident that the soldiers weren't going to let them pass without a fight.

The moment the gunner swung the imposing M2 Browning toward Hugo, Jack gently started to squeeze his pistol's trigger, stopping when the smuggler shifted his weight to the left—directly into Jack's line of sight. If the gunner opened fire, Jack's mission, as well as his and his team's lives, would be over.

Then, Hugo shifted his weight back to the right. *There!* Jack thought, getting his chance. The projectile buzzed over Hugo's left shoulder and struck the gunner in the head. Things went crazy after that. Luckily, the people he was working with weren't afraid to get their hands dirty. By the time Jack had exited the wheelhouse, the captain and the pilot were also dead.

The foursome was currently cruising toward a narrow tributary along the southern bank of the river. Unlike taking a ride on the highway, there were no signs out here on the water. You needed to know where you were going to get there. Jack turned and watched Miguel tap on a glowing screen.

Or you could have a navigation device.

"There is something up ahead," Miguel announced.

"How far?" Jack asked.

Miguel checked. "Fifteen miles—on the northern side."

"That's gotta be our excavation."

"I believe so. Okay, hang on," Miguel warned, "I'm going to open her up a little."

Manuel nodded, having already manned the machine gun. He used his lower half to successfully ride the rise and fall of the swiftly moving gunboat. He didn't even take off his backpack to do so. From the waist up, he looked as if he was riding a horse. Jack and Hugo joined Miguel around the single pilot's chair, clinging to the frame of its small canopy. Jack eyed the green screen of the navigation device as it read off locations and their coordinates. Hardly anything came up. The further they moved away from the outskirts of Calamar, the less there was to identify. Then, there was a long expanse of nothing except their own tiny green dot and the rivers themselves. They weaved through the chaotic *jungle* of waterways but steadily continued on an eastern trajectory. The GPS unit was the only thing keeping them from getting lost.

Up ahead, Jack spotted multiple sets of glowing dots—both on land and in the water. They were the eyes of the creatures that called the river home.

The motion of the gunboat skipping over the river's surface caused Jack's attention to fade. He thought back to everything leading up to this moment and was stunned at what he had learned so far.

And I'm still no closer to locating Matias or El Dorado.

Hopefully, the tomb at the heart of Aguilar's excavation would give them a little more insight into the City of Gold's location. Jack had his doubts, though. If the dig site had, in fact, provided the location, Aguilar would've already found it.

And is it really Diego de Ordaz's tomb?

Aguilar and his project leader seemed to think so. Whatever they had found at the site must've been enough evidence to identify it as such. Jack and the others had been so caught up in the mission that they had not properly inspected the photos on Jack's phone. The pictures of the map might hold some of their missing information.

He unlocked his iPhone and pulled up the first photo. The map—a piece of a much larger navigational chart—was incredibly detailed. Jack wanted to get these enlarged and printed one day. The next picture was that of the smudged writing. As Jack expected, it was in Spanish. Instead of struggling through the translation, he handed Hugo his phone.

"What does it say?"

Miguel's eyes darted back and forth between the water and Jack's phone. Hugo angled it lower so Miguel could see it better. He deserved to see it just as Jack and Hugo had. The three men conversed about what they saw and what it all meant.

"It says something about a place called the 'King's Room,'" Hugo said. "Also, it says that something called the Demon Heart guards it." Hugo tapped the bottom-left corner of the screen. "And here is Ordaz's signature. This unquestionably belonged to him at some point." Hugo's brow narrowed. "Where did a man like Aguilar get such a treasure?"

Jack and Miguel glanced at one another and recited the man's name in unison. "Suarez."

Hugo looked back and forth between them. "Who is Suarez?"

Jack shook his head. "We don't know, but I'd like to find out someday."

They quickly caught Hugo and Manuel up on everything Jack and Miguel had heard while spying on Aguilar.

"I would like to find this man too," Hugo said. "I want to know who is selling our history off to the highest bidder."

Jack might just take the man up on his offer.

"That is very honorable of you two," Miguel said, "but we have something else to take care of first." He pointed forward. Jack saw it. Sitting atop the pitch-black horizon was a light. As they approached, it grew in size.

The excavation was enormous.

"Holy shit," Jack said, seeing it for what it was. This wasn't just some two-bit operation. Jack thought back to what he and Miguel had heard while listening in on Agular's phone call. The drug lord had said that he had spent millions on this dig.

He wasn't exaggerating.

"Turn off the headlights and pull over up ahead."

Miguel nodded and did as Jack had said. He brought the gunboat over to the left-hand shore, grounding it on the first piece of cleared land he could find. Jack's eyes flashed down to the screen. The compass at the top of it said that they were still traveling due east, though this branch did turn south further ahead. After that, it was a messy spiderweb of offshoots.

And they aren't charted.

It gave Jack hope. No one in Aguilar's camp had made it any further than the excavation. If they had, they would've uploaded the locations into their shared mapping system. Regardless of their current position, they would huff it from here. The terrain was going to be terrible, but it would better than the alternative. There was going to be more than just three guys and a single boat here. From the looks of it, there was probably an army of workers and guards awaiting them.

Jack sighed. A wave of uncertainty washed over him.

This might not end well.

11

Aguilar's Excavation
15 Miles East of Calamar, Colombia

The bank was narrow and consisted of a bevy of broken tree limbs and clumsy wet earth. They tied off the gunboat to a healthy palm trunk and immediately got moving. For a moment, Jack had thought about sinking the vessel, as they had done to the fishing trawler, but he decided against it this time. If they needed a quick getaway—and an armed one at that—then they would have an option at their disposal.

Each of the four men held a flashlight low in the tall grass. Jack's was attached to the barrel of his M4A1 carbine. He kept it, and the barrel, pointed at the ground while carefully inspecting the terrain. He was 'reading the earth,' just as Bull had taught him. The Delta operator's training had seamlessly blended with the search and rescue aspects of his park ranger duties. Stutter-stepping, Jack held up a hand and knelt in the mud. There, just inches from his knee, was a track that sent a chill down his spin—not because they were in any real danger from it, but because he had never seen one out in the wild before.

Hugo joined Jack and peeked over his shoulder. He mumbled something in what sounded like Latin, when he saw what Jack was looking at.

"What?" Jack asked, glancing up at the smuggler.

"*Eunectes murinus,*" Hugo repeated, speaking Latin.

Jack didn't have time for this. "In English?"

Hugo's eyes met his. "Green anaconda."

The world's heaviest snake was primarily an aquatic hunter and reached weights above two hundred pounds. It had also been known to grow to lengths of nearly twenty feet. While it did possess a mouthful of dagger-like fangs, the green anaconda only used them as a tool to grip onto their prey before overwhelming them and wrapping its powerful body around its quarry to constrict—suffocate—them to death. Then, they swallowed the meal whole. Similar to Great White sharks, the anaconda had been labeled as a terrifying maneater while, in actuality, the extra-large serpents were very rarely the cause of a person's death.

Any other day, Jack would've killed to see one of the scaly monsters feed on a caiman or something like that. But now?

No freaking way.

He stood and started off again, doing his best not to accidentally step inside the coiled form of a living, breathing car compactor. Jack could've used a hug right about now. He would've liked to have someone hold him and tell him that everything was going to be okay.

Just not from an anaconda.

They picked up a game trail twenty feet from shore and followed it. Here and there, Jack heard a rustling of leaves and branches at the periphery of his light. It made sense since they were so close to the waterway. Rivers frequently saw heavy traffic from the fauna in the area. Whatever had made the path of crushed grass, it lived in the area. This was its home—its territory.

Please don't be a jaguar.

Thunder rolled through the rainforest. A storm was inbound. They moved in quickly down here. Jack remembered when a violent storm had hit him and his Delta team during an operation in Africa. It had been his first trip to the Dark Continent and a wet one at that. It had rained more than not during his stay.

Luckily for them, the rumble here was low and distant. They still had some time, but not a lot. The excavation looked expansive, but Jack prayed that the tomb itself wasn't. If they could get in and out without a lot of trouble, then they could make it back to their boat before they were hit by what he figured would be a torrential downpour.

The game trail veered off in the wrong direction, slowing them down significantly. Jack and the others were forced to high-step through the marshy undergrowth between the river and the tree line. It wasn't easy, but it was the fastest option. The trees were dense and contained entanglements of vines and roots. The water was the last possible path to take. The number of dangers lurking beneath its surface, in the middle of the night, were too many to count.

They moved in this manner for another hundred yards or so. Jack was the first to extinguish his light. The others followed his example. Together, they schlepped up a rise. The ground was already slick and nearly unnavigable. Jack couldn't imagine how bad it would get if, and when, it started to rain.

It probably did last night. Then again, the naturally wet air clung to everything.

Soon, the four men were at the peak of a tall hill. It overlooked the excavation as well as its entrance on the other side. Now, they had to somehow circumnavigate the entire dig site in order to enter the complex of tents and digging machines. Jack glanced back, unable to see what he was looking for. He visualized the game trail and the path of the river. Whatever creature had made the path, it had purposely steered around the bustling excavation. It was why the route suddenly darted off. The intrusive humans had moved in directly atop the animal's trail and its territory.

As far as the dig was concerned...

"Woah." Jack was impressed. He got down on one knee and took it all in.

Hugo knelt next to him. "I couldn't have said it better myself."

The rectangular excavation ran west to east, following along the edge of the river. Construction lights illuminated the grounds, much like the ones that were used throughout Aguilar's compound. And like the factory, this place was surrounded by razor wire-topped fencing. Jack estimated the cleared land to be the size of two football fields stacked next to one another. There were four large tents and various earthmovers—dump trucks, backhoes, and what have you—sitting between the eastern gate and Jack's position atop the hill.

And, of course, more soldiers.

They stood around and watched diggers shuffle in and out of a cave entrance directly below Jack and the others' feet. The team was nestled within a thicket of tall grass overlooking the action below. Even if they had the proper rappelling equipment, Jack would've advised against it. They would've been fish in a barrel if anyone with a gun had the wherewithal to look up. Staying low, Jack backtracked a bit, leading his team back down the embankment. Hugo stopped and headed south, in the wrong direction. Something in the dig had caught his eye.

"What is it?" Jack asked, following him.

They climbed back to the top of the rise but moved an additional one hundred feet to the south. The entire scope of the landscape changed. There was no grass here, and they now had an unblocked view at what Jack had previously thought was *just* a cliff face.

"It's a pyramid!" Jack said, stunned.

Hugo was equally as shocked. "A big one too."

Miguel and Manuel joined them. Their blank expressions matched those of Jack and Hugo. It was a sight to behold. The earth—dirt, grass, and trees—had reclaimed the ancient structure long ago. The slope they were currently on was the side of an ancient step-pyramid, not a naturally formed hill. Jack pictured its height and breadth and was amazed. It must've been enormous. So far, the entirety of the eastern face had been uncovered. Parts of the northern and southern faces were also exposed, but it was clear that the focus had been moved to the pyramid's contents and not the structure itself.

What a shame, Jack thought. He would've loved to have seen it in all its naked glory.

They descended the hill—the western side of the pyramid—and relocated the game trail. It led them around to the northeast corner and straightened out due east. They lost the dig behind the dense jungle—the light too. Jack switched his barrel-mounted flashlight back on and was startled when a snarling wraith jumped across their path. No one opened fire, thankfully. Even if someone had, they wouldn't have hit the jaguar anyway. In their combined light, the big cat showed off its power and agility by leaping onto the side of a thick tree trunk. Without pause, it scaled the growth with little difficulty. The four men stood perfectly still and waited for the predator to disappear back into the darkness. When it did, Jack released the breath he was holding.

"Okay... Well," Jack visibly shivered, "that was terrifying."

"Majestic too," Miguel added, still looking over to where the jaguar was last seen. "They were a symbol of power and strength in the ancient, pre-Columbian cultures of this part of the world."

"You could've been a historian, you know?" Jack said, stepping away.

Miguel stared longingly at the trees. It was obvious that the man loved history and nature and everything the two represented. So, why on earth did he get into the crime world?

"Why are you, well, you?" Jack asked, keeping his voice low.

Miguel turned toward him. The question came out wrong, but Miguel understood its intent.

"We do what we must at a young age to survive the streets. Not all of us grew up with the advantages of Bogotá's bustling business districts." He motioned to Manuel and Hugo. "We all grew up in the poor areas. Crime was an easy industry to slide into."

Hugo nodded. "Now, it's all we know."

"That's not true," Jack argued. "Everyone here has offered something different to his mission. The knowledge you two have on your country's history is awe-inspiring." He pointed at Manuel. "And you, well, you seem to be able to drive anything and can blow everything else to kingdom come. That's a skill in some professions. Believe me, I know. It's up to you to change. I walked away from the military because I made a choice." Jack turned away from them, took a step, but stopped. He glanced over his shoulder. "It was the right choice, but it was also an incredibly difficult one."

"Do you regret it?" Miguel asked.

Jack shook his head. "Not at all. Though, I do miss a few of the guys."

And with that, the group silently headed out. This time, they kept their lights on until they found an opening in the trees. After getting through the opening, they killed the lights and moved cautiously. Even though the excavation was lit up like a gaudy Christmas tree, they still needed to proceed with care. Any loud noise—any foul-up of any kind—could give away their arrival. Aguilar knew something was going on, but he didn't know what or who was responsible. Jack wanted to keep the man as confused as possible.

As he had done back at the compound, Manuel led the way and produced the foldable bolt cutters. He set about snipping the chain-link barrier one loop at a time. The perimeter was better guarded here than it had been at the factory. Every two or three snips, Manuel was forced to stop and take cover. Soldiers were combing the grounds, but they were doing so on a schedule.

Predictable, Jack thought.

Manuel got into a rhythm and finished cutting his way through. He left the right side of the square alone. It would act like a door hinge and hopefully give the illusion of nothing at all. They waited for the next guard to pass by before moving. Jack was the first through. He headed for the nearest cover—a dump truck—and slid beneath it with ease.

Another gunman strolled by. This one had a buddy walking alongside him. Hugo darted out behind them, keeping his footfalls light. He didn't make it to cover as gracefully as Jack did, but he still got there—and did so unnoticed—and that's what mattered most. Jack slid over to his right, toward the rear wheels, and gave the man enough room to roll underneath the hefty vehicle.

Miguel gripped his brother's shoulder and edged out into the dig site.

He hesitated for just a second and was forced to leap back through the cut opening. This caught the approaching soldier's attention, and he raised his rifle. Jack held his breath, knowing he needed to act. If the guy got too close to the fence, he would easily see their entry point. Jack held up his hand, telling Hugo to stay put. The smuggler nodded. Poking his head out, Jack confirmed that the coast was clear and then got to his feet. He matched the soldier stride for stride, and once the other man was close enough, Jack took off at a sprint. He collided with the guard's back and drove him straight through the chain-link flap. They landed together and rolled.

The soldier didn't stand a chance. Jack had planned on simply choking him out—not killing him.

Miguel and Manuel dove on top of the soldier before Jack could get to his feet. He died before Jack could get a single word off. The twins wiped their blades off on the man's clothing and sheathed their knives. The ferocity and quickness of the kill told Jack that the Arroyos might not ever be able to walk away from this life. Jack was trained to kill for his country—for freedom. Miguel and Manuel grew up killing people for their own selfish goals. Jack had never taken a life with that mindset.

He sighed. *But they had also killed to survive and protect one another.* That had to count for something.

Miguel dragged the body into the trees while Jack and Manuel reset themselves at the fence and did it all again. Eventually, everyone made it safely beneath the dump truck. From there, they would need to navigate the excavation as quickly and quietly as they could.

Jack moved first and rolled out of cover only to regain it again under a second dump truck. Hugo, Miguel, and Manuel followed him, and they were, once more, reunited. The next part was going to be tricky. Between them and the pyramid's entrance were three gigantic tents. They would either go around them or through them.

It was going to take a miracle for them not to get caught.

"So," Miguel said, "how are we doing this? I would like to avoid getting shot today."

Jack agreed. "You and me both."

Thunder rolled over the excavation, echoing against the exposed face of the ancient step-pyramid. Then, one by one, Jack spied large raindrops landing only inches away from his face, striking the earth with gusto. They gave Jack an idea. It was one that Bull had preached constantly back in

Yellowstone.

“Patience.”

“What?” Hugo asked.

Jack glanced back at his team. “We’ll wait for the weather to get nasty.”

12

In the rainforest, the weather didn't just get *nasty*. It got downright offensive. Occasionally, it got so bad that you'd think the planet had a personal vendetta against you. That's how Jack felt right now. Their position beneath the second dump truck must've been a low spot within the dig site because a muddy stream mixed with oil formed directly in front of him and his crew. The trickle morphed into a roar in seconds and spread the muck under the truck. Jack and the others were soaked, and they hadn't even been out in the rain yet.

Miguel growled and kicked Jack's foot with his own. "I blame you."

Jack didn't respond. He was too busy watching the soldiers scamper inside the tents for cover. And just like that, there was no one within earshot.

"Go!" he hissed. Jack crawled out from beneath their cover and took off at a dead sprint for a rectangularly cut hole in the pyramid's base. The rain was too heavy for him to get a good look at it. Was it as precisely cut as the rest of the structure, or had it been blasted open by Aguilar's men?

By the time they reached halfway across the expanse in front of the pyramid, Mother Nature had added erratically placed gusts of wind to her assault. Combined with the slick earth, Jack was having trouble staying on his feet. Hugo went down but was quickly scooped up by the Arroyos. Looking back at them was Jack's first mistake. His second blunder was lunging for the entrance. Jack's muddy boot hit the wet stone floor with zero traction. He lost his footing and went down on his ass, and jarred his lower back.

Then came the steps.

"Shit!" he shouted, riding them like some crappy funhouse slide. But before he could get too far, a pair of hands reached out and grabbed the straps of his shoulder holster. His bumpy descent suddenly halted. Just as they had helped Hugo up, Miguel and Manuel had stopped Jack from seriously injuring himself.

"Thanks," Jack said, slowly climbing to his feet. His back was killing him, but he would survive.

The corridor was tight and not built for people of Jack, Miguel, and Manuel's size. Hugo was fine. He could walk as upright as usual. The other three were forced to duck beneath the low ceiling. Jack slowly led them further underground. They kept their flashlights off until they were sure that they were out of sight. Then, one by one, they ignited them.

Better, Jack thought, picking up some speed. Still, he needed to be careful. His boots were a mess of mud and oil, and the stone was slippery.

"How far does this go?" Hugo asked.

"They can go on for a while," Jack replied, skipping a broken step. "Careful here."

"You..." Hugo grunted as he stretched his left leg over the crumbling stone. His smaller stature made the feat more difficult. "You have experience with stuff like this?"

Jack waggled his hand. "A little."

"Care to elaborate?"

"No," Jack replied, shaking his head.

Theoretically, Jack was free to talk about his adventures in Poland and Wyoming. He wasn't involved with TAC then. Now, he was sworn to secrecy regarding everything he found. It wasn't a cultish oath either. He had signed a Non-disclosure Agreement. No one outside of the Tactical Archaeological Command could know about his missions.

Except for Bull. Jack told his friend everything.

At the edge of his flashlight's reach, he spotted an opening. He wanted nothing more than to make a run for it. He badly needed to uncoil his sore lower back. But he put his practiced patience into motion and continued on at an even, steady pace.

Exiting the stairwell first, Jack was taken aback by how empty the tomb was.

"Uh..." he said, showing his light around the thirty-foot-square hand-cut chamber.

Besides a few skeletons dotting the floor, a handful of broken swords, and a dented helmet, there wasn't anything to write home about. The sarcophagus at the rear of the room had been opened. Jack and the others headed straight for it.

"Empty," Jack whispered.

"Did they take Ordaz's body?" Hugo asked, looking at Miguel.

Miguel glanced at his brother, unsure. Manuel shrugged, answering everyone's question. They had no idea what had happened to the Conquistador's remains. For all they knew, the bones could've been removed a hundred years ago.

No, I won't accept that!

The coffin itself was intricately designed but lacked anything else of significance. No gold. No jewels. Not even a corpse.

"Well," Hugo said, "Aguilar did say that he had wasted millions, right?"

Jack nodded. "Yeah, but I didn't want to believe it."

"So," Miguel said, "what happens now?" He thumbed over his shoulder. "Should we search the tents?"

Jack shook his head. "No." He wasn't giving up. "Search every square inch of this place."

"Okay," Miguel said, quickly doing a three-sixty. "Done."

Jack glared at him, and the local threw his hands up and backed away. "Fine, fine, but I don't know what you are looking for."

Jack sighed. "At this point, anything."

They spread out and combed the tomb. It didn't take long, as Miguel had so *hilariously* pointed out. Feeling defeated, Jack took a seat on a small ledge lining the foot of the coffin. He leaned his back against Ordaz's final resting place and closed his eyes, hearing a pair of feet stroll up in front of him. They stopped, but their owner didn't speak right away. Jack rubbed his forehead and opened his eyes. Hugo's attention wasn't on him. His eyes, and the beam of his flashlight, were focused on something between Jack's feet.

"Please don't tell me there's a snake or something between my legs."

Hugo shook his head. "No, look."

Jack did. He leaned forward and saw what Hugo had just discovered. Separating his feet more, Jack inspected a pair of grooves that had been cut into the floor. They were layered in grime, making it impossible to see without the aid of a light. Jack's mind leapt into motion, as did his body. He jumped to his feet, then knelt. Leaning in close, he took a deep breath and blew a puff of air into the nearest groove, uncaring that he was inhaling tiny particles of centuries-old grime. He coughed and leaned in even closer, nearly laying his cheek on the floor. The groove had been cut with precision. There was explicit intent behind its placement.

"It can't be..." Jack mumbled, climbing to his feet.

"It can't be what?" Miguel asked.

Jack whirled around on the sarcophagus and saw it with new eyes. He circled around to the other side and waved Manuel over. "Give me a hand, will ya?"

Manuel glanced at his brother. Miguel shrugged.

Together with the mute giant, Jack leaned into the coffin and pushed. Nothing happened, but Jack wasn't about to stop.

"Keep...going..."

"Oh, for God's sake!" Miguel blurted, stepping over to help. He and Manuel leaned into the outer edges of the coffin. Jack stayed sandwiched between them. Ordaz's empty sarcophagus started to move! Their combined strength had been enough.

"No way!" Hugo exclaimed.

"What?" Jack asked, in between breaths. "You've never seen a secret entrance...beneath a stone coffin...in the middle of a jungle...before?"

Face-flushed, Jack stepped aside and let the Arroyos finish the laboring job. If he had continued, he would've taken a nasty spill down the steps directly beneath him. Once the concealed passage was two-thirds of the way revealed, the sarcophagus stopped, unable to go any further.

Everyone except Hugo was out of breath, though he looked to be holding it now. Jack, Miguel, and Manuel took a minute to catch their air. The smuggler examined the entrance, showing his light all around the inside of the opening.

"I don't see much from here," he announced.

Jack pushed off his knees and stood erect. "No surprise."

Hugo gave Miguel a quick look before replying. "How do you mean?"

Jack stepped up to the opening and pointed his light down the steep, narrow shaft. "Whatever Ordaz hid down here must be valuable. Burying it up here, in the very first chamber, would've ensured its eventual theft."

"Makes sense," Hugo said, scratching his head. "Grave robbers can't rob you if there's nothing to take."

"*Nothing* is the ultimate deterrent."

As he had done so many times before, Jack led the way and entered first. He dragged his right hand along the ceiling, directly above his head. If Jack smacked his skull against the stone, at least his hand would be there to pad it. He pointed his small Maglite forward and down, keeping it on the steps directly in front of his feet. The only sound anyone emitted was their combined footfalls and their labored exhalations.

The ticking of dripping water disturbed Jack. The only thing that he could envision at the moment was the feeling of being deep underground with the room flooding. It wasn't the water that bothered him. It was the prospect of drowning in it that did.

His hand found the drip seconds later. The liquid was cold, and thankfully, not moving fast at all. It was a slow drip—nothing to worry about.

For now.

Eventually, the stone would wear down to the point of allowing a cascading stream to enter. One day, this whole place would be underwater unless the leak got plugged.

He heard Hugo shuffle his feet and groan. The drip had startled him.

"There's a leak," Jack said, too little, too late.

"Yes," Hugo replied, "I figured that out."

Another opening appeared at the edge of Jack's flashlight. He cautiously made his way to it, ducking under a low archway. On the other side, he unfolded himself, kneaded his lower back, stopping mid-rub. The next chamber was similar to the last one in that a coffin was situated near the back wall. But that was the only resemblance. This room was much grander—at least sixty or seventy feet squared with thirty-foot-high ceilings.

And it was plated floor-to-ceiling in gold.

Jack smiled. "Now that's what I'm talkin' about!"

"What is?" Hugo asked.

Jack stepped aside. "This."

Hugo's eyes went wide. "Oh, yes. Most impressive."

Miguel mumbled something in Spanish when he saw the gilded tomb. Manuel was silent, as expected. However, Jack was happy to see the boyish wonderment on Manuel's face. They all had that look.

The gold-plating reflected the beams of their combined flashlights so well that it lit up the chamber as if it had electricity. Beautiful artwork covered the walls and ceiling. Jack didn't understand most of it. The script was in a different language—and it wasn't Spanish. The hieroglyphs weren't even those of the Maya. Jack had seen enough of their language and art to recognize their handiwork. No, this was something else.

And at the rear of the tomb was something no one could've anticipated. Instead of artwork, the entire back wall had a map carved into it. Jack didn't know the country well enough to identify one riverbend from another. They all looked the same to him. He hoped that one of his three partners would understand what the hell they were gawking at.

Huh, a map led us to another map.

They were, quite literally, connecting the dots. Ordaz had separated the key and the lock well. He didn't want anyone to have all the information without looking for it with a fine-toothed comb. Jack's eyes fell from the wall-sized map to the sarcophagus. Like everything else in the tomb, it was made of gold. The value of the room must've been massive. *Even though it's totally empty, otherwise,* Jack thought. There wasn't a single piece of anything else lying around. The treasure here was the chamber itself.

"So," Jack said, heading off, "did Ordaz highjack someone else's tomb?"

"I'm not sure," Miguel replied, looking around. "If so, who was that someone?"

"What about the language? Do you guys recognize it?"

No one answered him.

But then, for the first time, Manuel spoke. "Musica."

Huh, he does sound like Elvis.

"Right!" Miguel said. "They were one of the four advanced civilizations from this area, along with the Maya, Aztec, and Inca."

Jack had heard the name before but didn't know much about them. "And the Musica people are significant to the El Dorado legend because...?"

Miguel smiled. "Jack, they *are* the legend. They are the ones that would cover their kings in gold dust and offer tributes to their goddess. When the Spanish came, they had heard of a City of Gold. Some scholars believe that it was a ruse to mislead the Spanish."

"Mislead them from what?"

Miguel grinned. "I'm not sure, but I think that the Musica people were hiding something extraordinary."

Hmmm. But what?

Miguel stepped closer to the sarcophagus. "This is positively Ordaz's tomb. His name is engraved below the lid." He squinted, reading something else. "Hmmm."

"What is it?" Jack asked.

"There's also a date."

Jack stepped up next to him. "And that troubles you?"

Miguel pushed off his knees and faced him. "Ordaz died in 1532, yet this is dated nineteen years after that."

"He faked his death?"

Miguel nodded. "To continue his search."

"Look," Hugo said, pointing to the far right-hand portion of the map.

Imbedded in the gold was a huge diamond. It was the only non-gilded item in the entire room. It must've been significant, or the builders wouldn't have included it in the design.

"I know where that is," Miguel said.

Jack stepped in front of him. "You do?"

He nodded. "Yes, our grandfather once told us about a place across the border. It's in a remote area of the Amazon in Brazil. He said it was a dark place. He said that no one who goes there ever returns."

"Sounds lovely," Jack replied. "Where is it exactly?"

Miguel looked genuinely frightened, but he bucked up and explained. "I should be able to input the location into the gunboat's navigation device, though there's no telling what awaits in between."

"It's a risk we'll have to take," Jack said, not liking the uncertainty.

"What about that?" Hugo asked, pointing at the oversized sarcophagus. Jack hadn't realized just how big it was until now. It was roughly twelve feet in length and as tall as he was.

Jack removed his phone from his pocket and snapped a few pictures of the map. He shook his head. "I seriously doubt we can remove the lid—even with the four of us pushing. That thing has to weigh a ton."

"And worth millions," Miguel mumbled, staring longingly at it.

Jack opened his mouth to say something, stepping back as he did. When his foot struck the floor again, something beneath it gave off a resounding *clunk*. He looked down and was startled when the area dropped a few inches. Then, like two sides of a vise, a pair of thick plates slid into view and ensnared his ankle. He fell to the ground and grabbed at his limb. The bone didn't break, but it did hurt like hell.

The room rumbled.

"Uh, guys?" Jack said, looking up.

They followed his gaze. The ceiling was slowly beginning to descend.

The weather had worsened significantly. The four large tents at the center of the excavation were jam-packed with people attempting to escape the storm. The only thing they had to worry about was the wind. If it picked up anymore, they could be in jeopardy of losing the structures. They were heavy-duty, built to withstand a beating, but not like this.

"Sir!" one of the soldiers shouted. "We've lost communications. The antenna has been knocked out."

Aguilar waved the man away without looking at him. He was staring at his backlit map. It depicted every known location within a hundred miles of the site. His project leader had said that the pyramid had been built by the Musica, which was odd since they weren't known to build grand stone structures. But nor was the pyramid that of the Maya, Aztec, or Inca. If the Musica people had erected it, then it was an anomaly.

"Or maybe," Aguilar said to himself, "history is wrong."

The ground beneath Aguilar's feet began to shake. Everyone stopped what they were doing and looked at one another for an answer. No one provided an explanation, except for a lone soldier in the far corner.

He yelled. "Earthquake!"

Aguilar gripped the sides of the light table and held on, riding it out where he stood. Others dashed outside to avoid being buried beneath the tent if it were to collapse. More and more of his men scrambled for cover.

But Aguilar didn't.

He looked up from the table and then back through the door. Something about the whole event felt off. It didn't feel natural. Something was causing the earth to shake, and it wasn't nature.

No, he thought, *this is something else.*

13

"Get me the hell out of this thing!" Jack shouted, trying desperately to yank his foot free. The rectangular plates didn't budge, though. No matter what he did, he couldn't get his boot to pop free.

Miguel and Manuel dug their fingers into the gap that held Jack's foot and pulled. Even with their combined might, they could only get the plates to fractionally separate. It wasn't enough. Jack was still stuck.

"Give me your rifle!" Miguel yelled. Jack unslung it and handed it to him.

Miguel shoved the barrel in between the plates and pushed.

"Do me a favor," Jack said, sweating hard, "don't shoot my foot, will ya?"

Miguel removed the weapon and ejected the magazine. He also manually removed the round sitting idle inside the upper receiver. Then, he rammed the barrel back into the gap and shoved. Manuel joined in the effort. Slowly, the plate began to move, but not fast enough. The ceiling was nearly halfway to them. It slipped past the map and the other walls freely. Jack also saw that it contained a cutout that was shaped precisely like Ordaz's sarcophagus. None of the priceless relics would be disturbed. The chamber's emptiness made perfect sense now. Everything that didn't belong in the room was meant to be turned into paste.

Jack continued to watch the ceiling lower while the others worked on his ensnared foot.

The plates shifted again and, miraculously, they didn't disengage. It seemed that, however much they moved them, they wouldn't automatically recoil back into place.

"Hugo," Jack said, sitting up, "help me with my boot. Get it off."

The smuggler nodded and dove into the gap. Jack felt Hugo work on his shoelaces. The compression around Jack's foot lessened some, but not the pressure around his ankle. He sighed. If the others stayed to help him, then their fates would match his.

"Go." The Arroyos stopped, as did Hugo. They all looked down at Jack. "Unless we cut off my foot, I'm not going anywhere by the time that thing crushes us." He pointed straight up. The ceiling was two-thirds of the way to them.

"No," Hugo said, "we will not leave you behind," he looked back and forth between the twins, "right?"

Miguel's eyes found his brother's, and both men stepped toward Jack, as opposed to the door. They weren't leaving him behind.

Huh, I guess there is honor among thieves, after all.

Manuel slunk out of his backpack and produced his trusty bolt cutters. He unfolded it and pointed its tip down at Jack's ankle. Jack grew nervous as the big guy stepped up to him.

"I was, uh, just kidding about the whole 'cutting off my foot' thing."

With zero emotion, as per usual, Manuel acted. He squeezed the handles of the bolt cutters tight, lifted them high over his head—tip down as if he was about to drive a stake through Dracula's heart. He brought it down on one of the plates. Beads of sweat rolled down Jackula's temple. Manuel struck the stone over and over again until a crack appeared. As he drove the bolt cutters into it again, Jack felt his foot shift. He tried yanking it free but couldn't—not yet.

Manuel was exhausted and gasping for air. Miguel tapped his shoulder and held out his hand, tagging himself into the fight. He took over. Miguel wasn't as thick as his brother, but he was still plenty strong.

"I don't mean to sound ungrateful," Jack nervously said, "but please hurry."

The ceiling was only ten feet above their heads now, and they were still sixty feet away from the one and only exit. Even if they got Jack free, it was going to be a close call.

With one final *whack*, the bolt cutters broke, but so did the stone plate! Jack wriggled free and climbed to his feet, limping hard. Miguel dropped the busted bolt cutters and ran for his life. Manuel was in hot pursuit, as was Hugo. Jack was still trying to get the feeling back in his lower leg and was having trouble keeping up. Hugo stopped to help him but was waved on.

"Don't—go!"

The ceiling was so close that Jack almost scraped the top of his head on it. He ducked down to avoid it. His lower back barked along with his left ankle. He was ten feet away from the exit when he fell. He clawed and scraped at the gilded floor, but his hands found no purchase. Spent, he glanced over his shoulder and closed his eyes. He was so close, but it wasn't enough.

A pair of hands reached out. Jack was pulled through the opening with a yelp of surprise just as the ceiling connected with the floor. He didn't care that he was lying atop Hugo—his rescuer—like a newborn baby. Jack stayed put and caught his breath, feeling the smuggler's—his friend's—chest rise and fall.

Jack was winded but managed a "Thank...you..."

Hugo gently patted the top of his head. "You're welcome."

Both men looked up the stairs but didn't see the Arroyos.

"Where are Miguel and Manuel?" Jack asked.

Hugo sat up, and together, they stood. "I'm not sure. Last I saw, they were running for the surface."

"Why?" Jack asked.

He got his answer moments later. Everything around them began to shake once more.

"Oh, hell no!" Jack shouted, pushing Hugo up the steps.

The local's short stature made the hike much easier on him. Jack was hustling along as best as he could. He kept moving, though. He had no intention of finding out what was about to happen next. The quakes grew to a crescendo by the time they reached the first chamber. Neither man paused to catch their breath. They ran straight for the next set of stairs and bucked up it.

Jack focused on the next step in front of him and nothing else. He was thankful to still have his small Maglite, though he had been forced to leave his rifle behind. They were too busy trying stay alive to remember it. Gratefully, Jack still had his shoulder holstered pistol and his knife.

They climbed higher and higher. Jack could make out the white noise of falling rain. The entrance into the pyramid was just up ahead. Thunder rolled through the tunnel. If it were possible, the storm sounded like it had gotten worse. Jack didn't care, though. As long as they got out and then got away, he didn't care how wet he was going to be.

Jack and Hugo spilled out of the ancient monolith, sliding through a shallow pool of mud. Hugo landed facing the pyramid. Jack didn't. He watched as several armed men came rushing out of the two closest tents. They didn't seem to notice the pair of intruders floundering in the muck. *Not yet*, Jack thought, knowing what he had to do. He stood and cringed. His ankle was sore as hell. Luckily, it didn't feel broken. Still, they needed to get away before they were spotted.

To their right was a row of oil barrels. They led around to the back of one of the structures. Hugo was only a few feet from it. Jack made a decision he hoped he wouldn't regret. He grabbed Hugo by the back of the shirt and shoved him forward. The smuggler fell head-first and clumsily slid behind the barrels just as the first soldier spotted Jack. He quickly threw up his hands in surrender. Hugo crawled forward but was shaken off. Jack nonchalantly waved him away.

Hugo didn't budge. It was admirable of him. He didn't leave Jack to die in the tomb, and he wasn't about to leave Jack now. But Jack needed Hugo to stay alive. If anything, he could contact TAC and let them know what had happened to him.

Matias too.

In the pouring rain, Jack was surrounded by a dozen gunmen. Some were Colombian military. Others were private contractors—mercenaries. All of them carried assault rifles with barrel-mounted lights. Jack was nearly blinded when they all turned on him. The two men at the top of the semi-circle stepped aside and allowed a well-built, spectacle-wearing gentleman through. He looked out of place, but Jack knew he wasn't. Jack knew exactly who *he* was.

Santiago Aguilar.

Jack slowly lowered his hands as the drug lord approached him. Aguilar was unarmed, not that he needed a gun. He had twelve of them at the ready. Jack was smart enough to avoid going for his weapon. It would've been a death sentence if he did. This was a battle he wasn't going to win with sheer brawn.

I'm going to have to figure something else out.

He and Aguilar were roughly the same size and weight. If this was a one-on-one fair fight, Jack knew he could take him, but bad guys didn't fight fair—ever.

"Hello, my name is Santiago Aguilar, and you...you don't belong here."

Jack shrugged, eyes darting from gunman to gunman. "I went out for a late-night Taco Bell run and got turned around."

"And that?" Aguilar asked, pointing to Jack's gun.

"You can never be too careful. There are a lot of assholes out tonight."

The corner of Jack's mouth turned upward. If he were standing next to himself, he would've given himself a high five for that one.

Aguilar's face hardened. "You find all of this funny?"

"Sorry, it's been a really long day—like Zack Synder's Justice League long. I get punchy when I don't go to bed at a decent time." Aguilar stepped closer. "But to answer your question... Yes, I do find all of this funny. I find it hilarious that you would willingly kill your golden goose." Jack stood tall—confident. "I'm your ticket to El Dorado."

"Liar!" The speaker was out of sight, coming up behind Aguilar. The gunmen's lights made it difficult for Jack to get a good look at the new guy until he marched right up beside Aguilar. "He knows nothing. He's just trying to save his own skin."

Aguilar turned away from the newcomer. "Excuse my rudeness. Let me introduce my project leader. This is Lorenzo Matias."

Matias! Jack was stunned. *So, he is a traitor.* But he hid the emotional outburst and shrugged it off.

Jack tipped his chin. "How's it hanging?"

"Is he correct?" Aguilar asked. "Are you lying to me and my men?"

The latter part of the question sounded like a threat.

Jack needed to convince them that he was valuable, and he knew exactly what to say.

"So, how 'bout that earthquake. Weird, huh?"

Aguilar's stern expression flipped to one of intrigue. He relaxed a bit. "Okay, I'll bite. What was it?"

Before he told them, Jack needed to divide and conquer.

"Why doesn't your know-it-all project leader tell you?"

Aguilar glanced at Matias. The turncoat stepped away from Aguilar and glanced back and forth between his boss and Jack.

"How could I possibly know what—"

"See," Jack interrupted. "I can tell you. Would you like to know too, Mr. Matias?"

Jack recounted precisely what had happened, excluding his team's involvement. He told Aguilar everything, leaving no stone unturned. He even mentioned the pictures of the map he had taken. His word wouldn't be enough. He needed to provide proof, and the images on his phone were that proof. If he wanted the drug lord to trust him enough not to kill him, he needed to come clean.

Aguilar didn't say anything.

Jack pushed him. "It looks to me that you require an upgrade to your project leader position. Your current guy seems a bit inept."

"Shut up!" Matias shouted. "You are nothing!"

"Am I?" Jack asked. "Then how come I've found more in the last hour than you have in the last month?"

Matias lashed out and kicked Jack in the stomach. Jack fell to his knees, gasping for air—and he didn't fight back. Jack needed Matias to look like the guy in the wrong here, not him. If Jack wanted to slide into the role of project leader while also staying alive long enough to screw Aguilar over, then he needed to play ball.

"I think I've struck a nerve." Jack laughed off the blow, coughing and inhaling greedily. He looked up at Aguilar. "You said you spent millions on this, right?" Jack got to his feet. "How much more are you willing to fork out with inferior help leading the way?"

"I am not inferior!" Matias shouted, drawing his pistol.

"Enough!" Aguilar boomed, burning holes in Matias.

Both Jack and Matias quieted. Aguilar was in charge here, and Jack needed to stay in his good graces. It was obvious that the guy was already thinking over Jack's proposal. He was desperate to find El Dorado. But was he desperate enough to put his faith in a man that had just broken into his dig site—the same man that had also killed several of his men and destroyed a large chunk of his factory?

Aguilar's eyes opened wide. "So, you were in my office?"

Oops. Jack winced. He shouldn't have mentioned that Aguilar had spent millions on the operation. He had said that while on a private phone call in his office.

Jack came clean. "Yes, that was me."

"And my factory?"

"Um," Jack said, "there were other parties responsible for that."

Technically, Jack wasn't lying. He didn't physically have anything to do with the explosives that decimated Aguilar's compound. And as far as Jack knew, no one outside of him and Hugo knew the Arroyos were involved. Their presence here was still veiled.

"Hugo Nunez," Matias said. "It has to be."

Jack needed to deflate that thought. "Come on; Hugo? I mean, he's your best friend—well, he was anyway. Do you honestly think a nice guy like him could do all that?"

Aguilar didn't speak.

Matias was going nuts. "You can't seriously be thinking about trusting him?"

"As of now, I trust no one. But he's right. He has found more in the last hour than you have in nearly a month."

Matias looked hurt...and angry. He squeezed his fists and stepped toward Jack, looking very ready to hit him again.

Jack had enough of him. "Touch me again, and I'll put you in the ground."

Matias's expression transformed from rage to uncertainty.

"Who are you exactly?" Aguilar asked.

"Call me Jack."

"Jack what?"

He shook his head. "Just Jack."

Aguilar relaxed his posture. "Well, 'Just Jack,' I must ask. What is in this for you?"

Jack shrugged. "That's easy. Don't kill me."

Aguilar stepped up close to Jack. Now, he was only feet from him. "Unfortunately, that is something I cannot guarantee you."

Jack winked. "Don't worry, pal. After all of this is over, we'll be laughing it off over an ice-cold *cerveza*."

Aguilar actually cracked a smile. "You are a very confident man, Jack."

"You have to be in my line of work."

"And that is?"

Matias stepped around Aguilar. "You're Jack Reilly, aren't you?"

Jack snapped his attention to Matias. The only way he could know his name was if he still had contacts inside TAC. That mole would have to be dealt with when he got back.

If I get back.

"You were sent here to rescue me, weren't you?" the traitor asked, smiling wide. He was enjoying the moment.

Jack had no reason to lie. "We were worried about you."

"I'm sure you were," Matias snorted. "How are Raegor and Eddy, anyway?"

"They're good."

"And where's my friend, Hugo Nunez? I expected to see him here as well."

Jack shook his head. "He's not here."

Matias smiled. "You're a terrible liar."

Now, it was Jack's turn to smile. "And you're an asshole."

He looked at Aguilar and thumbed over to Matias. "See, I told you they were out tonight."

Matias launched a straight punch at Jack's face. The former Delta operator expertly ducked it, side-stepped his aggressor, and kneed him in the stomach. Then, Jack brought his elbow down on the base of the man's skull. Matias flopped to the muddy ground. Jack and Aguilar stood over him, watching him roll over onto his back with a groan.

"So," Jack said, speaking to Aguilar but still looking at Matias, "do we have a deal?"

Aguilar eyed him. "You've proven to be a very capable man, Jack Reilly, but," he snapped his fingers, and Jack was swiftly apprehended and disarmed, "let's see how much else you know."

Jack didn't like the sound of that. "But I thought we were on the same side now? What about the ice-cold *cervezas*?"

"For now, yes, we have aligned interests, but I also want a little retribution for the damage caused to my facility." Aguilar spoke to the soldiers holding Jack's arms. "Bring him to my quarters. I'll handle his interrogation myself."

14

Hugo watched a man step around Aguilar. His identity, however, was still a mystery to him. The gunmen's lights were making it difficult to see anyone's faces. But whoever he was, he was someone important. Like Aguilar, he carried no weapon.

"Excuse my rudeness," Aguilar said. "Let me introduce my project leader. This is Lorenzo Matias."

Hugo's world came crumbling down. His childhood friend had been working against them—for the man responsible for his sister's death. It took everything within him not to step out and shoot both men. But if he acted too rashly, he and Jack would also die. If he died because of his thirst for vengeance, then so be it, but Jack's fate shouldn't be tied to that decision too.

"And where's my friend, Hugo Nunez?" Matias asked. "I expected to see him here as well."

Jack shook his head. "He's not here."

The American had just lied to protect Hugo. It was a gesture that he wouldn't forget.

Hugo waited to move. He thought about heading back to the hole Manuel had cut in the fence but refrained. It had probably been discovered by now. No, Hugo would have to find another way out.

Jack was marched away from the pyramid.

Staying low, Hugo followed them from afar, remaining behind the row of oil barrels. Jack had saved his life after pushing him behind them. If Aguilar had spotted Hugo, he would've surely executed him on the spot. Hugo wondered whether or not Matias would've stepped in on his behalf.

Lorenzo... Hugo thought. He couldn't believe it. His close friend had betrayed him—Jack too.

Hugo continued behind the first tent, stopping when he reached its edge. He leaned out and took in the action. Several soldiers had been ordered to stay in the rain instead of being allowed to seek shelter. Two men escorted Jack into a smaller tent on the other side of the excavation. There was nothing Hugo could do for Jack. He looked around, hoping to spot the Arroyos hiding somewhere. But they were gone.

"Where are you?"

The wind picked up again. It allowed Hugo to make a run for the next tent. The soldiers at the center of the dig cowered away from the conditions, covering their faces. He ran and slid to a stop, taking a minute to collect himself. He was close to the excavation's front gate now. Oddly, it had been left unguarded. Exploiting the opportunity given to him, he stayed low and headed for the exit, quickly slithering between the sagging chain-link gates. The gap between them was just large enough for a grown man to fit through.

Hugo slipped on the wet earth but stopped almost immediately. His foot struck something as soon as it lost traction. He knelt and examined the find. The grass concealed it to his right. He flicked on his flashlight, covering most of its beam with his other hand, and was startled to discover the body of one of the soldiers.

A hand wrapped around Hugo's mouth. Its owner swiftly dragged him deeper into the trees. He tried to fight against his abductor but was unsuccessful. Whoever had apprehended him, the individual was freakishly strong.

A second light blinked to life.

"Shhh. Easy, my friend. It's us."

Miguel?

Manuel released Hugo and nodded to him. It was the closest thing to a hello, or possibly even an apology, that Hugo would get. The smuggler wheeled around on Miguel and berated him.

"Friend? You left Jack and me to die!"

Miguel put a finger to his mouth and led his brother and Hugo deeper into the growth. They kept their flashlights covered and continued.

"That was self-preservation. We had no chance."

Hugo knew he was right. He was just angry at what had recently transpired.

"Lorenzo is a traitor."

Miguel nodded. "We know. We saw him walking with Aguilar before they confronted Jack."

Hugo chuckled, feeling exhausted. "You must be loving this."

Miguel's face soured. "No, I would never wish this upon you." He sighed. "We all used to be friends—you, me, and Manuel. When are you going to trust us again?"

Hugo's shoulders dipped. He had instantly thought the worst about them. He was so sure that they had ditched him and Jack. In reality, they had escaped as soon as they'd been given a chance. If not, they might have been caught and most likely killed.

"I'm sorry. I do trust you." He patted Manuel on the shoulder. "You too."

"Good," Miguel said. He turned to leave but was stopped by what Hugo said next.

"I'm going to have to trust you for us to rescue Jack."

Miguel looked at his brother. Then back to Hugo. "Excuse me? Did you say that we are going to rescue Jack?"

Hugo nodded and hiked back up to the road. "We owe him that much." He pointed through the gates, back toward the tent that Jack had forcefully entered. Its lights came to life at that moment. "No one deserves what awaits him." He turned and faced the Arroyos. "After Aguilar gets what he wants, he'll kill him."

Something awful was about to happen—something Jack had never experienced a day in his life. He was about to be tortured for information. Then, if life could get any crueler, he was expected to work for the torturer. Jack didn't know which was worse, torture or being forced to submit to the person responsible. It's not like Aguilar had some psycho asshole that was the "torture guy." Aguilar *was* the torture guy! He truthfully was the judge, jury, and executioner.

They stripped off Jack's shirt and threw him up against an upturned metal bedframe. It was straight out of a scene from Rambo: First Blood Part II. In that movie, John Rambo had been tortured with electrocution by Lieutenant Colonel Podovsky.

"You know," Jack said, trying to make light of the situation, "if you have any Jiffy Pop pans, now's the time to break them out."

"Always a joke with you," Aguilar said, flicking on a switch. A large steel box to Jack's right powered on, humming loudly.

He smiled nervously, trying not to show his fright. "Seriously, all you'd have to do is hang one around my neck like Flavor Flav, and *pop*, movie time!"

Aguilar stopped what he was doing and gave Jack a look that questioned his sanity. Jack's adrenaline was pumping as hard as ever. He'd need it to survive what Aguilar had planned for him. The drug lord adorned a pair of thick rubber gloves and picked up a set of worn jumper cables. Whatever this device was, it was plain to see that it was homemade.

You didn't typically find stuff like this on Amazon or eBay. Aguilar connected the ground to a random steel rod next to the power box and then held up the *hot* end in front of Jack's face.

"What should we talk about?"

The red end of the jumper cable was so close to Jack's face that his eyes crossed while looking at it. "Favorite nineties hits? You look like an *MMMBop* kind of guy to me."

Aguilar growled and clipped the jumper cable on the frame, sending a jolt of torment through Jack's body. He experienced a pain like he had never felt before. Getting shot had never felt so good until now. Then, just like that, it was gone. Aguilar removed the red clamp from the frame, but he didn't put it down.

"Okay, okay..." Jack gasped. "What do you want to know?"

Aguilar shrugged. "Nothing I don't already know." He leaned in close. His breath smelled of methylated cigarettes. "I want to watch you squirm."

Jack looked up at the ceiling and closed his eyes. "Squirm. Yeah. No problem."

Aguilar hit Jack again. It lasted only a second, but like before, it was a pain that no man should ever have to endure.

Except for, maybe, Aguilar.

"How," Jack said, barely getting the words out, "does someone...turn out like, well, you?"

Jack was surprised when Aguilar didn't quickly reattach the jumper cable. Instead, the psychopath set it down and opened a bottle of water. Jack stared longingly at the drink and was stunned when Aguilar offered him some. Jack accepted the tip of the bottle as if he were a helpless calf. At the moment, he felt like one.

He's trying to keep me alive, Jack thought. Aguilar wanted to hurt him—not kill him. *Well, he's succeeding.*

Aguilar sat on a barstool, facing Jack. Jack could've lashed out and kicked Aguilar in the face but didn't. His legs felt like Jell-O. He was too weak and knew such an act would lead to nothing except more torture.

"Like your friend Hugo, I grew up on the streets of Bogotá. But unlike him, I didn't have a loving mother and father." His eyes locked onto Jack's eyes. "I watched my father shoot my mother in the head, in cold blood. Then, he stared at me as he took his own life."

Geez. No wonder this guy is so screwed up.

"My older brother couldn't handle what happened, and he left one night. I haven't seen him since." His head dropped, and he stared at the floor. "I was seven when all this took place."

Jack sighed. "My parents died when I was six."

Aguilar looked up at him with watering eyes. "How did you get through it?"

Jack couldn't believe that he was having a heart to heart with the man who had been torturing him. He was okay with it too. He would do whatever he had to do to keep himself from being electrocuted again.

"My grandparents took me in and raised me."

Aguilar nodded, understanding. "My grandparents died during Chavez's reign in Venezuela. The only family my brother and I had left was here in Colombia."

"Who cared for you?"

Aguilar looked away from Jack.

Damn, Jack thought. *He raised himself—on the streets.*

"I'm sorry for your losses."

Aguilar stood and picked up the jumper cables. He faced Jack. "Me too."

Everyone within earshot heard Jack's shrieks, including his team who were just outside the perimeter fence. Jack's cries broke something inside Hugo. He openly wept for his new friend. Miguel's hand found his shoulder. Neither Arroyo showed the emotion that Hugo was showing, but it still pained them to hear Jack suffer.

"Come," Miguel said, "I have a plan." He pulled Hugo away from the gruesome scene, and the trio headed back toward the water, eventually picking up the same game trail they had used earlier. They followed it back to the gunboat and pushed it off the shore and back into the water. With Manuel at the helm, Miguel explained what he was planning.

"Head upriver. Keep the lights off."

Manuel nodded and got them moving. They chugged along and headed around to a makeshift dock that had been built on the northern shore. There were already four other boats tied off there. The gunboat was one of Aguilar's and would blend in just fine. Manuel slowed them to a crawl and maneuvered the craft in line with another similar vessel which was also armed. Hugo and Miguel quickly tied them off. The trio then crept up the dock toward the front entrance to the dig site.

"Okay," Miguel said, kneeling. Hugo and Manuel followed his example and ducked down. "We each have to take out one of Aguilar's men and replace them. Luckily, we're all locals and fit the bill."

Hugo nodded.

Miguel unsheathed his knife and held it up. The moonlight reflected off of the steel. Hugo's eyes locked onto its smeared surface.

"Hugo." He looked away from the blade and returned his attention to Miguel. "Can you take a man's life with nothing more than your hands because we're going to have to be quiet for this to work?"

Hugo swallowed and nodded. "Yes."

Miguel gave his brother a quick look and tilted his head toward the excavation. There were two plain-clothed men currently guarding the docks. *Mercenaries,* Miguel thought. One turned and looked their way, just now noticing their arrival. He slapped his partner on the shoulder, getting his attention.

"Stay hidden," Miguel said, "these two are ours."

Hugo nodded and climbed back into the gunboat. He got low enough that only his head could be seen. Miguel and Manuel vanished in the blink of an eye. Just as they began to move, a pair of flashlights bloomed to life further ahead. Both men leapt onto the decks of adjacent boats and hid. The gunmen sauntered forward, conversing in low, hushed tones. They hadn't noticed where Miguel and Manuel were hiding.

Good.

Miguel could just make out their words.

"That storm was crazy," one of them said. "I'm soaked!"

"Yeah! Thankfully, it has slowed," the other man replied.

Their radios squawked to life.

"Dock team. Be on the lookout for intruders. We believe that the American was not alone."

The guy on the right answered. "Copy that. Over." He waved his partner on. "Come on. Let's recheck the docks."

Damn, Miguel thought. Their plan was about to get infinitely harder. So, Miguel changed it. He held out hope that most of the men here didn't know each other all that well.

"Manuel, follow my lead." It was time for Miguel to do some talking.

He stepped out of cover and climbed back onto the docks. His brother did the same thing, and a pair of bright lights instantly accosted them. They lifted their rifles and stopped.

"Who are you?" shouted Righty.

"Where did you guys come from?" Lefty asked.

"Woah, there," Miguel said. He stepped forward. Manuel did too. "Do you know who you almost shot?"

Righty and Lefty gave Miguel a set of confused looks.

"We are Santiago's cousins." The twins took two more steps closer. Now they were within ten feet of the mercenaries. Miguel stuck out an accusatory finger at Righty. "Do you know what would've happened to you if you had pulled that trigger?"

Righty glanced at his partner. For a second, both men dipped the barrels of their rifles. "But we were told to look out for intruders."

"Not us, idiots!" Miguel roared.

Lefty stammered back, further away from them.

Not good.

Miguel raised his hands and apologized. "I'm sorry. It's been a crazy night, no? What—with the break-in here, and the attack back at the factory..."

"The factory?" Righty asked. "What happened at the factory?"

Now, I've got you. These men hadn't been informed of what had taken place in Puerto Esperanza. Miguel had just used it to his advantage.

"Yes, an attack. Many of our men perished. Him..." he said, pointing toward the dig site. They took two more steps forward. "The American killed our friends—our brothers!"

Lefty was pissed, but Righty didn't look like he was buying the act. Miguel and Manuel took one last giant step toward the mercenaries. If they acted fast enough, they could reach them both before the gunmen opened fire.

But Righty stalled their approach as he asked a question that Miguel had no answer to.

"How did you get here?"

Miguel laughed and glanced at his brother. He tipped his head toward the gunmen. "How did we get here? You hear that? He asked us how we got here. It's simple, really."

"Yes?" Righty asked, slowly raising his rifle.

"We swam!"

Miguel kicked the barrel of Righty's AK-47 away. Manuel lowered his shoulder and bulled into Lefty. Miraculously, no shots were fired. Miguel disarmed Righty by quickly drawing his knife and slashing at his lead arm. The mercenary's reaction was to defend himself with the rifle, using it as a bow staff. Miguel, once more, went for his appendages—this time it was the man's fingers. He connected and forced Righty to relinquish his weapon. That was all Miguel needed to finish him off. He leapt inside his range and drove the blade deep into his gut.

After the third such strike, Righty was dead.

Manuel had his man in a rear chokehold. He dropped Lefty while Miguel cleaned off his knife on Righty's pant leg. Both men quickly began to gather the guards' belongings. As they did, a third light flicked on. Neither twin had noticed the man that was coming down the embankment to check on the dock team. He was as surprised as the Arroyos were. Lefty Jr. fumbled to bring his rifle up. It had been laxly slung around his shoulder as he discovered the gruesome scene. Neither Miguel nor Manuel was quick enough to act.

But Hugo was.

The smuggler rushed in, moving extraordinarily fast. He ducked his head and took the third gunman off the ground. Both men went down but rolled to their feet and squared the other up. Hugo had his back to the twins, making it impossible for either of them to line Lefty Jr. up in their sights.

Taking a page out of both Hugo and Manuel's books, Lefty Jr. ran at Hugo and pushed him back toward the water's edge. Hugo tripped on a loose plank and fell. He grabbed a hold of the third merc's shirt and brought him along for the ride. The pair plunged into the murky river. The depth was shallower near the shoreline. Neither of the men fully submerged. Hugo landed atop Lefty Jr. and used his position of leverage to his advantage. He seized the gunman by the back of the head and pushed.

The mercenary's reaction was instantaneous. He thrashed as if someone was attempting to drown him, and for a good reason because someone was doing just that. Hugo shouted and cursed at the guy, tossing every expletive he could muster. It was an atrocious act, but Hugo was victorious in his efforts. Miguel and Manuel met him down on the shore. While Miguel checked on Hugo, Manuel stripped the dead man of his possessions. Then, he dragged the body beneath the dock.

"Well, my friend," Miguel said, nodding his approval, "that's one way to do it."

15

Jack fell to the floor of Aguilar's tent as he was released from his bonds. He was barely cognizant and in excruciating pain. Jack also had a numbing sensation throughout his extremities. It was the oddest feeling he had ever experienced. His bare back felt like it had been torched.

Two men entered the structure.

"Clean him up. He's no use to us dead." The soldiers rushed over and plucked Jack off the floor like a ragdoll. He allowed them to manhandle him, mainly because he didn't have the strength to fight back.

He mumbled something incoherent.

Aguilar removed his glasses and turned around, wiping his face with a towel. "Excuse me?"

"Valentina."

The drug lord paused mid-wipe, replaced his glasses, and faced Jack. He got close and leaned into his face.

"Never say that name."

"Why not?" Jack asked, feeling like a bobblehead.

Aguilar snarled and punched Jack in the stomach. The air left Jack's lungs. He would've collapsed if Aguilar's henchmen weren't supporting his weight.

Jack blinked away unconsciousness. "You loved her, didn't you?"

Aguilar went to hit Jack again, which proved the point he was trying to make. Instead, Aguilar balled his fist, but relaxed. He, once more, removed his glasses and wiped off his sweaty face.

"My feelings are inconsequential. She is dead, and nothing will change that."

The way he said, "my feelings" and not "what I used to feel" struck Jack.

He still loves her.

It was clear to Jack that Aguilar blamed himself for her death. Hugo held him responsible too. It was becoming more and more palpable that Aguilar was, indeed, accountable for the woman's death—more than Jack had initially believed. He had blamed Valentina more than anyone. Personal choice was king, not the pressures of your peers. But in this case, if the two had been that close and deeply intimate, then maybe it wasn't all on her.

"You're going to pay for this—all of it."

Aguilar put his spectacles back on and smiled. And it wasn't a happy smile. His stare was blank as if he was living in both the present and the past. He was thinking of Valentina.

"We will see. We will see..."

Aguilar barked a string of rapid-fire Spanish at the soldiers. They nodded and removed Jack from the tent, dragging him across the excavation. The rain had nearly stopped, but there was just enough to repeatedly strike Jack's aching back. The cool water on his overcooked flesh calmed him some. It relaxed him so much that he almost passed out in the soldiers' arms. They dragged him into a second tent and laid him down on a cot, placing him on his side. As instructed, one of the men cared for Jack's wounds, slathering a white goop on the injuries. Jack didn't feel any of it. He was out cold. His body and mind had gladly accepted exhaustion.

Jack awoke the following morning in the same position he had been placed—not that he remembered any of it. Keeping his eyes shut, he stayed still and listened, mentally examining the room. Jack was able to pick up on random noises that bled into the tent from the outside world. Men were shouting, and machinery was being moved. In Jack's opinion, it sounded like Aguilar's people were leaving. The information Jack had given them had been enough for Aguilar to decide to move onto the next phase of his plan.

El Dorado.

"You can open your eyes now. I can see that you're awake."

"How'd you know?" Jack asked, drawing open his eyelids.

Lorenzo Matias smiled at him. "Your breathing changed."

Jack sighed, lying still. He didn't know the state of his back, and he wasn't in the mood to find out yet.

Matias was sitting on a wooden folding chair six feet in front of Jack. He had watched Jack while he slept. The former TAC agent had done exactly what was expected in a situation like this: Never watch a person's physical movements—or lack thereof—to confirm whether the other person was asleep or not. Focus on the individual's breathing instead.

"Great. You. I was hoping it was Aguilar."

"Why?" Matias asked, leaning forward on his knees.

"Because he's not a backstabbing liar. I know where he stands."

Matias huffed and got to his feet. Jack decided it was time to get up. He would rather do it himself—at his own speed—than have someone tear him away from his relative comfort and pain-free state. *Huh?* Jack felt surprisingly good.

He inquired about it. "What did they give me?"

"A topical remedy," Matias explained.

"A topical remedy?" Jack asked, pushing himself up. The skin on his back was sore but nowhere near as bad as he thought it would be. It felt like he had been given nothing more than a bad sunburn. Jack's shirt hung on a hanger dangling from the low ceiling of the tent. He stood to retrieve it, cringing, but not from the burns. His lower back was still killing him from the fall inside the pyramid's entrance.

He slipped his shirt off the hanger and noticed a small, wall-mounted mirror. Turning, Jack inspected the damage and was shocked to find very little evidence of the torture. There was a small amount of scarring but no welts or blood. Whatever concoction they had given him, it had healed him in a way that no modern medicine should've been able to.

Impressive, he thought, carefully putting his long-sleeve thermal back on.

"Aguilar keeps the good stuff to himself," Matias explained, stepping around the cot. He grinned. "He's not only in the narcotics business, you know."

Jack had figured Aguilar was involved in some shady stuff. The steroidal injections his men had given themselves outside Abuelita's were proof enough. And now, this magic ointment. Jack was beginning to feel like Sean Connery in the Medicine Man. The world's rainforests have been known to contain fruits, flowers, and roots able to treat all sorts of ailments. In the acclaimed adventure drama, Connery's character, Robert Campbell, successfully found a cure for cancer but was having trouble synthesizing the serum. During the film's climax, Campbell discovered that an indigenous ant species that lived on the flower, not the flower itself, was responsible for the lifesaving properties. It wouldn't have shocked Jack to know that Aguilar had gotten a hold of something similar and had not revealed it.

The morning sun hurt Jack's eyes and his brain. It seemed that the ointment did, in fact, only work on his skin. He needed a handful of ibuprofen and a cup of strong black coffee to get the feeling of a hangover to subside. He sighed. Jack doubted there was any of either around here.

He followed closely behind Matias. A detail of two armed soldiers picked them up but hung back some. They were giving Jack some leash, not that he had anywhere to go if he escaped. He didn't know where he was. Even if he found a boat, Jack doubted he could get back to civilization without some assistance.

Where are you guys? Jack asked himself, searching for any signs of his crew. If they were smart, they would've left him here and scrammed. *Fat chance.* Since they hadn't left him below in the golden tomb of Diego de Ordaz, then they weren't about to ditch him now. Jack was confident in that. They were out there somewhere. Plus, there was the whole thing about getting rich.

Matias led Jack over to an open-topped Jeep. They climbed in and were whisked away, straight through the wide-open front gates. Not everyone left with them, though. It looked like a team was staying behind to continue to work on the excavation. The wealth beneath the surface was absurd. Aguilar would've been a fool to leave it behind.

Jack just realized that he had forgotten to mention the pressure plate trap to Aguilar—the cause of the earthquake. *Oops.* He shrugged and hoped that there were more traps to come. That room was way too big to have just the one. What if two people triggered them at once? Jack and the others had been fortunate to activate only the single plate.

He lowered himself into the seat behind the driver. Matias sat up front. Beside Jack was a thick, powerfully built mercenary. He was a monster—bigger than Manuel even. The ride back to the river was a short one. It only took them a couple of minutes. The tree line had been forcibly cleared, and a makeshift docking system had been installed over the water's edge. Five boats in varying shapes and sizes were parked there. The largest of them was also the newest looking. Jack's Jeep parked in front of it. A well-dressed, spectacled man exited the wheelhouse to greet them.

"Good morning, Jack." He grinned. "You seem well."

"Yeah, I'm surprisingly okay, I guess. Besides the kidnapping and torture, of course."

Aguilar's right eyebrow rose. "I thought we were working together now?"

Jack rolled his eyes. *Just you wait...*

The boat was similar to Captain Lopez's trawler, only larger, and it had a machine gun mounted on its roof. The weapon was a newer version of the one Jack's gunboat had possessed.

He lifted his leg to board the vessel and noticed something that made him smile. *His* gunboat was tied off at the end of the dock, and there were three men busily working on something aboard it. If Jack had to guess, the trio didn't belong to Aguilar's crew.

"What's so funny?" Matias asked, noticing the smirk.

Jack stood. "I was just thinking of you wallowing in the mud like a pig. How's the neck, by the way?"

Matias squeezed his fist.

"That's enough, you two," Aguilar said. "If we're going to find El Dorado, we're going to have to play nice."

Jack gave Matias a wink and stepped away, heading for the stern of the boat. He crossed his arms and watched as they pulled away. They slowly bypassed two other vessels and took the lead. As they did, Jack gave the three men aboard the gunboat a small salute. He couldn't see their faces from here, but he recognized the Arroyos' bald heads and muscular builds, as well as Hugo's stockier physique.

Their presence gave Jack the ace up his sleeve he desperately needed. And when the time was right, he would gladly draw it. Until then, patience would be paramount. The trek was going to be a long one, from the looks of it. Six heavily armed men and four gasoline barrels accompanied Aguilar and Matias aboard the vessel. The barrels were a clue that Jack picked up on to learn that they were in for a long-distance trek.

A figure stepped up beside Jack. He glanced over and saw that it was Matias. Jack had to know why he betrayed TAC.

"Why did you do it?" he asked, keeping his eyes on the landscape.

Matias turned his back to the railing and leaned up against it. "Have you ever fought for something for so long that you questioned whether or not you believed in it anymore?"

Jack knew what he meant, but he wasn't going to give the man the satisfaction of agreeing with him. Instead, he stayed quiet.

"Raegor and TAC believe that history is sacred—and I respect that. But I also see it as a way to increase the size of my bank account. I've seen so much wealth in my time with TAC and have very little to show for it." He turned and looked down into the water. "El Dorado will change that."

"That's awfully selfish."

Matias leaned sideways with his elbow against the railing and looked at Jack. "Not everything is about honor and integrity, Jack. We—humans—are inherently self-centered creatures. I'm just following my instincts. You,

Jack, are the oddity here, not me."

Jack nodded, looking out into the trees as they passed by them. "For once, we agree on something."

They traveled like this for hours on end. The sun had begun to set before Jack finally picked up a chair, spun it around, and sat, propping his feet up against the railing. With that, he shut his eyes and decided to get some additional rest. Whatever concoction they had given him to heal his body had done very little for his mind. Jack was still exhausted. Trouble was on the horizon, and he needed to be at his best when it reared its ugly head.

The chugging of the engine and the rocking of the boat gently coaxed him into a beautiful siesta. He had no idea how he was going to find El Dorado—or if it even existed. The diamond embedded in the wall of Ordaz's tomb was pointing them to a specific location deep in the Amazon. Was it the City of Gold, or was it something else altogether?

Jack had no idea what time it was when he awoke. That was the least of his worries, however. The cries of men on the defense caused him to leap to his feet and reach for his gun. But he didn't have one. One of Aguilar's men had confiscated it. Automatic gunfire erupted, aimed at the tree line to the north—to Jack's right. He spun and ducked as a projectile whizzed past his head. He followed its path and was stunned to see an arrow embedded in one of the soldiers' chests.

What the hell?

Bullets were sporadically fired into the trees. Jack tried, but he couldn't see if the rounds were doing much of anything. To Jack, it seemed like a waste of ammunition. If it were up to him, they would've sped up and left the aggressors in the dust. He didn't mention it. Instead, he kept his mouth shut and his head down. Sometimes the "thinning of the herd" was a good thing.

But the arrows kept coming. Whoever these people were—these natives—they were well-armed and came to play with solid numbers. Jack scrambled across the deck of the boat and dove behind a barrel of gasoline. It wasn't the greatest of places to hide, but he was confident that it would hold up against simple arrowheads.

Matias had taken up position behind a similar barrel. Jack spotted Aguilar just inside the wheelhouse. He was armed. Everyone was, except Jack.

"Give me my gun!" Jack shouted, spotting his pistol in the back of Matias' pants.

Matias scoffed at the demand. "What? No!"

Jack turned to Aguilar. The drug lord had overheard his demand. He locked eyes with Aguilar and yelled, "You need my help!"

Matias glanced over to his boss.

"Do it!" Aguilar shouted.

The TAC traitor growled and reached around to the small of his back and pulled the Glock 19 free. He tossed it to Jack with a venomous glare. The former Delta operator plucked the weapon from the air, racked the slide, and swiftly popped up to one knee. Movement caught his eye. He squeezed off a pair of rounds, timing the trigger pulls with the rise and fall of the boat. The aberration was knocked back, just as a trio of arrows whizzed past him.

He dropped back down to his butt, startled when the volley took down a second soldier. Two struck his chest, and a third hit him in the gut. He fell to his knees, catching a fourth arrow just below his Adam's apple.

Jack was about to reengage but didn't. Aguilar finally ordered his pilot to speed up. They quickly left their attackers behind, slowing down a mile further downriver. Jack, Matias, and Aguilar assembled around the first soldier who had been injured. The other man was already dead, lying in a pool of his blood. The first one was sitting up against the railing on the other side of the deck. Surprisingly, he appeared to be in pretty bad shape even though he had only taken one arrow in the shoulder.

Matias produced a knife and cut free a section of the man's shirt. After just a few minutes, the wound, as well as the skin around it, started to blacken. Darkened blood vessels became clearly visible beneath the soldier's skin.

"What the hell is it?" Jack asked, stumped.

Matias was quiet. He had no idea.

"I've heard stories," Aguilar said.

"What kind of stories?" Jack asked, watching the soldier's breathing rapidly increase.

But before Aguilar could explain, the soldier broke into a fit of wet coughs. His eyes rolled into the back of his head, and he slumped to the side. The arrow had killed him in a matter of minutes.

Aguilar carefully plucked an arrow out of the rail behind the dead soldier and examined its head. It was slathered in a black, inky substance.

Jack knew it was some sort of poison, but what? He had never heard of something capable of killing a man *that* fast.

"It is said to derive from the toxic skin of a rare species of poison dart frog."

"A poison dart frog?" Jack asked. "I mean, sure, they're deadly, but not like this." He pointed to the blackened wound. "You typically have a few hours to seek medical attention after any contact with the poison, not minutes."

"Trust me," Aguilar said, "I've researched this."

Of course he has. Jack could only imagine what a man like him would do with a synthesized version of this stuff. He had already experimented with pain-suppressing steroidal injections. Why not a quick killing venom too?

"It means we're close," Matias said.

Jack agreed. The fact that a tribe would come out of the woodwork like this told him that they were most likely guarding something that they valued immensely. They hadn't come here to wound anyone either. They had come to kill the intruders—Jack and the others—not drive them away. Luckily, Aguilar and his team had modern weaponry on their side. But this was the natives' territory. Everyone aboard the small convoy of boats was at a serious disadvantage. Jack's survival skills were about to be tested, as were his combat abilities.

He turned and faced Aguilar. "I'm going to need more than just *this*." He held up his sidearm. Before Matias could object, Jack slipped the firearm into his empty shoulder holster.

Aguilar was smart enough to know that arming his captive wasn't a good idea, but he was down by two men and would need all the help he could get.

The drug lord spun and glanced at Matias. "Do it. Give him what he wants."

Jack crossed his arms in victory as Aguilar re-entered the wheelhouse. Matias wasn't happy, but nor did he defy his boss' orders.

"Fine," he said, jaw tight. "Follow me."

16

It wasn't much, but Jack was given a like-new AK-47, along with a couple extra of its signature banana-shaped magazines. The rifle was currently slung across his back. The ammunition went into a canvas pouch on his hip. Jack also received a machete. It, like the Kalashnikov rifle, was on his back, safely sheathed in a protective scabbard. Last but not least, Jack received a walkie-talkie, clipping it to his belt. The device contained ten channels to communicate through.

"Channel one is off-limits, except to Santiago and me," Matias explained. "Channel two is for everyone else." Jack nodded, grinning. "What?"

"You must hate this."

Matias growled and shoved past him, stomping away. Jack didn't react. He was enjoying the show of petulance too much. Jack's presence threatened Matias. He had exposed the man's ineptitudes at every turn, showing Aguilar that he was better at Matias' job than he was—as a hostage, no less. Jack had willingly offered to help Aguilar, but there were no illusions about what was going on. Jack would only be useful until they found El Dorado.

Jack stepped up to the bow of the boat. He refrained from whooping into the air and shouting, "I'm the king of the world!" The breeze whipping by him felt great. He closed his eyes and enjoyed the moment, dissecting the smells and sounds of the remote jungle atmosphere. His radio crackled to life, causing him to sigh in disappointment. He unclipped it from his belt and lifted it to his ear.

Everything was in Spanish, but he did recognize a few words.

"*Un día más,*" the speaker announced.

Jack's shoulders slumped. If his translation was correct, they still had another full day of travel to go before they reached their destination. Typically, Jack didn't mind being out in the middle of nowhere for days on end. This was a different situation, though. It was an environment he had been trained to survive in, but not one he was particularly familiar with or fond of. Jack had spent most of his military career in the Middle East's sunbaked deserts, not the wet rainforests of South America.

He was comfortable with the desert's arid, scorching days and its cold-ass nights. Even now, Jack had done very little physically in over a day's time, and yet, he was drenched in sweat and exhausted. The temperature wasn't the problem here. It was the ungodly thick, equatorial air. Unless you were a native in a loincloth, you didn't belong here.

Jack looked down at his clothing and sighed. He was clammy, but at least he was covered. The bugs in this part of the world were as vicious as the people that had just attacked them. The insects weren't picky, and they took no prisoners.

The river widened a bit up ahead. Situated directly at its center was a jagged rock taller than their boat. It resembled some space-age shark fin—slicing through the ever-growing current.

Growing current!

Jack spun in time to see the other soldiers disappear behind the wheelhouse. Jack instantly knew what was coming. Men shouted in fright all around him. Jack ran for the back of the wheelhouse, staying calm while doing so. He planted his back against the wall but had nothing to hold. He looked up and grabbed the edge of the wheelhouse's roof. It would have to do.

The bow of the boat tipped forward, causing the stern to rise. Every part of Jack's body clenched in response. After tilting to a near forty-five-degree angle, they quickly righted and leveled-out as the front of the hull struck home. The waterfall was short but still dangerous enough to capsize a vessel of this size. Jack blew out a long breath and glanced to his left. Matias was also plastered against the back wall of the wheelhouse. But Aguilar's project leader looked infinitely more scared.

Jack laughed and playfully nudged him with his elbow. "Woah! Did your butthole pucker too?"

Matias didn't think the latest events were worth giggling over. Jack had learned to laugh-off danger—it was his natural reaction to do so. But that didn't mean his adrenaline hadn't spiked. His skin was still broken out in goosebumps. The rush—the high—was all the same for him. Matias staggered away and wretched over the stern railing.

Jack turned to the nearest soldier, motioning to Matias. "Probably doesn't like rollercoasters either."

The soldier couldn't hold back his smile.

A pop and a bang startled Jack. Thick black smoke billowed out from the rear of the boat. Something devastating had happened to the engine. Without it, they would be set adrift at the mercy of the river. A pair of men came rushing by Jack, headed straight for the damaged engine.

More shouts arose and got Jack moving. He headed back around the wheelhouse, finding Aguilar standing at the bow of the boat. The drug lord lifted his walkie-talkie and started yelling into it, pointing straight ahead while he spoke. Jack stepped around him and figured out why he was so frantic and heated.

There was another waterfall up ahead.

And from the sloshing, rushing water, it must be a lot bigger.

And we have no engine.

"Can we tie off somewhere?" Jack asked.

Aguilar shook his head. "How? We have no engine or oars, and the trees are too thick. There's nowhere to go!"

"Do we abandon ship?" Jack asked. He wasn't a sailor. He was unsure of what to do. Aguilar didn't answer him either. The man's eyes were locked onto the precipice up ahead.

The power of the river revealed itself and began to spin the boat. The pilot tried desperately to keep them straight but was having trouble doing so. Their speed picked up immensely. If they were going to abandon ship, it was too late now. Jack was a strong swimmer, but even he wouldn't be able to fight the raging waters beneath his feet. If he entered the water now, Jack would surely drown before being tossed like a ragdoll over the falls. So, he headed for the bow's railing and held onto it with all his might. Jack wanted to see it coming. When the time came to act, he would do whatever he needed. Either way, Jack knew he needed to separate himself from the boat before they hit. Timing the division was going to be the tricky part.

"You're really going to do this, aren't you?" Jack asked himself, laughing at the ridiculousness. "You're going to leap from a boat while it tumbles over a waterfall in the middle of a godforsaken Colombian rainforest?"

He didn't get to answer his own questions. The edge of the falls came quickly. Jack locked his right ankle around the rail post, feeling his body being lifted away from the much heavier boat as it fell. There wasn't anyone else on the deck with him this time. Either they were in the wheelhouse—a soon-to-be watery coffin—or they had all gathered along its back wall again. They, once again, passed the forty-five-degree mark. But this time, instead of the boat leveling-off, it kept going.

This was one of the craziest things Jack had ever done. He'd been transformed into the figurehead of Aguilar's vessel. In a matter of seconds, Jack gauged their height and his potential landing spots. He waited to see if the boat tilted to one side or the other. It did! The stern of the ship started to edge right. So, Jack readied himself. Just as the entire boat slipped off the waterfall, Jack unwrapped his ankle from around the rail post. He lifted his foot and planted it on the banister. Then, he shoved, jumping as far to the left as he could.

Jack and the vessel went their separate ways. Each fell a good thirty or forty feet before they both pierced the surface of the large plunge pool below. Jack entered feet-first. He tucked his arms into his chest and straightened his body into the aerodynamic shape of a torpedo. The boat, however, wasn't so agile. It clumsily crashed into the sloshing waters, landing on its side with a thunderclap of splintering wood.

Fully submerged, Jack stayed under until he calmed down. He also wanted the debris to settle before swimming through a sea of serrated shanks. The last thing Jack needed was to get an arm-sized fragment of wood in his eye while beneath the surface.

Nearly out of breath, Jack decided to surface and survey the scene. When he did, he was immediately forced back under. Jack kicked as hard as he could—straight down—chased to the bottom by the shadow of a second free-falling boat. He struck the floor of the shallow-ish plunge pool in seconds. Turning around, Jack watched the smaller vessel slip through the surface. Its pointed bow nearly made it down to him. He witnessed the pilot smash against the inside of the windshield as his momentum was violently halted. If Jack had wanted to, he could've reached out and touched the tip of the boat's hull. Its buoyancy took over, and it began to rise. Jack didn't, though. He waited, dumbfounded by the events of the last few minutes.

Finally, he pushed away from the floor of the plunge pool and surfaced. The smaller of the two boats had fared better than Aguilar's vessel. His had been completely obliterated from the hard fall, settling against the right-hand shoreline. It lay on its side, showing off a pair of prominent fractures in its hull. The wheelhouse had been split open like a burst soda can. There were no signs of movement. Jack doubted that everyone aboard had died, but he was confident that people had, in fact, perished. The damage to the boat was too significant.

Jack swam over to the boat just as a body was swept further downriver. There was also another man lying down face-first in the shallows. Neither were Aguilar or Matias. Both of the men wore military fatigues. Jack sloshed to confirm the second soldier's fate. He checked for a pulse and found none.

Jack waded onto shore and fell to his knees. His body was still in shock over the entire ordeal. He took in a few breaths to regain his composure before struggling back to his feet. Miraculously, he still had all of his gear. Both his AK-47 and his machete were strapped to his back, and his Glock was still tucked under his arm. Besides being waterlogged, Jack was okay.

The same couldn't be said for Aguilar's men.

Jack rounded the capsized boat, beholding a grim scene. Another of the soldiers was slumped forward but still in the air. He had been thrown from the ship but never landed. A large, spike-like chunk of wood had been driven deep into his chest, exiting through his back in a bloody, gory mess.

There was still no sign of Aguilar or Matias. Had Jack hit gold? Were the drug lord and his hound dog dead? A rustling sound picked up somewhere inside the wheelhouse. Jack stopped and reached for his pistol, stopping when he saw that it was Aguilar. Miraculously, the man's glasses were still on his face. He was drowsy, and the left lens was cracked.

"Matias?" he asked, spotting Jack.

"No idea," Jack replied, tossing his hands up. "You're the first person I've seen alive."

Aguilar staggered out of the diagonal structure. "How many dead?"

"Three or four so far," Jack replied. "Two boats as well." It took everything in him not to draw his gun and shoot the bastard in the head. But Jack needed help. He wasn't going to find El Dorado alone. Plus, Aguilar's brain contained a wealth of knowledge on the subject.

Aguilar turned and looked back up the falls. He raised his radio and attempted to hail the others. While the expedition's leader tried to contact his men, Jack searched the area for survivors. He spotted the second boat, resting up against the opposite shore. It was fully capsized. Two soldiers knelt in the sand nearby. They were tending to a third, presumably injured, man. The pilot was, no doubt, dead. Jack had watched it happen while he was underwater.

A moan caught his attention, as did movement. Matias sat against the opposite side of a nearby tree. He was holding his side, desperately trying to stymie the blood flow. The amount was nominal, which was good. But in an environment such as this, any minor injury could turn into a fatal one in time.

Matias spotted Jack. He shut his eyes and leaned his head back against the tree. Jack stopped a few feet in front of his toes but didn't say anything.

"Enjoying the view?" Matias asked.

Jack crossed his arms. "Not at all. None of this is fun to me. Even an asshole such as yourself getting hurt doesn't *amuse* me, in the least." Jack scratched his head. "Is it bad?"

Matias shrugged. "I'm not sure."

Jack grumbled out a curse and kneeled. "Let me have a look."

Matias nodded and allowed Jack to inspect the wound. Something had slashed Matias' side—probably shrapnel from the boat. Whatever had caused the injury; it wasn't present now. The cut itself wasn't all that deep, but it was long and would still need to be properly attended to, or else he would bleed out. The jungle was a terrible place to suffer such an injury. Typically, you'd want to put your feet up and relax, and if you had to move, you'd prefer to avoid scaling uneven terrain.

Jack looked over his shoulder. The world around them was utterly uneven.

"Any idea on how to close the wound?" Matias asked, cringing as Jack poked around his side.

"Yeah, I have a few." Jack stood and wiped his hands on his pants. He sighed. "But you're not gonna like any of them."

Everyone watched the two lead boats go over the waterfall. Hugo even thought he spotted somebody leap away from the deck of Aguilar's vessel. The smuggler was impressed with the jumper's strategy. He had separated himself from the boat.

It had to be Jack.

Three of the five boats had been able to run aground on the southern shore. They had witnessed the rapidly increasing current sweep the other two vessels away in a hurry. Aguilar's boat had been damaged by the first fall and was unable to correct course. Hugo didn't know why the second boat's pilot had been so close.

Now, it was just Hugo, Miguel, and Manuel, along with ten other men. Luckily, the trio didn't recognize any of the men that were with them. Now, they wouldn't have to disappear, as planned, into the trees to fend for themselves.

"No," Hugo countered, "we need them." He grinned. "Come on, Miguel, don't you want an army for yourself?"

"What do you mean?"

Hugo pointed at the other two boats. "These men have no leader here. You are dressed as one of Aguilar's men—not a soldier. You could take command." Hugo waved at the nearest boat. Two of the soldiers awkwardly returned the gesture. "Let's face it... We need whatever help we can get."

Miguel turned to his brother. Manuel nodded and spoke. "Good plan."

Hugo beamed with pride. Manuel had only spoken twice since they had gotten together at Abuelita's. Once when he had identified who the Musica people were. And now, to praise Hugo's plan.

"Fine," Miguel said, grabbing the radio. "I'll do it, but if things go badly, we all agree to make a run for it, okay?"

Hugo and Manuel nodded.

Miguel took a breath and depressed the call button on the corded receiver.

"Hello, do you copy?"

The trio turned and watched both boat pilots pick up their radios at once.

"We copy," one said.

"We hear you," said the other.

Miguel stood, making a show of it. "We need to gather our gear and find Aguilar and Matias."

Multiple voices grumbled in response.

"Listen to me!" Miguel shouted, quieting everyone. The outburst even gave Hugo goosebumps. "The job is to locate El Dorado, and if you do not comply," he drew his pistol, "I'll shoot you myself. Do you understand?"

Hugo smiled when both pilots replied with, "Yes, sir."

They're taking the bait!

Miguel's eyes flashed down to Hugo. He gave the smuggler a wink.

"Good job, my friend." Miguel looked back to the other boats and then returned his attention to Hugo before speaking again. "Now what?"

"Now," Hugo said, "we find Jack."

"We'll have to wait until morning," Miguel said, motioning to the dimming sky. "It's going to get dark very quickly out here."

Hugo didn't like the idea of them waiting an entire night to get moving again, but he agreed with Miguel's assessment. The rainforest wasn't a place to take lightly—ever—especially at night. The pause in their mission would also give them more time to put together a better plan of attack and to rest. Hugo was starving. Everyone must be hungry.

"Okay," he said. "We'll camp out in the boats tonight." He looked over the edge of the gunboat. The water scooted by them quickly, yet quietly. "Sleeping on the bank of a water source is never a good idea."

17

Jack hated the idea of setting up camp near the edge of the plunge pool. He knew better than to do something so foolish. But they didn't have any other options. Aguilar's boat would've made the perfect shelter, but it was listing heavily and far too unstable to re-enter. The deck had nearly collapsed beneath the drug lord when he attempted to call for help. Unfortunately, he had failed to reach anyone. His radio had been damaged in the wreck.

But Jack's squawked to life in a lively discordance of static. The man on the other end was speaking in rapid-fire Spanish, repeating his words over and over again. Jack happily handed off the device to Aguilar and waited to see what the boss man heard. He depressed the call button and spoke, quickly quieting the man on the other end. After twenty seconds of conversation, Aguilar gave Jack the lowdown.

"They're also camping for the night," Aguilar explained. "They're going to move forward in the morning and try to catch up with us."

Probably Miguel's idea, Jack thought. He didn't know whose plan it had been—Miguel's, or maybe Hugo, Manuel, or even one of Aguilar's other men. Either way, it was a good one, and his team now had a small army traveling with them.

Jack's present group was much more disheveled. As of now, he and Aguilar were in the best shape physically. Except for his nerves being a little fried and his back being sore as shit, Jack felt pretty good. Matias was injured, but, thankfully, he could still walk. Jack had closed the wound to the best of his abilities using a needle and thread from a first-aid kit that he had found inside the second boat. At first, Jack had jokingly offered to cauterize the wound with a red-hot knife blade, but as expected, Matias had denied his request.

"It'll only hurt for a minute," Jack explained.

"No, thank you," Matias replied. "The smell of my seared flesh might attract some unwanted attention."

Wouldn't that be a shame, Jack thought, hiding his smile. In doing so, Jack reacquired his sodden cellphone. As of now, it was useless, but it contained valuable evidence—evidence he was confident the TAC could recover once it dried out.

Matias' comment reminded Jack that they needed to do something with the dead. They needed to play it safe and remove anything *enticing* from the scene. The rainforest was home to many dangerous predators. Leaving Matias to rest, he and Aguilar grimly dragged the deceased soldiers' bodies back into the water and released them. The current swiftly hauled away the buoyant cadavers without any trouble. Soon, they were out of sight, disappearing downriver where they would surely be torn to pieces. The only body they couldn't retrieve was that of the second boat's pilot. He was still inside the watercraft's submerged wheelhouse.

One of the six soldiers from Aguilar's boat had survived both the attack by the natives and the fall. And only a pair of men from the second boat had walked away with their lives. By Jack's count, that now made their group a total of six.

Six, he thought, looking up at the dimming sky.

A pair of gunshots rang out behind him. Jack dropped to one knee, spun, and lifted his AK-47. Shouldering it, he stared down its sights and waited for the attack. It didn't come. One of the soldiers called out from the edge of the clearing, waving for someone to come over and help him with something. Another man ran over, and together, the pair dragged a large, furry lump out of the tree line.

It took a moment for Jack to recognize the creature. "Is that a capybara?"

Matias slowly climbed to his feet, keeping his left arm pinned against his side. He squinted and nodded. "Yes. They are a delicacy around here."

"So," Jack said, not looking happy, "we're having a giant rodent for dinner?"

Matias shrugged. "Better than going hungry, no?"

Jack sighed, but he agreed. If they were going to survive in the jungle, the first thing they would need to do was forage for food and collect water. The latter would be the easy part. The rainforest contained thousands of miles of freshwater tributaries, and it rained constantly. There was no going thirsty here.

The capybara must've weighed over a hundred pounds. The best description of the animal that Jack had ever heard was that it was nothing more than a gigantic guinea pig. Now, Jack was about to dine on one. He left the locals to prepare the rodent and continued his walk of the area. The plunge pool narrowed and transformed back into a river further ahead. As its width shrank, the current picked up. He stopped at a hundred yards, and for a moment, contemplated making a run for it. His survival training was as good as it got. There was no doubt that he could stay alive for a long time on his own, but he had no reason to leave. If anything, like his friends above, he had a small army at his disposal. Jack would've been an idiot to leave that behind.

It was getting darker, and Jack had yet to make his way back to camp. He knew he needed to, but he was enjoying his alone time away from the drug lord and the treacherous TAC agent. Jack drew his sidearm and checked it. He had made it a habit to check his weapons regularly whenever he had been out in the field and that applied to his Delta and National Parks Services stints. Satisfied, Jack gave the clearing one last look. He let out a long exhalation and turned and came face-to-face with a man he didn't know. The stranger was one of the natives that had attacked him! Or was he?

He lifted his pistol but didn't pull the trigger.

The guy looked a little older than him, and he was dressed in a pair of ragged cargo shorts with no shirt or shoes. He was a blend of both worlds, the civilized and the wild. The local was short, lean, and muscular—perfectly built for a life of living among the trees. What struck Jack the most was that he was so docile. The others he had encountered had acted violently for no reason. Aguilar's crew had not posed a threat to anyone. At the time, they were just passing through when a bombardment of poisonous arrows fell from the sky.

Jack's eyes darted downward. He smiled. Unbeknownst to him, the native was holding a spear to Jack's throat. The guy could've killed Jack easily.

But you didn't.

The native spoke slowly as if he knew Jack wouldn't understand him. And he spoke Spanish, not some unrecognizable dialect. Jack didn't quite follow him either way, but he did memorize the words. Shouts of surprise picked up from somewhere behind him. Jack looked over his shoulder and spotted Aguilar and two soldiers running toward him. They had also spotted the newcomer.

"You need to leave before..." Jack said, facing the native. But he was already gone. "Um... Hello?" Jack spun in a circle, finding no trace of the guy. He flicked on his flashlight and didn't even see any tracks.

Did he vanish into thin air?

"Who was that?" Aguilar asked, pistol at the ready. The soldiers kept watch, embedding their rifles into their shoulders.

"I...I don't know," Jack replied. "He kinda just appeared out of nowhere."

"Did he say anything?"

Jack nodded, still peering into the trees. He repeated the words.

Aguilar's forehead scrunched. He was troubled, not liking what he had mentally translated.

"What does it mean?" Jack asked.

"'The guardians show no mercy.'"

Jack's right eyebrow rose. "What guardians?"

Aguilar shook his head. "I don't know, but we need to be cautious."

"Ya think?"

Within the aura of the firelit campsite, Jack and Aguilar spotted Matias waving at them.

"Come," Aguilar said, "we'll discuss the possibilities over dinner."

Unsurprisingly, the meal was simply prepared. The capybara had been expertly skinned, and only the leanest meats had been chosen. It was apparent that the men here had done this before. Oddly, the camp smelled of pork and fish. Jack looked around and saw no fish present. Matias handed him a large leaf with a half-dozen cubes of medium-rare rodent meat. Jack was too hungry to question it.

He sat and picked up a small piece. Jack pinched the cube and found it to be firm and juicy. *Oh,* he thought, sniffing it. *So that's where the fishiness is coming from.*

Jack held it up to his lips. *Here we go...*

He bit the chunk in half, and after two chews, popped the rest of the helping into his mouth. It wasn't his favorite—far from it—but it was edible and would fill his gut. The only seasoning he could detect was salt. The other flavors were entirely natural.

Needs some A1.

"So," Jack said in between chews, "the 'guardians...'"

Aguilar nodded and swallowed. "It could mean several things. I believe it might point to the sacred animal of the rainforest."

"A jaguar?" Jack asked, recalling the one he had seen outside of the excavation.

"No," Aguilar corrected, "*jaguars.* The native warned us of *guardians*—plural. It would only make sense that there would be multiple guardians out here."

Everyone took another moment to eat. Matias spoke up next.

"What if there are different guardians? Not a singular species."

Jack shrugged. "At this point, anything is possible." He shoved a large, savory piece of capybara meat into his mouth. He was starting to warm up to it. Juices flowed with every bite. A little dripped down his chin. Jack wiped it away, getting a smile out of Matias.

"Enjoying yourself?"

Jack shrugged. "It's not bad, though I could do without the fishiness."

Matias grinned and took another bite. "Agreed."

"What about the locals that attacked us on the river?" Aguilar asked. His eyes were intense and locked onto the fire. "Could they be the guardians?"

"If they are," Jack said, "then the warning was a hair too late to matter much. No, I think there is something else waiting for us. How close are we anyway?"

Matias tossed his leaf-plate aside and dug a small GPS device out of his bag. He powered it on and flicked through a few images. "If the location displayed inside of Ordaz's tomb is accurate, then we are within a two-day walk."

Two days? Jack groaned but didn't vocalize his disappointment. He had signed up for this mission and had no one to blame but himself. He could've just as easily denied the assignment—the job altogether—and stayed in Wyoming.

"Jack?" Matias asked.

"Huh, what?" he asked, blinking hard. He had zoned out, thinking of home.

"What do you think about following the river?"

"Oh, yeah. That's fine." He stretched. "Okay, guys, I'm done." He stood. "I suggest that everyone gets as much rest as possible. We have a long hike ahead of us." He stepped away but stopped and held up his rifle. "And keep your weapons close while you sleep. There's no telling what's out there."

The others stayed close to the fire. Jack didn't. Instead, he found a grassy spot up against the base of a tree at the light's edge. He sat, slinking down until he felt somewhat comfortable. Jack laid his AK-47 across his chest, placing his right hand atop its grip. The smells and sounds originating from their camp would surely attract a creature of some kind, and he didn't want to be in the thick of it if it did, indeed, show up.

Hopefully, for everyone, it would be nothing more than another capybara coming to check on its friend.

Do they know they smell like fish?

Aguilar stood and held up his radio. He told the men to do something, but Jack didn't know what. He no longer had one of the devices. Aguilar had confiscated his. He watched Aguilar turn one of the knobs on the top.

He turned it off. Conserving its battery was a good idea, but the strategy also had its downfall. Now, they would be unable to contact the others back upriver, and vice versa.

Jack licked his lips. The taste of fishy pork was still fresh. He unclipped a canteen from his belt and unscrewed the cap. One of the soldiers had filled them before they had sat down to eat. Jack greedily drank half of it without the blink of an eye. He was twenty-five feet from more. He was also twenty-five feet from whatever nasties lived beneath the water's surface.

Back up the waterfall, Hugo, Miguel, and Manuel, and the other soldiers all settled into their respective boats. Hugo curled up in the pilot's chair, nodding on and off. His back was aching, but he was so tired that he barely noticed. Miguel was collapsed on the floor next to him, using someone's backpack as a pillow. His brother had decided to sleep outside under the stars. It wasn't because of his love for nature either. Manuel wanted to stay as close to the M2 Browning as possible.

Half-asleep, Hugo felt the gunboat begin to rise and fall beneath him. Most of the vessel was still out in the river, so it was only natural for it to still bounce around a little. If anything, the motion was soothing. Hugo nestled lower into his seat. Finally, he found the perfect upright-to-horizontal ratio and felt consciousness slip away.

But then the boat rose again. This time it felt as if the current had picked up. That was impossible, though. The only time the intensity of the water changed was during flood season—and it wasn't flood season. Groaning, Hugo opened his eyes and struggled out of his seat. He stood, stepped over Miguel, and stumbled to the stern of the gunboat. Blinking awake, Hugo clicked on his flashlight and aimed it at the surface of the water.

"Miguel, Manuel... Wake up." The twins mumbled something. Hugo spun and hissed at them. "Wake up!"

They must've sensed that Hugo was serious because both men leapt to their feet, guns drawn. They joined Hugo at the rear of the boat, peering over the edge. In the beam of his light, they could just make out a shape moving beneath the river's surface. It was too dark, and the water was too murky to see much of anything else.

"What is it?" Miguel asked.

"Nothing good," Hugo replied.

Miguel pointed downriver. "It's headed for the waterfall."

Hugo nodded, his attention never leaving the entity. "And for Jack and the others."

"What can we do?"

Hugo shrugged. "We can try to warn them, I guess."

Miguel headed for the wheelhouse and attempted to raise someone below. After a third unsuccessful try, he gave up, slamming the hand mic down. Either everyone was asleep, or they had had also turned their walkie-talkies off. Jack and the others were about to get some unwanted company, and they had no way of warning them.

The endless roar of the waterfall, and his full belly, were enough to lull Jack into sleep. When he was out in nature, Jack never worried about his night terrors. He rarely suffered one while camping, or in this case, shipwrecked and semi-enslaved. Jack had been given a sizeable amount of freedom recently. His weapons were proof of that. The partnership would be mutual until Aguilar decided that it wasn't. They needed Jack as much as he needed them.

Other than the sound of rushing water, everything was silent.

Then, the screams came.

Jack opened his eyes just as one of the soldiers was being yanked off of his feet. The guy had been standing on the water's edge. Jack had no idea why. He jumped to his feet and aimed at the assailant but couldn't see anything. The firelight had dimmed, and the *thing* had moved too far away, retreating out into the middle of the plunge pool. Aguilar ordered the others to open fire, but the soldiers balked at the command. Jack understood why. Their own man was too close to the action to risk it.

A flashlight ignited, but it was too late. The guy got pulled underwater before anyone got a look at what had attacked them. It didn't take long for the pool's surface to return to its calm self. Unless you had seen what had happened, you would've been completely unaware that a man had just lost his life.

"What was he doing?" Jack called out, hustling over to the firepit.

Aguilar asked another soldier. "He says that Rodriguez had gone to relieve himself."

"Did anyone get a look at what got him?"

No one answered. Like Jack, they had all been caught with their pants down. Rodriguez in particular. Jack felt stupid. His group had let down their guard in the middle of one of the most dangerous environments in the world. Aguilar shouted at one of the remaining soldiers. There were only two of them left.

The soldier nodded and took up position in between the fire and the water.

"I'm guessing that was one of our guardians?" Matias asked.

Jack wasn't sure that the guardian was truly guarding anything. The natives may have just thought that they were because of their people's natural superstition. Animals didn't protect treasure. This wasn't Smaug from *The Hobbit*. Wildlife defended things like their territory, a recent kill, and their families, not gold.

For good measure, Jack threw more wood and a couple of dried palm fronds onto the fire. The fronds acted as a natural accelerant. You could make a bonfire reach the heavens if you had enough of them. This time, everyone stayed as close to the fire as possible. Jack smartly lay down on the opposite side of it, keeping the flames between him and the pool. After what he had just witnessed, he'd take his chances with the things living amongst the trees.

Jack took another headcount and sighed. *And then there were five.*

But little did Jack know what lurked beneath the water's surface also spent a large chunk of its existence on land. And the closer he and the others got to their destination, the deeper they would find themselves in its territory.

18

The fifteen heavily armed men marched through the rainforest in a single-file line. Manuel led the way, keeping the pace steady. If they moved too fast, they would tire quickly and have to stop. And no one wanted to stop. Everyone was already drenched with sweat, even in the early minutes of the morning sun. Nights in the jungle were much cooler than the days, but they were still plenty humid.

Hugo had fallen in line between the Arroyos, gawking at how easily Manuel was carrying the M2 Browning. At first, the eighty-pound machine gun seemed like it would be impossible to heft through the winding terrain, yet here Manuel was, doing it with little trouble. The quiet giant had removed it and its tripod from the deck of the gunboat before the group headed off in search of Jack's group. Miguel carried the weapon's tripod and ammunition in his pack.

"Whatever we saw last night..." Miguel had explained, "Manuel wants to be prepared if it shows up again."

Hugo was thinking the same thing. But what could they do against something that big? They still didn't even know what *it* was. Miguel's radio crackled to life. He answered it but kept the group moving.

Aguilar was on the other end. He quickly went over what had happened to them last night. Hugo was stunned. A soldier had been attacked and dragged into the water without a single shot being fired. The assault had happened fast and without warning. It sounded like they also had a cryptic, nonthreatening visit from one of the natives.

"We're still up on the ridge and trying to find a way down to you. We'll call you back in a couple of hours. Over."

The column weaved their way through the dense foliage for over an hour, seeing nothing except green. The canopy above them was impenetrable, barely allowing the sunlight through. It kept the temperature reasonable, but it also blocked the airflow. The air was stale and smelled of leafy rot. Occasionally, Hugo spotted the bones of something half-buried in the dirt. Very little grass grew here. One of the skeletons looked like it was a human, but he wasn't one hundred percent sure.

Manuel held up a closed fist. Everyone mimicked the gesture to the person behind them. The line stopped. Then, Miguel motioned for them to get down. Everyone followed his command and knelt, shouldering their weapons as they did. Just Manuel got back to his feet half a minute later. He methodically skulked toward a triangular cut sliver in a wall of green. Leaning forward, he poked his head through. As Manuel drew the heavy vines away, Hugo was blinded by sunlight.

The silent twin must've been satisfied by what he saw because he swiftly unsheathed his machete and hacked at the green curtain until a grown man could step through unperturbed. Manuel waved the group forward, waiting for them to catch up before leading them through.

Hugo shielded his eyes, stepping over a pile of cut vines. He dropped his line of sight to the ground so he wouldn't trip. When he looked up, the world around him had changed dramatically. There was a peaceful, gently sloping valley. A slow-moving stream cut directly across the middle of it. For some reason, the trees did not grow as eagerly here. The landscape was serene, except for a flock of birds jumping and pecking at something near the center of it all. Even from this distance, Hugo recognized the animals as Andean condors. They were a member of the New World vulture family and were one of the world's largest flying birds, weighing in at thirty pounds and owning a wingspan of ten feet.

He counted eight of the massive birds in all. Whatever they were feeding on must've been large enough to support their numbers. Without a word, the line of men plodded down the grassy knoll. Manuel led the train to the left, around the disturbance. Even though Andean condors were a scavenger, feeding exclusively on carrion, Hugo agreed with Manuel's choice to avoid them. If the condors decided to become rowdy, they could cause Hugo's group some problems.

"We must be getting close to Brazil," Miguel said, keeping his voice low.

"Makes sense," Hugo replied. "All of this would've been nothing more than loose-bordered territories in Ordaz's day."

Hugo glanced over his shoulder and spotted Miguel rustling through his bag.

"What are you doing?" Hugo asked.

"Finding out exactly where we are."

Miguel removed the gunboat's GPS device and powered it on. When he did, it let out an annoying squeal. The birds reacted to the sound as if it were a gunshot or train horn. They stopped feeding, one by one, and took in the long line of newcomers. This new attention on them made Hugo nervous.

Miguel gave Hugo and his brother an apologetic look before returning his attention to the condors.

The group, however, made it to the narrow, knee-deep stream unscathed. Manuel didn't stop, sloshing through the cool water. Once he made it across, the birds took flight. Each of the condors began to circle them. Hugo had never seen such behavior before.

"Is this normal of them?" the soldier behind Miguel asked.

"No," Miguel replied, looking up, "it is not."

A series of low grunts and grumbles picked up overhead. Hugo watched in awe as the immense birds communicated with one another. The feeling of wonder transformed into one of horror as all the condors dove straight for them.

"Run!" Miguel shouted, shoving Hugo forward.

The smuggler splashed through the stream and took off at a sprint. Manuel was already in motion, heading for the nearest tree line, but it was over a hundred yards away. Bullets tore into the sky, some of them finding their marks. A loud squawk and a thud announced the arrival of a wounded, possibly dead, condor. Hugo decided to conserve his ammunition and drew his machete, taking a page out of Manuel's book. The larger man was currently hacking and slashing at anything near him.

The screams of a soldier nearly made Hugo skid to a stop, but he was pushed along by Miguel instead. He did look back and watch as one of the soldiers was taken down beneath a quintet of hook-billed birds. Together they bowled into the off-balance man with their combined 150-pounds of body weight. They also had a healthy amount of downward force at their disposal.

Hugo turned away from the carnage, cringing as the soldier's cries for help morphed into wet gasps. Then, nothing. The condors were quickly doing what they did best. They tore into their meal with fevered excitement. One of the men stopped and opened fire. One of the birds got clipped, and the gunfire brought the rest of the animals' attention to him now. He ran but headed in the wrong direction. Suddenly, more of the condors swooped down from the heavens, joining in on the fray. Now, there had to be sixteen or seventeen of them.

Oh my God, Hugo thought, biting his lip as he ran. This was going to be close.

Manuel reached the trees seconds before Hugo. When he did, he spun and cocked back his machete, aiming for Hugo's head as he did.

"Hugo—down!" Miguel shouted from behind.

Hugo did as he was told and dove forward. Manuel's blade impacted the fast-descending condor, connecting with its throat. After three more strikes, he removed the bird's head from its body, huffing for breath while helping the smuggler to his feet. Soon, the remaining soldiers followed each other deeper into the tree line. The birds did not follow, returning to their fresh meals instead. Ten of the twelve soldiers had survived the ordeal. The two that didn't were now being stripped of their flesh.

The thought made Hugo shudder.

"Thank you," he said, nodding at Manuel. The twin returned the nod with one of his own. "You too," he said, holding out his hand to Miguel. Miguel took it and pumped it twice, smiling wide.

"What?" Hugo asked.

Miguel laughed. "How many are you going to owe me by the time we're done here?"

Hugo rolled his eyes and noticed that Manuel was inspecting the dead condor's severed head. He and Miguel joined him and immediately noticed that something was wrong with the bird—besides its body no longer being connected.

"What's wrong with its eyes?" Hugo asked.

The bird's irises were bright red. They looked downright demonic.

"Another of our guardians?" Miguel asked, using the name the native had used.

"Possibly," Hugo replied. "What do you think caused it?"

Miguel shrugged. "I don't know, but I bet we'll find out soon."

"How do you know?" Hugo asked.

Manuel stood, getting everyone's attention. He faced the not-so-serene valley. "There is evil here. I feel it." Then, he turned around and headed off.

Hugo and Miguel got to their feet and followed Manuel deeper into the trees. They found the ten remaining soldiers in various postures of relaxation. Some were sitting. A few were lying down or leaning up against trees. All of them looked scared.

"Is that what you think too?" Hugo asked, looking at Miguel.

Miguel didn't look so sure. "I don't know, but I have learned to trust my brother's instincts. If his gut says that there is something evil inhabiting the rainforest, then, well, I'd rather believe him, and have it not be true then the other way around." He sighed. "Either way, there is something unnatural going on."

Hugo agreed. "And we are headed right into the heart of it. Jack too."

"Yes," Miguel said, worried. He checked his shotgun. "You ready?"

Hugo nodded and fell in line behind the Arroyo twins. The soldiers followed his example, and they all quickly moved on. As he had done before, Manuel kept the pace even and steady. They still had a long way to go based on Miguel's initial calculation. They would be forced to camp overnight in the jungle again before they stumbled upon the large green dot on Miguel's GPS device.

El Dorado, Hugo thought.

He was questioning whether it was still worth discovering. So far, they had lost countless men on this expedition, and all of them within a short time. If Hugo watched all of this unfold on TV, he would've laughed at how unprepared the explorers had been. Highly trained, well-armed soldiers and people like himself and the Arroyos were still no match for Mother Nature.

Hugo was the least capable out of all the people looking for the City of Gold. But he was skilled at surviving. He figured that Jack was having better luck than his people were. A man like Jack could take care of himself.

19

After hiking for nearly three hours, Jack, Aguilar, Matias, and the two remaining soldiers came across another game trail. He decided to avoid it and stepped off the worn pathway. He didn't want anything to do with the beast that had created it. The terrain around it seemed fine. So, Jack did the intelligent thing and stepped off the trail.

His foot found nothing but air.

"Shiiit!"

Jack fell, landing a few feet later on a steep grade of muddy earth. He tumbled down it, desperately trying to snag a tree branch or a deeply rooted shrub—anything! Jack righted himself, riding out the fall in a seated position. He locked his jaw in anticipation, expecting the descent to end abruptly. They always did, in his experiences. But this time, the slope slowly leveled off, and he finished the trek in an upright, sitting position. He stayed seated and looked back and up the way he had come, unable to see the rest of his party. Jack doubted any of them would willingly follow him. If it were Hugo and the twins, maybe. But not Aguilar and Matias. For now, he was on his own.

A tree branch cracked.

He swiftly got to one knee, paying no attention to his barking lower back. He swung his mud-covered AK-47 around, shouldering it, waiting to see if he had attracted the attention of something nasty. He kept perfectly still for a couple of minutes before standing. Nothing had come to greet him. It surprised him too. Jack held his breath as he stood, listening carefully. Typically, rustling sounds greeted him—the kinds that were always present in the rainforest—the sway of tree branches and the scurrying of tiny, nonthreatening critters. At least, Jack hoped they weren't a threat.

Jack closed his eyes and focused, picking up on something else. It was the faint sound of running water. A river was nearby. He wasn't sure that he wanted to see another body of water after what had happened last night. Watching that soldier get pulled under wasn't a memory Jack enjoyed replaying over and over again in his head. He grumbled incoherently. Nevertheless, Jack headed towards the sound.

A river would be a perfect place to meet back up with either of his groups. They had all agreed to follow the tributary but were forced to divert based on the unnavigable landscape they had encountered. The ground beneath his feet rose slightly. Jack veered around it, heading right, deeper into the trees. Luckily, the river was still within earshot.

He stepped over a log and nearly lost his left boot in the mud. Jack couldn't count the number of times that had almost happened. The ground was incredibly soft here. The rainwater seemed to collect worse in some spots. He figured that the elevation was lower here than in other places, though he had no real idea. He was just making an educated guess at this point.

The river grew louder as he marched on. Pushing aside a palm frond, Jack was taken aback by the beauty of the water. He wanted nothing more than to take a dip in it and rinse off the layers of sweat and filth from his sore, bruised body. Jack stopped just feet from the water, satisfied that he was alone. He looked up at the sky and closed his eyes, enjoying the silence. The only sounds he could hear were the running water and the gentle breeze whistling by his ears.

A metallic creak forced his eyes open.

Dropping his head, he looked to the right. There, pinned against a pair of large boulders, and spanning across the entire river, was the last thing he expected to see in the jungle.

"Uh..."

It was a World War II-era German U-boat.

He sighed. "Great, more Nazis."

Jack had read about Hitler sending submarines to the Amazon in search of artifacts and gold, but he had never expected to see one here. This thing had easily been here since the forties. It was rusted out and had a large hole in its flank. Jack suspected that it had been torpedoed, but if it had, then why had it made it all the way here? From what Jack knew, most of Hitler's U-boats had stayed up on the northern edge of Brazil, not down here.

Jack could just barely make out the submersible's identification number.

"U-590," he read aloud.

The name sounded familiar. It took him a few seconds, but Jack remembered where he had heard of it before. A friend of his grandfather, Dan Thompson, was in the U.S. Navy during the Second World War. After retiring from the service, he became something of an expert on the war's maritime history, happily discussing it on nearly all of his visits to the Reilly home. Jack would sit in on all the conversations, soaking up the information like a sponge.

U-590 had supposedly been sunk back in 1943 by U.S. aircraft via depth charges. The current evidence proved otherwise, though. *U-590* had obviously survived the attack and had somehow made it across Brazil and into Colombia. Jack had no idea how, but here it was, its entire 200-foot length visible for all to see. The only thing Jack could think of was that floodwaters had guided it to this spot. Then, it had gotten stuck, pinned up against the massive stones on either side of the narrowing river.

Using what little "beach" there was, Jack headed for the watercraft, still in awe of seeing it in person. It was, understandably, in dreadful condition. The U-boat had been here for decades, assaulted by the jungle's sweltering heat, humidity, and constant rainfall. Most metals didn't take too kindly to this kind of environment, and *U-590* fared no differently.

"What a mess," Jack said, slowing as he approached. He heard a continuous booming of water on the other side. "Great, another waterfall."

The U-boat's bow was on his side of the river. Years of water level changes had buried the bottom section of the hull deep into the embankment. Essentially, the vessel had been glued in place. *U-590* had become an artificial dam of sorts. Jack attempted to bypass the discovery and continue onward, but he couldn't. The trees were too dense to cut through, and the earth was loose, wet, and unnavigable. Plus, it dropped out of nowhere.

"No shit, Sherlock," he said. "It's a waterfall, after all."

Still, he needed to properly scout the area beyond the submersible, just in case.

Jack climbed up the boulder holding the U-boat's bow in place, reaching its peak in seconds. From there, he could nearly reach out and touch the historic vessel. Under other circumstances, this discovery would've been worth all the hassle. This was an incredible find on its own. But Jack had a maniac's lust to satiate. If Jack didn't find El Dorado, he was a dead man. He doubted the drug lord would settle for a 200-foot-long, rusty doorstop.

"Dammit," he mumbled, still unable to do much of anything. The trees had grown out over the water, blocking his view.

He bit his lip and thought of what to do next. He turned and came up with another idea. He lined up the five-foot distance between himself and the U-boat.

"Thank God for Tetanus shots."

He leapt and grabbed the corroded railing with ease. His boots swung forward and connected the hull with a solid *bong*. Wincing, Jack waited for the U-boat to crumble to pieces. When it didn't, he pulled himself up the rest of the way. Standing atop the World War II-era submarine was a surreal feeling. The flat deck made it easy to maneuver, but the angle of it didn't. And it leaned toward the drop. Jack tested the integrity of the deck a little before venturing too far out. He stomped his foot. Nothing happened. Jack went as far as jumping up and down in place. Again, nothing. The vessel was solid and unmoving.

And he saw a pathway on the other side.

The opening in the tree line had been hidden from his view earlier. Stepping lightly, Jack crossed the deck with ease. The breeze was stronger out in the middle of the river. The jungle wouldn't be so bad if the wind were able to make it inside the trees.

The only thing he could hear was the deafening roar of the falls. It was the tallest one he had seen so far. Its power would've been even more impressive if it didn't have the U-boat holding some of it back. If the "dam" ever broke, it would send a miniature tidal wave through the rainforest beneath it. This area had not seen the full force of the falls in nearly eighty years. The plunge pool and river below would quickly flood and change the landscape in minutes.

"Jack!"

He spun and looked for the voice's owner. But the sun was directly in his eyes, making it difficult to do so.

"Jack!"

There, he spotted a lone man running further down the sandy bank. It was Aguilar. Was the drug lord coming to his rescue? It felt out of character for the man to do so.

Standing in the middle of *U*-590's deck, Jack hurried over to the starboard side and raised his hand to wave. He stopped himself when he saw Aguilar vigorously pointing at the water. Aguilar was trying to warn him of something. Jack followed the other man's hand but didn't see anything of note. Jack had expected to witness a wall of water rushing at him or even a convoy of armed natives in canoes. Instead, all he saw was the river's current.

Jack lifted his left hand to shield the sun's rays. That's when he saw it.

Just below the surface of the water was a lengthy, shadowy aberration. Jack had no idea what it was. His mind went back to the thing that grabbed the soldier who had been taking a leak. Was it the same creature?

He moved back toward the bow but only made it two steps before the submarine let out a hollow, echoing bellow. Jack took another step and received the same result. His presence was altering the integrity of the makeshift dam.

And he had an undisclosed behemoth bearing down on him.

The U-boat moaned again. Its call caused the incoming threat to speed up. It had to be some kind of snake, but Jack didn't know of any snake that would be this big. Even the green anaconda didn't reach lengths of this magnitude. Aguilar made it to Jack first. He stayed on the shoreline and yelled as loud as he could.

"Get out of there, Jack!"

Jack laughed. "Oh, really?"

"Move! It's coming!"

Jack looked at the local with his hands out to the side, trying to keep his footing. "What's coming?"

Aguilar looked terrified. Whatever it was, it was scaring Aguilar. In turn, that frightened Jack.

The U-boat was struck with the force of a pissed-off African elephant. The *bong* shook Jack's teeth and violently assaulted his skull. He held on to the rail as the submarine tipped toward the waterfall. Jack was ripped away, thrown back, landing in the center of the deck. He staggered to his feet and shuffled back to the starboard railing. He needed to see this thing—whatever it was.

He gripped the rail and pulled himself up to it. Slowly, he leaned over the side and looked straight down, just as the enormous head of a black and green serpent broke the water's surface.

"Titanoboa!" Aguilar shouted, backing away from the river's edge.

"What?" Jack replied. *Titanoboa?* It started climbing the hull without issue. "You have got to be shitting me!"

"Unfortunately, I'm not!"

Jack took a step back. "I thought they were extinct!"

"They are!"

He laughed. "Tell that to him!"

The Titanoboa was an extinct species of colossal snake and was indigenous to the region. The largest specimen ever discovered was just over forty-feet-long, weighing an estimated 2,500 pounds. The one Jack was watching climb his U-boat beat that by over ten feet—maybe more. Locked in fright, Jack made eye contact with the beast.

Its irises were blood red.

"What the hell?"

He readied his AK-47 and carefully stepped back toward the middle of the deck. There, he waited for the monster to show itself. When it did, Jack knew that his bullets weren't going to do a damn thing to its armor-plating—and that's what its scales looked like to Jack. Its head cleared the rail by fifteen feet, blocking out the sun. It reminded Jack of a cobra "standing up."

"Holy crap," he said, stepping back again. His ass bumped the portside rail, and he stopped. The inadvertent contact made *U-590* cry again. The movements by both Jack and the Titanoboa were making the submarine list further towards the falls.

Jack got an idea that might work provided that the enormous animal's girth would slow it down once it was out of the water. Snakes of this thing's ilk were excellent swimmers but sluggish on dry land. Jack needed that to be true of this *extinct* species.

"Come on, you scaly bastard!" he shouted, trying to antagonize it. "Come and get me!"

He pulled the trigger of his rifle and harmlessly peppered its belly. That did it. The Titanoboa lowered its massive head and opened its jaws. Its fangs looked like rows of over-sized fillet knives. It didn't so much as launch itself at Jack, but rather, it fell and landed with a boom atop the teetering submersible's deck. Jack ran for the stern of the U-boat, slinging the AK-47 around his back. He would need both of his hands free for what he was planning to do.

U-590 tilted again as the snake fully emerged from the water. Jack looked back. The thing was closer to sixty feet in length and must've weighed at least 3,000 pounds. He was shocked. He had seriously underestimated the creature's size.

And speed! The Titanoboa moved just fine across dry land.

But all of its girth was doing what Jack had hoped.

The bow of the submarine broke loose first, and when it did, the river's power took over. It pushed the 200-foot-long U-boat over the edge. The stern lifted as the bow dipped. Jack hustled up the incline, nearly getting taken out by a section of debris. He vaulted for the ten-foot piece of railing and leapt out over the falls. He stretched both hands out in front of him and snagged the nearest tangle of vines, swinging out over the drop like an uncoordinated Tarzan. But unlike the movies, the vines didn't miraculously hold his weight. The Titanoboa, *U-590*, and Jack fell like a trio of bombs. Suddenly, a few of the remaining attached vines held long enough to swing him back in the direction of the cliff just to the right of the cascading water. He slammed into the rocks and was knocked loose. He scrambled for anything to hold onto and blindly grabbed hold of a second tangle of vines.

Jack quickly wedged the tips of his boots into place in some unseen crevasse and gasped for air. He shook with adrenaline and started to laugh. Looking between his feet, Jack spotted *U-590* lying on its side in the shallows, but he couldn't see the creature anywhere. An animal the size of the Titanoboa should've been easy to see from this high vantage point.

"It survived?" he asked no one. He looked up and screamed as loud as he could. "Of course it survived!"

But so had he.

"Okay, Jack, calm down. You're alive."

The sky above him darkened. It was too early for the sun to set, which meant another storm was rolling in. Jack needed to get off this cliff face before he was forcibly torn away from it and laid to rest beside the decimated Nazi U-boat.

Santiago Aguilar couldn't pull his attention away from what he had just witnessed. Jack Reilly had just gone toe-to-toe with a sixty-foot-long Titanoboa—a species of constrictor snake that was supposed to be extinct. The massive black and green serpent had slunk up the side of a Nazi-era U-boat like it was nothing. Then, its weighty girth forced the submarine, and Jack, off the edge of a tall waterfall.

Presently, Aguilar stood still with his mouth agape. He replayed the encounter in his head once more, picturing the creature in the flesh. The Titanoboa was *the* apex predator of prehistoric Colombia, though this one was much larger than anything ever recorded. The jaguar might have been the most well-known and revered in the country's history, but the Titanoboa, like its cousin, the anaconda, was the largest.

He heard footsteps come up behind him, but he didn't move. He was too engrossed in what he had seen to look—or care. Aguilar had just seen—with his own eyes—the single greatest spectacle of nature's might in all his life. It was a memory he would never forget.

"Reilly?" Matias asked, stopping next to him. The man was breathing hard.

Aguilar shook his head. "There's no way he survived that."

Matias stepped in front of Aguilar, finally getting the man to blink. "What are you talking about? Survived *what*?"

"You didn't see it?" Aguilar asked, turning his attention back to the falls.

"What the hell are you talking about, Santiago?"

"A god."

Matias' right eyebrow rose. He looked back and forth between the drug lord and the water. "You saw 'God?'"

Aguilar shook his head, slipping back into a trance-like state. "No, not God. I just saw Jack take on *a* god—the god of the rainforest. And it was beautiful."

"You're not making any sense," Matias said. "Are you feeling okay?"

Aguilar smiled maniacally. "Me?" He faced Matias—who took a step back. His gaze slowly returned to the water. "I've never felt better."

20

Jack let go of the cliff face, reaching out with his right hand to test another jumble of thick vines. He pulled on them hard, happy when they didn't tear away. Jack breathed a sigh of relief. He released his left hand from the wall and discovered that they did hold his weight. Leaning away from the cliff, he slowly walked backward down it.

Feeling more confident in his situation, he loosened his grip on the growth and jumped, rappelling down another twenty feet. He brought his feet up and braced himself for impact. But it never came. Jack's forward momentum swung him through the carpet of greenery and into a dark void beyond it. His hands slipped, and he went down, landing flat on his back on the stone floor. The air was swiftly expelled from his lungs, causing him to break into a fit of coughs.

Catching his wind, Jack groaned and sat up. He could just barely see what lay beyond. Behind him, a section of vines had torn free as he made his entrance. The small opening allowed a sliver of sunlight inside. The scene in front of Jack was a dreadful one.

Two bony corpses greeted him. The pair had decomposed long ago. Between their feet was a small, improvised fireplace. There were still unused pieces of wood stacked atop one another near the rear of the room.

"Well," Jack said, fishing through his pocket, "at least I'm not alone." He removed his flashlight and clicked it on.

Both bodies were dressed similarly. They had been sailors in the *Kriegsmarine*—the navy of Nazi Germany. "Aboard *U-590*, no doubt," Jack said to himself. The demise of the submarine had been greatly exaggerated. It may have been damaged back in 1943, but it most definitely hadn't been sunk.

And it made it all the way here.

The cave was more of a shallow alcove than anything else. It was barely twenty-feet-deep and ended at a hefty pile of boulders. The two seamen, Bert and Ernie, were laid up near the rear wall. Jack stood and noticed something in his flashlight's beam. The guy on his left, Bert, held something in his right hand. The German was flopped over on his side, nearly concealing it from view. And if he hadn't been primarily tatters and bones, Jack would've missed it.

The low ceiling forced Jack to walk with a slight hunch. He swung his light over to the second man. Ernie was sitting upright against a flat boulder. From what Jack could tell, he held nothing of value, though the man's right hand was presently veiled from sight.

Jack knelt and inspected the object in Bert's hand, seeing a glint of gold beneath a thick layer of grime. Jack pried the item free from the German's gnarled digits. The man's fingers audibly cracked in the process.

"Sorry, Bert. I guess that means no piano scholarship."

The artifact was a type of ceremonial dagger, but it was unlike anything Jack had ever seen. Its construction was similar to that of the Maya, resembling an elongated arrowhead. The base of the blade was what caught Jack's attention the most. Inlaid right where it connected to the handgrip was a sizeable purple gemstone. The jewel itself was cut into the shape of a star or possibly a flower. It was beautiful, and it had, no doubt, come from El Dorado—he just knew it! With all that had gone on—everything that had tried to kill him and the others—it was nice to have the first tangible evidence of what it was they were looking for.

Jack's hands shook as he stood. Lost in that moment, he forgot where he was and smacked the top of his skull on the ceiling. "Ow!" He rubbed his head, checking his hand for blood. Finding none, he turned and headed for the cave entrance. It had started to rain now. Jack held onto the dagger tightly and stuck it out in the growing maelstrom. He rubbed decades of filth away with great enthusiasm, going as far as using his shirt as a rag. He performed the chore twice more before being satisfied with its condition.

Jack smiled and faced Bert, slipping the dagger into his belt. Then, he shined his light over the second man.

I wonder...

He, once more, knelt. This time, he inspected Ernie's remains. "Whatcha got there?" Jack asked, spotting something in Ernie's right hand. This time, the object wasn't some priceless artifact. It was a pistol—a Nazi-era Luger.

"Oh..." Jack swung his light back over to Bert. The way the man had been positioned now made sense. Jack slipped his flashlight into his mouth as if it were a horse bit and grabbed Bert by the shoulders. With both hands, Jack turned him over. "Yikes," he mumbled, speaking around his flashlight.

Bert had a hole in his forehead. The sailor had been executed by his partner.

Just inside the boundary of his light, he saw why Ernie might have done it. His left ankle had been broken.

Jack snapped his head back over to Bert. "You were going to leave him behind, weren't you?" He closed his eyes and rubbed them. "But Ernie didn't let you leave."

Jack reached out and turned Ernie's face toward him. There was a hole in his right temple. Ernie had killed Bert and then had shot himself. It wasn't uncommon for people to go batshit crazy when they were lost in the wilderness for extended periods of time. This grisly scene was a prime example of just that. Bert had wanted to leave—maybe even to get his friend some help—but his partner, justly or not, had thought differently. He had probably assumed that Bert was going to desert him and leave with the valuable dagger.

And now, with the weather outside worsening, Jack wasn't sure if he'd get the chance to escape either. Storms could last for days here. It was called a "rainforest" for a reason.

Jack had no food—no supplies of any kind. All he currently held in his possession were his rifle, pistol, a waterlogged cell phone, a canteen, and two knives, one of which was dull and nothing more ornamental.

He looked back outside. "At least I have water."

Before Jack searched the two men for anything of use, he chugged the rest of his canteen, then refilled it with rainwater.

"Okay, buddy, what else do you have?"

Inside Bert's shirt was a folded piece of something. It wasn't paper. With great care, Jack unfolded it, recognizing it as an evasion chart, or drift chart. These maps were intended to be used if a soldier was caught behind enemy lines and needed an escape route. They were constructed of Rayon acetate materials, making them impervious to water damage. The worn map opened to four times its original size, revealing a bird's eye view of the surrounding rainforest. There had been an X drawn on four separate locales. A string of German script accompanied each of them. He recognized one word, "gold." It meant the same thing in both English and German. It confirmed that the Nazis had been searching for the City of Gold. They weren't just trying to escape the Allies' bombardment.

Jack traced his finger down *his* river and found no X's present. Based on this evidence, and the wrecked U-boat, Jack assumed that the Nazis never found El Dorado.

Good, he thought. The last thing Jack wanted to discover was a pillaged city of nothing. After everything Jack had been through so far, this mission needed to be a success.

He sighed. "Well, at least I'm not cold *and* wet."

Behind him, the wind shifted and blew inside the alcove, drenching his back in cool water. The temperature had dropped significantly since he had entered the hideout. *Great. You had to say something, didn't you?* Jack shrank away from the wriggling opening. He needed to find a way to pin down the vines and close the door. As of now, they were wildly blowing around with the wind. He spun and apologized to both sailors. He dragged their remains over to the entrance, stripped them of their clothes, and tossed them outside. Their dry wears could be used to start a fire later.

Jack leaned out and watched Bert and Ernie smash against the rocks beneath him. If Jack didn't survive this, he might have to explain himself to the sailors in the afterlife.

"So," he would say, "the reason I desecrated your remains was..."

With more room to work, Jack took stock of his surroundings. The rocks that Ernie had been lying against were large, but they were also loose. He gripped the edge of the biggest one and pulled it free. Inch by inch, Jack pushed it toward the precipice. He paused just long enough to jam the thickest vines beneath it. Jack smiled when the covering held in place. Most of the wind had been successfully blocked.

Step one was finished. He had blocked the wind and rain from entering. Now, Jack needed to do something about food. But he didn't see anything. So, he went about trying to make a fire instead. Jack gathered together the remaining firewood and prayed it would still light. He wadded up Bert's soiled shirt and placed it beneath the kindling. Jack drew his sharp, modern-day tactical knife and picked up a flat stone the size of his palm. He struck it several times, grinning when a spark ignited and fell atop the German's shirt. After six more tries, the clothing caught. It wasn't much, but it was a start. He laid down on his stomach and got close to the small flame. He gently blew on it. It was so close to catching the wood, but the vines came loose again. He and the wood were doused in a spray of water.

"Argh!" he snarled, climbing to his feet.

Jack was pissed, wet—slightly irritable. He grabbed the biggest boulder he could find, one at the back of the shallow cave, and pulled. But it didn't budge. Gritting his teeth, he pulled harder. This time, it shifted slightly, and he and the large stone fell *towards* the wall.

The alcove wasn't so shallow after all. Jack tumbled forward, rolling to a stop a few feet later. Something in the past had caused a cave-in, concealing the rest of the space from sight.

He laid flat on his belly before rolling over and looking up, noticing something strange. Jack had dropped his flashlight during the spill. It was lying on the ground somewhere and was now pointed to the ceiling at an odd angle. Like the ceremonial dagger, the ceiling was made-up of beautiful purple gemstones.

Jack grunted and sat up. "Well, that's not what I expected."

He plucked his flashlight off the ground and pointed it deeper into the cave. It narrowed significantly, but it also seemed to go on forever. With nowhere else to go, Jack continued forward. Thirty feet later, Jack was forced onto his hands and knees. Then, onto his stomach. He didn't stop. Jack army crawled with his flashlight out in front of him. Jack wasn't sure how far he had traveled before the floor gave out beneath him. He flipped and landed on his back a few feet later. As soon as he struck the hard stone, Jack began to slide headfirst back the other way.

Suddenly, the grade tilted violently, but his momentum was halted just as quickly as it had started. The earth leveled off, and he was deposited rather nicely onto a smooth floor of another larger chamber. Jack was lucky not to lose his flashlight this time. Above him, the likewise-purple ceiling seemed to glow.

He sat up and showed it around the cavern. Pockets of the same purple jewels were present, but they didn't cover the entire surface as they had in the smaller cave above his head. Rocky rubble lay on the ground beneath the cleared sections.

"They mined it!"

Jack leapt to his feet and swung his light around, seeing the remnants of a primitive mining operation. Several large dried-out leaves sat on the floor. A few of them held loose stones. But one of them had a single, baseball-sized purple gem sitting atop it. The plants were used to carry the jewels! Jack rushed over and discovered a trio of woven baskets near the center of the space. And like the leaf, one of them held a pair of the gemstones.

Jack shrugged. "You never know..." He pocketed a few of the raw, unfinished jewels. He stretched his lower back and looked around the circular room. "Now, how the hell am I going to get out of here?"

He looked up, tracing the beam of his flashlight down from the ceiling to the base of the far wall. The rocks didn't look right. He headed toward them and noticed something.

The stones had been stacked there. It wasn't a natural formation.

They sealed the quarry. Why?

What he did know was that if someone had blocked the entrance, then he could unblock it. It would take some time, but Jack was confident that he could move enough of them to make it outside. He slipped out of his shoulder holster, setting it down next to his machete and rifle. Last was the ceremonial dagger. For now, all he would need was his tactical knife and his flashlight. His other possessions would only be a nuisance as they banged around on his back and sides.

He tried like mad to dig out even one of the stones but failed. He needed both of his hands, and he really didn't want to stick his filthy flashlight back in his mouth. Jack stood, rubbed his neck, and looked up. He closed his eyes and thought hard of a way to make this work. Then, it came to him. He opened his eyes and spotted a cluster of the jewels directly above the impassable entry. Jack pointed his light down and found a torn basket. Kneeling behind the basket, he positioned it and his flashlight so that the narrowed beam connected dead center with the gemstones.

When it did, the rear portion of the cave bloomed to life in deep shades of purple. It wasn't much, but it was enough for Jack to see what he was doing. He scaled the rubble to the uppermost rocks. There, the light was the brightest. He quickly jammed the tip of his blade into a crack and got to work.

Lorenzo Matias wanted to get moving, but Aguilar didn't. No, *didn't* wasn't the right word. Aguilar *couldn't* get moving. He was locked in place. Matias was still having trouble believing what the drug lord had described. Aguilar had said that a sixty-foot-long snake, a Titanoboa, had emerged from the river and forcefully detached a German U-boat, as well as Jack Reilly, from their perch above the waterfall.

This is ridiculous, Matias thought, getting antsy.

He stepped up next to Aguilar. "Santiago, we have to go."

Aguilar either didn't hear him, or he was purposefully not paying attention to him. He was still locked onto the now empty falls. Matias could just make out the man mumbling to himself, but he couldn't understand the words. *Did he go mad?* Matias hoped that wasn't the case. All that was left of his team was him, Aguilar, and two soldiers. Matias wouldn't admit it out loud, but they were at a severe disadvantage without Jack around. Matias was injured, and he doubted he'd be any good in a fight if another should arise. He could move just fine, but not quickly.

They were going to have to backtrack too. The river was too strong for any of them to swim across. Matias pictured what Jack had been trying to do. The U-boat would've made a perfect bridge across the water. Now, it was gone, and Matias and the others were out of options.

"Santiago?"

Aguilar didn't respond.

Matias sneered, drew his pistol, and fired it into the sand. Aguilar wheeled around on him, fists balled, ready for a fight. Typically, Aguilar was always in control of his emotions. Matias had never once seen the man express fear or even anger. He was the most level-headed person Matias had ever met, even when he was brutally beating another human being. But now, the man displayed a combination of both terror and rage. His eyes darted back and forth, and his breathing was labored.

Matias didn't holster his weapon—not until Aguilar proved he was back to being himself. He would shoot the drug lord, here and now, if he proved otherwise. There was no time to babysit a grown man while trying not to die.

"Santiago."

Aguilar finally looked at him.

Matias uttered two words that he knew would get the guy moving again.

"El Dorado."

Aguilar's attention zeroed in on the former TAC agent. Some of his resolve returned, but his eyes were still wild. His posture began to relax, and he unclenched his jaw and quivering fists. Without another word, Aguilar pounded back up the shore. Now, it was Matias' turn to gaze at the falls. Aguilar was confident that Jack hadn't survived.

Matias wasn't so sure.

21

Jack didn't know how much time had passed, but it must've been a couple of hours. His hands were killing him, and his knife blade had dulled significantly. He checked his watch and confirmed that he had been digging for just over two hours. A speck of wavering light could be seen. Either the weather was still bad, or he was about to come out directly behind a veil of cascading water.

He unscrewed the cap to his canteen and took a sip, but nothing came out.

"Wonderful..."

Flashlight in hand, he stood and climbed back up the pile of rubble, stepping over stones that he had personally dislodged. Jack was as careful as he could be. There was no way of knowing how unstable the pile was—the wall too. Jack craned his neck back and, once again, made sure that there were no signs of it all coming down on top of him. He panned his light back and forth until he was satisfied. When he was content, Jack ducked down and crawled forward on his belly.

He figured he would pop out behind the waterfall. It would've concealed the quarry's entrance perfectly. It was a cliché thing to presume, yet here he was. With his knife in his teeth, Jack scurried through the tight opening. He would've made a good pirate in a past life—an honorable one. He would've been one-part Jack Sparrow and one-part Robin Hood. Jack could see himself robbing from the rich and giving to the poor, but using the *Black Pearl* to do so.

He shook his head and refocused. His concentration was slipping away. Instead of focusing on the task at hand, Jack found himself contemplating the name of his ship.

Renegade Reilly's Revenge.

Jack sighed. He needed a proper nap.

He slithered into a small hollow. It was just large enough for him to sit up. Settling in, he gently retrieved his knife from his mouth and jammed the blade into a small space between two flat stones. They were each the size of a square manhole cover but twice as thick. Someone had purposefully stacked this pair together. The entire pile had been intentionally created and not just by some random cave-in. He didn't know why someone had gone to all this trouble. No one would've found this place regardless of it being blocked.

Jack dug and dug, but to no avail. He spun around and jammed his shoulder up against the flat stones, and pushed. Surprisingly, one of them shifted, ever so slightly. With newfound energy, Jack reset his stance and got his legs directly beneath him. In a perfect three-point stance, Jack leaned into the rocks and, once more, pushed. The top stone slid across the surface of the one beneath it. Jack gritted his teeth and held his breath. He put as much as he had left into the effort.

"Woah!" he yelped, spilling headfirst along with a half dozen boulders. He got his arms up and covered his head. Jack turned and barrel-rolled down a small embankment of rocks, feeling every single one of them poke and prod his body. He took an edge of one of them between two ribs. The hard shot made him cough and wheeze, and he landed on his side, eyes closed. After a few deep breaths, he opened them and gazed into the empty eye sockets of another corpse.

"Gah!" he shouted, rolling away.

He collided with the blockage, dust flying everywhere. Blinking it away, he turned back toward the body. It, as well as four others, were scattered all around the quarry's entrance. Behind them was a semi-circle of rocky earth, and beyond that, the foot of the booming waterfall. Jack's hypothesis had been correct. Sort of.

He looked back and forth between the remains, recognizing the uniforms of the Nazi submariners. These men had been a part of Bert and Ernie's outfit. The Germans had concealed the quarry—*not* the natives! They had hidden their discovery from anyone that might have stumbled across it. Jack was confident in his assessment. Like Bert, each of these sailors also possessed gunshot wounds to their heads. Jack even spotted a bullet casing near one of the corpses.

"Geez, Ernie... What the hell, man?" The seaman had gone on a killing spree before finally offing himself. No one had lived long enough to report the discovery. Ernie's psychopathic behavior had inadvertently concealed the find from everyone, including the Nazis.

Before Jack ventured any further, he climbed back up into the hole and reclaimed his belongings. He returned to the backside of the waterfall and filled his empty canteen. He guzzled down the entire thing before refilling it once more. With his thirst quenched, Jack went about searching the dead. Unlike the drift map he had found with Bert, Jack found nothing of interest here. No weapons either.

These men had been treated as prison camp workers.

"How long were you guys here?" Jack asked the bodies.

The evidence—and a bit of Jack's imagination—told a grim story. Ernie had taken over command and forced his comrades into labor. One after the other, his men would've collapsed from exhaustion. And one by one, once they had completed their chore, Ernie had executed them.

He looked up and pictured Ernie's body. "Bert was the last to defy you, wasn't he? But you acted rashly and killed him and left yourself with no one to help."

Jack slipped back into his shoulder holster. Then, he slung his rifle and machete over his shoulder. The only thing he was sorely missing was food. And he was starving. The capybara, while not a preference, would've been a Godsend right about now. Jack needed something else.

He licked his lips. "Mmm... Nona's pizza." He shook his head and berated himself. "Cut that shit out, Jack."

To his right was a small gap between the cascading water and the cliff face. He made his way to it, relishing in the cold spray that struck him. It was refreshing, and it woke him up some. He put his back against the wet stone and sidestepped his way around the blinding spray of the falling water. Jack closed his eyes but kept moving. Soon, the barrage subsided, and he reopened them.

"Ouch," he said, seeing U-590.

The submarine was on its side and cracked open like a tin can. Luckily, there was no sign of the creature. Jack had no idea if the snake actually was a Titanoboa or not. Either way, it wasn't meant to be trifled with. He would actively avoid a second run-in with the beast. The memory of its devilish eyes made Jack's skin run cold. It had been a chilling experience for sure.

There was no rain, but the air was wet with moisture. Jack didn't think the humidity could get any worse than it was before. It was insufferable—challenging to breathe. He took the trek slowly, navigating the wet stones surrounding the base of the falls with care. Jack descended the ten-foot-tall rock formation, purposely keeping his distance from the circular plunge pool. As of now, Jack would assume the serpent was beneath the surface, waiting for him to drop his guard. Moreover, he wouldn't be turning his back to the water for any length of time.

If he had the time, Jack would've figured out a way to explore the U-boat. It had to have been full of all kinds of historically significant artifacts. He still had the drift chart, though. That would be enough to prove that U-590 hadn't been sunk as stated in the history books.

He frowned. Jack wasn't going to be able to reveal this great find. There was no way to do so unless he gave up the presence of TAC. His discovery was going to have to remain his for now. The thought of not being able to tell anyone about a Nazi submarine in the middle of a South American rainforest hurt.

He'd tell Bull, of course. Jack told Bull everything.

Which makes him vulnerable, Jack thought.

He pushed the thought away and followed the natural bend of the river. As much as he wanted to move his hike into the trees, Jack knew the plan. Their destination was on this river somewhere up ahead. Jack estimated it would take him another day to reach it, at most, as long as he didn't run into any more obstacles. Unfortunately, it seemed like he couldn't do anything *but* run into additional obstacles.

"Okay," he said, ticking off a list with his fingers, "you've battled mercenaries and soldiers. You've been welcomed to the neighborhood by the locals—both good and bad. You've also run into a jaguar, ate the largest guinea pig you've ever seen, and stared into the demonic eyes of a snake that would make St. Patrick shit his pants."

He took a breath and stopped.

Jack needed to calm down before he had a panic attack. He allowed himself to close his eyes. He focused on the rainforest and let it speak to him. It was beautiful. The waterfall dominated the area's other noises, but he could also hear the calls of random birds and the squeaks of small animals. In a way, it reminded him of home. It reminded him of Yellowstone.

That was what eventually eased his tension. Jack knew what he was doing. He was more comfortable in places like this nowadays than out in the *wilds* of humanity. Here the river was dangerous, but Jack knew he must continue to follow it if he wanted to find the others, as well as El Dorado. He tried to stay near its bank but was occasionally forced inland here and there. At least the sound of running water was always easy to relocate.

He decided to arm himself while he walked. His AK-47 packed a mean punch but wasn't all that accurate at long ranges. Luckily for him, any attack would take place up close, if at all, based on the most recent events.

Jack hefted his rifle higher. He'd be ready for anything.

It had been hours since the two soldiers were torn to ribbons by a flock of diseased Andean condors. At least, Hugo thought they were diseased. Miguel agreed with him. Neither man could come up with another name for it. They were all confused about what was going on here. Some of the rainforest's inhabitants were going ballistic and acting out of character. Condors weren't typically aggressive hunters despite their impressive size. They ate carrion, and rarely did they ever eat anything else. Vultures were the garbage disposals of the natural world.

But the men had all witnessed the birds violently attack two living, breathing human beings.

Hugo couldn't get the scene out of his head. Something was seriously wrong around here, and they were stuck in the middle of it—marching toward it. Everyone in their group agreed that whatever lay at the center of Ordaz's tomb's map was the origin of this...this sickness.

"Why would you point us to it, though?" Hugo asked himself. He shook his weary head and yawned. His mind was wandering now. "We should stop."

"Not yet," Miguel replied. "We go as far as we can."

Hugo couldn't argue with the man. He was too exhausted to do so. Hugo looked over his shoulder and was impressed by what he saw. Each of the ten remaining soldiers was still moving steadily onward. Like in the movies, Hugo half-expected to only see nine of them when he turned around. He figured that the guy at the end of the line would fall behind and get lost, or perhaps get picked off by something hungry without anyone noticing.

His stomach grumbled. So far, they had all been surviving on rations. They each had enough to last them another day—tops. Eventually, they'd have to go out and hunt for their dinner. Hugo thought about what the rainforest had to offer in terms of a meal. There was a bevy of things you could safely ingest, but there was also a laundry list of things that could kill you.

I think I'll wait for one of Aguilar's men to take the first bite.

Hugo completely lost track of time. He bumped into a mass of flesh and stumbled backward, crashing into the nearest soldier. Miguel turned and grabbed Hugo's shirt sleeve before he could fall. Miguel steadied him, then patted him on the shoulder.

"We're stopping."

Hugo nodded and shrugged out of his backpack. Everyone that had one did. A few of the soldiers had lost theirs over the last day for various reasons. Manuel didn't carry one since he was still hefting around the M2 Browning. His brother carried it on occasion too, but it was Manuel's baby, and he didn't let it out of his sight for long.

Manuel eased the hulking weapon to the ground and swiftly began to set it up. He unfolded its tripod stand and went about reconnecting the armament to it. In minutes the powerful machine gun was ready. And like Manuel had done on the gunboat, he made his bed directly beneath the weapon.

"He sure loves that thing, doesn't he?"

Miguel looked over. He shook his head. "No, not really, but he knows it's our best defense against whatever attacked Jack and the others."

"You come up with anything yet?"

Miguel shook his head. "Nothing I can believe, no." He perked up and unclipped his radio. "But I can try to find out."

Hugo began to unpack his things while Miguel attempted to radio Aguilar and Matias. He was unsuccessful at first but connected with the traitor TAC agent on a crackling connection. The poor signal would help to continue to hide Miguel's identity. He had met Matias several times, though it had been a few years since, now.

Miguel relayed that they were stopping for the night.

"We're doing the same," Matias replied. "Santiago needs some rest."

Miguel eyed Hugo. It was a weird comment to make. So, Miguel pushed for an explanation.

"Come again?"

"Santiago... He says he saw a Titanoboa if you can believe it. He said it attacked a beached German U-boat and took it, and Reilly, over a waterfall." Hugo and Miguel cringed at the thought of Jack being dead.

"Where is Aguilar now?" Miguel asked.

"Why does it matter?" Matias asked, sounding suspicious.

"The men—we—are worried and could use some assurances."

Matias sighed. "I have no guarantees to give you. But if it makes you feel better, he is further ahead of our camp. He insisted on being alone tonight."

Hugo needed to know. He mouthed Jack's name.

Miguel nodded and asked. "Your thoughts on the American's status?"

“I don’t know. Unfortunately, I wouldn’t count him out. He’s like a cockroach. He just won’t die.”

That made Hugo smile.

Miguel finished up with Matias, doing his best to relay their exact position. But he was the one with the GPS device. Matias didn’t have one. Not anymore.

“The device failed,” Matias explained. “I think water got inside of it. No matter, though. We’re still following the river.” He let out a tired laugh. “I hope it’s the right one.”

I hope it’s not, Hugo thought. He wished for Matias and Aguilar to stay lost forever.

And with that, the receiver went silent. To conserve its battery, Miguel turned his radio off, then clipped it back onto his belt.

Something in the trees shifted. Hugo and Miguel both scooched closer to Manuel and the M2, just in case.

22

Minutes turned into hours. Since the incident with the Titanoboa, Jack's solo romp through the rainforest had taken a turn for the better, and he had been left alone. Occasionally, he would spot movement in the trees, but when he stopped to look, whatever creature had caused the commotion was already gone.

He smiled when he heard an agitated howler monkey go off somewhere behind him. Their bellow was easy to recognize. Several more joined in. They were like the wolf of the jungle. Once one got going, the others were bound to start up too.

The bugs grew worse the further downriver he traveled. He could almost see their swarms stop, locate him, and move in for the kill. His long sleeves and pants were mostly keeping them at bay. Unfortunately, his face and neck were exposed. So, he did what was needed. He paused, knelt by the river, and scooped up a handful of mud. Jack slathered his exposed skin with a healthy layer of muck, instantaneously noticing a difference. The pests no longer cared for his flavor.

Jack felt like he was ahead of everyone else, but just how far ahead was he? It wasn't a bad thing. He could scope the place out before Aguilar and Matias arrived.

If they arrived, Jack thought.

That was the best-case scenario. Even if the two men didn't die, Jack needed them to get lost, or at least, delayed until he could find whatever they were searching for. At this time, they still didn't know if El Dorado existed, and if it did, was it a city? The golden tomb's map pinpointed the location of something special. For now, Jack would continue to assume it was a city constructed of gold.

What else could it be? And what's up with the red eyes?

They reminded Jack of a strung-out druggy, except they usually had bloodshot whites, not blood-red irises. It was a mystery, for sure. And he was getting the feeling that he'd solve it soon. He stood, catching movement to his right. A pair of furry blobs appeared from behind a cluster of palms. They entered the shallows and circumvented the growth, wading straight toward Jack. More capybaras. Jack kept still and watched. When they were thirty feet from him, they stopped and looked up at him.

"Oh shit," Jack said. Their eyes were red.

Just like the Titanoboa.

Both animals squealed and charged him. Jack didn't let either of them get close enough to do any damage. Their teeth were similar to all rodents, just more prominent. He swung his rifle around and carefully lined up the capybaras. Jack held his breath and then released it, squeezing the trigger of his weapon four times.

Each of the two-round bursts found their intended targets, and the animals dropped.

Jack didn't check to see if they were dead. He stood and re-entered the trees before something else could come and investigate the noise. The sun was getting low, and so was the temperature. It wasn't a significant drop, but he welcomed it. He needed to find somewhere to crash for the night. Staying on ground level wasn't an option—not with the Titanoboa still lurking.

Demon capybaras too. Whatever was infecting the animals of the rainforest, it possessed the ability to jump species which made it all the more dangerous.

It took Jack a few minutes of searching to find a good spot. He eventually located a tree with thick branches and long vines. Being a skilled free climber, it took Jack no time at all to scale the tree. Thirty feet up, he sat on one of its heavy-duty branches and drew his knife. It was much duller than before, though it was plenty sharp enough to cut through the vines. Jack got as comfortable as possible and began wrapping the climbing plant around the branch and his thighs. They would keep him in place while he slept.

Jack kept his AK-47 slung around his shoulder but held the weapon in front of him. He crossed his arms on top of it and leaned back. The tree trunk was rigid and unforgiving.

"Not too shabby," Jack mumbled. He had slept on worse before.

It didn't take long for Jack to doze off. The gentle swaying of the trees and the vocalizations of the rainforest's nocturnal species lulled him into dreamland. He figured that the events of the last few days would keep him awake, but they didn't. The rainforest's song overpowered it all.

Jack awoke. It was pitch-black except for the random rays of moonbeams that made it through the canopy. Just for a moment, Jack forgot that he was tied to a tree branch. His back ached. It was primarily because of the handful of bumps and bruises he had suffered and not because of the lack of cushion the tree offered him. He checked his watch and saw that he had only been asleep for a couple of hours.

He grumbled incoherently and adjusted his incline, closing his eyes again. They snapped back open when something moved below and behind him. The sleep drained away from him in an instant. He shouldered his rifle and leaned left, looking back around the tree trunk. It was too dark to see much of anything.

There!

Beneath one of the small openings in the canopy, he witnessed the ground move. No, not *move*. It slithered.

Jack's eyes opened wide. The Titanoboa was directly below him. It moved slowly and was almost totally noiseless. Its stealth was impressive considering its size. The creature's body only made the slightest grinding sound. Its movements harmonized perfectly with that of the white noise of the jungle. Jack barely noticed it now. He waited until the tip of its tail passed through the light before shifting his line of sight. He found another small opening forty feet ahead. The Titanoboa's body had already engulfed it.

Then, it and the grinding noise was gone. Jack was, once more, left to his thoughts. He knew he wouldn't be sleeping again tonight, but he needed to try. Jack closed his eyes. His mind ran wild with images of the giant serpent staring into his soul. He couldn't describe the sensation he had felt when he looked it in the eye. It was the closest thing to evil he had ever seen.

Most civilizations, at one time or another, regarded snakes as symbols of evil. Jack knew it was nothing more than primitive superstitions. But some cultures revered serpents as symbols of fertility and rebirth. The Hopi tribe of North America was one of them. The Hopi people went as far as dancing in celebration with snakes. The creatures had never bothered Jack, but this one did, chiefly because it was big enough to swallow him whole with little trouble. He regularly avoided anything that could pull off such a feat.

Jack sat up. The grinding sound had returned. This time, it came from in front of him. He was convinced that the serpent was searching for something—for him. Jack was overdue for a shower, but his human scent still stood out. Luckily, his stink was faint.

At least, Jack hoped it was.

Snakes owned an incredible sense of smell. One this big must be able to track everything in the area, stretching for miles. Something foreign had entered its territory recently. That something was Jack and Aguilar and their teams. The Titanoboa was doing its best to expel, or even kill, the perceived threat.

The red eyes still concerned Jack. The behemoth was acting way more hostile than he ever thought possible. Like the capybaras, something was affecting the serpent's amygdala, causing it to act aggressively. Toxins and natural defects were common causes. Jack was leaning toward a toxin of some kind since it wasn't just the snake that was acting oddly.

Suddenly, the Titanoboa stopped. Jack looked for it but was unable to. The sixty-foot-long monster had vanished into thin air. Jack frantically searched the area around him, using what little light there was, but he failed to locate something that should've been too big to lose.

Unless... Jack shuddered.

The Titanoboa's lair was nearby. It was the only explanation. Jack had unknowingly stumbled into the heart of its territory. "Son of a bitch," he mouthed, scared to death. He didn't know what was worse, having the beast slithering around directly below him or knowing that he was right on top of its nest. It must've been an enormous burrow too.

The one thing he had going for him was that the Titanoboa hadn't discovered him. And now, it looked like it was retiring for the night. Jack inhaled deeply, slowing his pulse. He laid his head back against the tree and closed his eyes. He was coming down off an immense adrenaline spike and was starting to feel tired again.

Jack spent the rest of the night trying to get comfortable enough to sleep. He did, but for only a few minutes here and there. He never once passed out for more than half an hour. Jack watched the sunrise from his perch. He couldn't actually see it, but he did watch as it subtly penetrated the canopy. The illumination stopped at a stage just brighter than dusk.

He yawned and went about untying his legs but didn't get up. He needed to get the feeling back in his lower body first. The pins and needles sensation in his feet was unbearable. He rode the pain in silence, knowing it would pass. While he waited, he searched the grounds for the Titanoboa. The animal was nowhere to be seen.

"Okay," he muttered, standing.

He kept his back to the tree and stretched out the rest of his body. As he expected, his lower back was killing him. He rotated his upper body to the left and then the right, pausing the motion. His eyes found something directly behind his position. Jack spun so fast that he nearly fell out of the tree. He wrapped his arms around the trunk, hugging it tightly. Slowly, he leaned around it. Not thirty feet from the base of his tree was the entrance to the serpent's nest. It was a natural cave opening at the bottom of a small hill. If Jack had to guess, the entry was barely large enough to fit the Titanoboa. If it continued to grow, it would eventually outgrow its own home.

Jack hadn't heard it emerge in the middle of the night. It must still be in the home. But he couldn't wait to find out. He needed to get moving. He eased himself down the tree, stepping onto the ground lightly. Not only did snakes have an acute sense of smell, but they also had a highly developed sense of hearing—not that they had ears. They listened to the world around them through skull vibrations. If Jack didn't watch his step, the Titanoboa would *hear* his presence through the earth.

He backed away from the tree, keeping it in between him and the cave. Every couple of steps, he glanced at the ground behind him. Falling wasn't an option. His weight hitting the earth would be like a signal flare soaring high into the sky. He continued in this manner for a hundred more yards before turning around and speeding up. He didn't run, however. Jack did his best morning mall walker impression and turned on the jets.

Jack weaved through the trees, keeping the river on his left. The farther away he got from the Titanoboa's nest, the more relaxed he became. Soon, Jack slowed and found a steadier rhythm. Interestingly, the dense cluster of trees and grasses thinned out as he moved. They did the exact opposite along the river. Jack tried to keep the water in his sights but couldn't do so. He stopped and headed straight for it. Hands on hips, he inspected the growth, trying to find a way through.

"Dammit," he mumbled, feeling something crawling on his arm as he ducked through a tangle of vines. He brushed the creature away without identifying it.

His next step found water. Jack looked down, cringing at his submerged boot. The river's bank had been completely swallowed. There was no bank here. It meant that Jack wouldn't be walking along it without taking a dip.

He shook his head. "No freaking way." He knew what was hiding beneath the surface and was actively trying to avoid it.

Jack backtracked and planned his next move. If he couldn't keep the river on his left, he would keep the trees along the river on it.

Easy enough.

But it wasn't that simple. The brush grew so dense that Jack couldn't push his way through. Nor could he cut it with his machete. Tree limbs grew into one another, and the mosses and vines became intertwined with one another and merged down into grasses. Jack was forced around the impasse. He continued his hike, visualizing the river's position in reference to his own. The trees thinned up ahead and revealed his next obstacle.

A cliff.

Jack followed it up, spotting an anomaly near its peak. It was too high to see precisely what the irregularity was, though. A tree branch snapped behind him. Jack made the call and began to free-climb the crag. Anything was better than what he had come across last night. Keeping three points of contact on the cliff face's surface, Jack steadily made his way higher and higher. He found a narrow ledge forty feet up and stopped to catch his breath. Typically, he wouldn't have to stop so soon, but he was tired, and his hands were killing him. The skin was raw and covered in tiny, annoying cuts. A loud crack preceded a falling tree. Jack was just high enough to witness the top of the tree disappear below the green canopy.

Jack shot to his feet and continued his climb. Twenty-five feet later, he came upon the anomaly he had seen from the rainforest floor. Short, wooden spikes had been driven into gaps in the rock. They dotted the façade and were spaced at random distances from one another.

To keep something away, Jack guessed. He looked straight up. *From whom?*

He paused to inspect one of the spikes just as a second tree came crashing down below. Jack looked between his feet but saw nothing. He knew what it was, though.

The Titanoboa had emerged from its den.

A breeze picked up and almost dislodged Jack from the cliff. He leaned into the rocks and held on. Once it subsided, he got moving. Jack knew what awaited him below if he decided to retreat. He was pretty sure he knew what awaited him up top too. But he held out hope for something else.

Twenty feet from the top, Jack was forced to stop again, unable to find a proper handhold. He gawked at the six-inch-thick spikes here. Their bases had been fitted into hand-carved holes. Not only were the people that installed them capable of scaling the cliff, but they also possessed the ingenuity to build tools that were tough enough to chisel through solid rock.

He gripped one of the spikes and pulled down. It held. Jack took a deep breath and pulled himself up, planting his foot on a second spike. It, too, supported his weight. He continued upward, using the pointed shafts as if they were a set of primal monkey bars. Jack was now at the mercy of the spikes' positioning, zigzagging back and forth up the rest of the way. The protrusions thinned out near the peak. The last leg of his trip would have to be done the old-fashioned way. Jack stood with his feet on separate spikes, balancing with his chest up against the cliff face. He reached as high as he could, grazing the ledge with his fingertips. The sound of another tree crashing to the forest floor spurred him into action even though he wasn't currently in any danger from the Titanoboa.

At least, I don't think I am.

Jack's foot slipped, and he fell, yelping in fear. He landed spread-eagle on the shaft of a protruding spike with a thud and a groan. He reflexively squeezed his legs together, ignoring the ache in his crotch. Regathering his wind, Jack pulled himself back up, finding a handhold to grip.

"Wow..." he said, taking a deep breath. "Really could've done without that."

He rescaled the distance he had lost. He went for gold this time and jumped, clutching the edge before he slipped and fell again. Holding tight with both hands, Jack pulled himself up with the last of his strength. He got his right knee up and rolled his way back onto solid ground. Flat on his back, Jack turned his head to the left and spotted the river. Jack saw that the tributary broke off into three smaller waterways from this high angle. They each moved off in three different directions. If Jack had followed it, like he had planned on, he would've become lost—probably forever.

"At least," he said, panting, "I don't have...the snake...to worry about...anymore."

But Jack wasn't out of danger yet. He turned away from the cliff and felt the blood drain from his face. Someone had to have built the spikes, and Jack had just found their village.

"Oh crap."

23

Jack got to his feet, expected to be overwhelmed, and slaughtered where he stood. He didn't even draw his pistol to defend himself. He was that hopeless. But miraculously, death didn't come. He listened closely for the pounding feet of his would-be executioners. Still, there was nothing. Jack's luck was at an all-time high.

Anyone home?

Like a stealthy cat burglar, Jack stepped lightly and tiptoed through the center of the primitive settlement. It was an eerie feeling. It made his skin crawl. Sandwiched between every other heartbeat, he expected an attack. But, like before, death didn't come.

"Don't question it," Jack told himself.

He kept moving, spotting the edge of their small village up ahead. The trees had been cleared in areas, making way for circular huts built of whatever the builders could get their hands on. The nearest shelter had a roof comprised of layers of palm fronds, and its walls had been constructed of cut tree trunks. The architecture was impressive, bearing in mind what these people had to work with. Not only had they built their own homes from scratch, but they would have had to construct the tools they used too.

Jack slowed at the center of the village. There was a communal firepit, and it was subtly smoking. It had only recently burned out. The inhabitants couldn't have gone far. Jack headed around the hearth, rechecking his surroundings.

The place smelled of pork and fish. Jack wrinkled his nose.

Capybara.

He passed three more huts before coming across something he didn't expect. Right on the outskirts of their village was a cemetery. Jack counted over two dozen oval-shaped mounds. Each one of them was lined up next to the other. A few were relatively small.

Kids. Damn...

Unfortunately, young people's deaths were part of living in a place like this. Modern medicine didn't exist out here, and neither did the practices of its doctors. If you caught a cold in a third-world country, it could kill you with little trouble.

The flu? See yah.

God forbid you stubbed your toe. Boom! Gangrene.

Further ahead was another river. This one was different than the others. At its center was a small rocky island. Spanning the gap between the land masses on either side were bridges. It roared as loud as any that Jack had come across so far. He hustled over to it and skidded to a stop.

"Oh, come on!"

The paths across weren't bridges. They were logs.

The natives had cut down a few of the more sizeable trees and used them as rudimentary bridges. Jack knelt and inspected the first one's base. Before laying the trunk down, they had dug out the ground directly beneath it. Jack estimated that six inches of it had been buried. The earth was acting as an anchor, keeping the log from rocking and rolling. It was similar to how *U-590* had been buried in the sand. Jack couldn't help it. He whistled and stood upright. It was roughly twenty feet across the first section and only a foot above the water's surface. The second expanse looked to be the same distance.

Both *bridges* were wet from the river's spray.

"Yeah, this isn't sketchy," Jack muttered, weighing his options.

He glanced back and felt there was only one option—forward.

Eight natives appeared from the ledge that Jack had just surmounted. They quickly spotted him and communicated the sighting within their ranks.

Jack mounted the first log before they made their move. He didn't have the time to test it properly. Luckily, the felled tree didn't budge. Turning around, Jack shuffled backward a few feet. His position atop the tree trunk was entirely exposed. He wanted nothing more than to shoulder his AK-47 and empty it into the advancing horde. Jack refrained from doing so because the only ammo his rifle had was inside its only magazine. He needed to conserve his bullets, no matter what. There were more dangerous things out there than eight loincloth-wearing men armed with nothing except bows and arrows. He finished crossing the first log just as the natives approached the river's edge. In unison, they drew back their bows.

Jack noticed a horrifying similarity between them all. Their eyes were red.

Them too?

Their eyes were the same color as the Titanoboa's. They didn't attack Jack, thankfully. He peered over his shoulder and saw why they had not, immediately, slain him. Jack was stuck halfway across the raging river—right in the middle of *two* gangs of natives. A second, larger group had silently moved into position behind Jack, unannounced. Something about the latest newcomers caught his attention. Unlike their loincloth-wearing brothers, these people wore an unusual combination of both traditional and modern-day garbs.

Jack recognized one of them. It was the man from the plunge pool—the one who had warned him about the guardians. Jack gave the guy a courtesy wave. The twenty, non-red-eyed natives answered him by drawing back their bow strings.

"Seriously, guys." Jack nervously laughed and raised his hands. "Can't we all just get along?"

The leader of the regular tribe shouted across the raging waters in a language Jack had never heard before. One of the red-eyed men stepped forward and pounded his chest in defiance. He spouted off a raspy, hissing reply, venom dripping from his words. These two knew each other well.

The red-eyed man turned back to Jack and jabbed a finger in his direction.

Uh oh.

The other chief quickly stepped forward with what Jack hoped was a commanding "No!"

Nothing immediately happened. Jack didn't know if that was a good thing or a bad thing. Either way, he prepared for the inevitable. He turned his head and closed his eyes, waiting to become the world's largest porcupine.

But no one loosed a single arrow.

He took a quick glimpse and watched the eight red-eyed, loinclothed men back down. They lowered their weapons and allowed Jack to continue across the second log. Jack turned around and sprinted across the last five feet. The other party leader greeted him with a handshake, grasping Jack's forearm in a crushing vise grip.

Jack winced. "Easy there, buddy. It's been a rough couple of days."

His new friend didn't understand a lick of what Jack had just said. The language barrier was going to be a big problem if Jack was going to try and get him to help. Hopefully, the minuscule amount of Spanish he knew would be enough.

Jack turned back toward the river. The red-eyed tribe was gone.

"Well, that's not creepy."

He was ushered into the trees and away from the water. They snaked their way through the throng of vegetation for half an hour in complete silence before stopping. When they did, Jack was led into a second settlement. This one didn't appear as permanent as the last one. He looked around and realized that it was more of a campsite than anything else. At the center of it was a small fire. The tribal leader—the chief—motioned for Jack to sit. He nodded and sat—everyone did except for one man who began preparing some kind of drink instead.

Alright, let's get down to business. Jack needed answers.

"Thank you," he said, bowing slightly. Chief looked at him oddly. "Right," Jack said, feeling foolish, "this isn't Asia." He held out his hand and, for a second time, grasped forearms. "*Gracias.*"

The native gave him a curt nod in return.

Jack pointed back the way they had come. "Guardians?" His new friend nodded. Jack made a side-to-side slithering motion with his right arm. "Guardian?" Again, the tribal leader nodded.

So, the Titanoboa is also a guardian, Jack thought. *What else?* He needed more information about what he was fighting.

It came to him. He pointed at both of his eyes, recalling the word for *red* in Spanish. "*Rojo.* Guardians?"

Chief looked uncomfortable, but he nodded once more. It seemed that everything with crimson irises was considered to be a guardian. Matias' assessment had been correct after all. The sickness—whatever it was—could cross species.

Small, wooden bowls were passed around the group. Even Jack received one. It was of simple construction. Its worn surfaces, both inside and out, told Jack that it was old and had been used many times. He was the first to be offered a drink. He was a stranger, but he was being treated as a welcomed guest.

The liquid was warm, and it owned a powerful floral aroma. *Tea?* Jack thought. It might have been a ceremonial drink—a beverage that was consumed after a successful mission. But what was their mission?

"*Gracias,*" Jack said again, attempting to use what little Spanish he knew. He held up the bowl and bowed his head slightly, doing what he could to show his appreciation.

Chief held up his drink and began to speak the same language Jack had heard at the river crossing. The other men quickly joined in. It was a chant. They each raised their bowls to the heavens. Jack followed their example and also lifted his. He had no idea what these people were praying to, but he would show them respect and honor their customs.

After three seconds of silence, everyone drank. Jack paused and closely inspected his tea before taking the first sip. It was unsweetened and slightly bitter, but no more than a typical India Pale Ale. Floral and herbal notes exploded on his palette. Jack was pretty sure he was drinking a combination of mulled flowers, herbs, and roots. It wasn't his thing, but he drank it all anyway, earning a smile of pride from Chief.

A pleasant warming sensation engulfed Jack. He instantly felt his rising anxiety wash away, as well as the ache in his back and legs. Jack felt pretty damn good. He glanced down into his drink and raised an eyebrow.

He needed to get the recipe before he went home.

"What's your name?" Jack asked Chief. "*Nombre.*"

The native put a hand on his chest. "Gaspar."

"Gaspar?"

He nodded.

Jack reached out his hand and clasped forearms with Gapsar. "I'm Jack."

"Jack," Gaspar repeated, pronouncing it *Jock*.

Gaspar stood. Jack did too, but no one else followed. "Uh," he said, watching Gaspar step away from the fire. "Am I supposed to come with you?" Gaspar stopped and waved him on. "Okay, I guess that's a yes."

Jack and Gaspar were the only ones that hiked back into the trees. They were on a trail too, but Gaspar didn't look all that concerned about it. Jack had been actively avoiding them since arriving in the rainforest. The native obviously knew this land, and Jack was going to trust his judgment.

"Where are you taking me?" Jack asked, speaking softly. Even then, his voice sounded like he had just spoken through a megaphone. The jungle was eerily still here. The only thing Jack heard was the crunching of his footfalls. Gaspar's feet were silent. His light steps and bare feet allowed him to travel unheard.

Checking his watch, Jack saw that twenty minutes had passed. Gaspar led him to a small, cleared section of land that was no greater than the size of his living room. A single boulder sat up against a rise in the dirt. Gaspar motioned for Jack to stand on one side. He gripped his end and looked over at Jack. He nodded.

"We're lifting this thing?" Gaspar didn't answer. How could he? "Alrighty, let's do this. *Uno, dos, tres.*"

The pair put everything they had into it. Slowly, the large round stone moved. Jack spotted darkness behind it. When it was halfway removed, Gaspar said something and shook his head. Jack eased up, and they stopped. The two men took a moment to catch their breath. Gaspar stretched his back and yawned, and since yawns were contagious, Jack yawned too.

Gaspar ducked and slipped headfirst into the void. Jack followed him and produced his flashlight. He wasn't sure if Gaspar had ever seen one. He clicked it on, covering most of the lens with his hand. The native turned and held out his hand, unafraid of the "magical device." This led Jack to believe that Gaspar's tribe had experienced more contact with the outside world than most Amazonians.

It begged the question.

Why continue to live like this if you know what else is out there?

These people—Gaspar's people--were here for a very specific reason. They possessed a purpose that was far greater than living more comfortably and acquiring nice things. After traveling on their hands and knees for a time, the cave grew taller and broader. Gaspar showed Jack exactly why he and his people had stayed put.

"Oh," Jack said, dumbfounded.

The flashlight's beam stopped on the back wall of the two-car garage-sized hollow. It displayed a pictograph of unknown origin. It was apparent that one of Gaspar's people had drawn it, but it was impossible for Jack to assess how long ago it was completed. Jack wasn't in that business.

The base of the image showed a wave of people moving up toward a beautiful purple star. Jack realized what it was, and he pulled the ceremonial dagger from his belt. Gaspar took a step back. Whatever the blade embodied, Gaspar wasn't thrilled that it was present. Jack held it up and compared the cut gemstone implanted in it to the one represented in the drawing.

"They're the same," Jack said.

When the people neared the star, they split down the middle. Half went right toward a light source of some kind. The other half headed left and were engulfed in inky darkness.

Jack didn't need to be an anthropological expert in cave art to know that this pictograph signified the paths of good and evil. Maybe it was the tribe's belief system's origin! If so, Jack had just been shown something amazing.

And why me?

The stone bothered him too much to celebrate the discovery.

"What is it?" he asked, pointing at the purple star.

Gaspar didn't reply.

Jack needed to break it down into its simplest form. He pointed at the people moving into the light.

"Good? *Bueno*?"

Gaspar nodded.

Jack stepped left and pointed at the people moving into the abyssal cloud.

"Evil?" Gaspar didn't understand. Jack stuck out his forefingers and lifted them to his head. He mimicked Satan's horns. "Evil. *Diablo.*"

Gaspar's eyes widened a bit. He nodded. "*Demonio.*"

"Demon?"

Gaspar nodded.

So, it's not the Devil, per se, Jack deduced, scratching his head. *The darkness just represents 'evil,' in general.*

"*Corazón.*"

"What?" Jack asked, looking away from the artwork.

Gaspar tapped Jack's chest. "*Corazón.*"

Jack didn't comprehend what he was trying to tell him. The only thing he knew about Corazón was that it was a tequila brand, though he didn't know what the word translated to.

"Chest?" Jack asked. "Demon chest?"

Gaspar shook his head. He gently clutched Jack's hands and placed them over his sternum. Then, he made a thumping sound, mimicking the sound of Jack's heartbeat.

"*Corazón de demonio.*"

Jack figured it out. "Heart? Demon heart? You call the purple thing the 'Demon Heart?'" Gaspar nodded. "Well," Jack said, "that's comforting..."

Hang on, Jack thought. Ordaz's map warned about something called the Demon Heart. It was supposed to be protecting the King's Room.

Gaspar stepped up and tapped both sides of the star, one at a time. He faced Jack and waited.

"What are you—" But Jack understood. "You want me to choose sides, don't you? You want to know where my heart lies."

That was an easy answer. Jack tapped the people on the right.

Gaspar nodded and turned and left. Jack was forced to follow quickly.

The native still had his flashlight, after all. While they moved off, Jack took in everything he had learned here.

These people believed that there was a star—or gemstone—that could change the hearts of men. Humans, as a species, already possessed an inherent darkness inside of them. But they also had good in them too. If there was some kind of relic that could alter a person's heart—or maybe their way of thinking...

Jack was on to something. The Demon Heart must've been a radioactive ore of some kind, and when exposure occurred, it stimulated the amygdala to the tenth degree. It explained the increased violence of the infected. The crimson irises were nothing more than a side effect.

A good one too. Red eyes screamed, "I'm a bad guy!"

It all sounded preposterous, but Jack had seen enough to know something strange was going on. The Demon Heart was unquestionably responsible, though he still didn't know what the thing was and how it related to the legend of El Dorado.

24

Hugo yawned and blinked awake. He checked his watch and saw that everyone had slept in later than planned. That was acceptable. They needed the extra rest. No one was thrilled with the idea of moving out at dawn. Even now, Hugo still felt exhausted. He sat up and clipped the barrel of Manuel's M2 machine gun with the top of his head.

"Ow!" He rubbed the top of his head. "What a nice way to wake up."

His outburst stirred the Arroyos. Miguel and Manuel both sat up but were aware enough not to hit their heads.

"What was that noise?" Miguel asked, sliding his hand down to his holstered pistol. Eyes glued onto the tree line, he powered on his radio and raised it to his lips, but he didn't speak.

"That was my cracking skull," Hugo said, gently prodding his head with his fingertips.

"No, not that," Miguel said, looking past Hugo. He lowered the receiver and pointed. "That."

Hugo heard it too and spun. The trees behind him shook violently.

Then came the hollering barks of dozens of howler monkeys. Their vocalizations were unmistakable. By now, everyone was on their feet, quickly packing up their belongings. The only one that wasn't packing up to go was Manuel. Instead, he racked the loading handle of the belt-fed .50 caliber machine gun.

"Ready your weapons!" Miguel shouted, following his own order. He shouldered his shotgun. Hugo carried a rifle, and he pointed it in the direction of the sound, filled with uncertainty.

The vocalizations built up to an intolerable volume before—in an instant—the entire rainforest went silent. The howls cut off all at once, which was more frightening to Hugo than the noise itself. At least before, he knew where the animals were coming from. Now, he had no idea. The howlers could've headed behind them, and they would never know.

No one moved.

No one made a sound.

Thirty nerve-wracking seconds went by, and still nothing.

The soldier directly behind Hugo took a shaky step backward and snapped a twig with his boot. In the stillness of the jungle, it sounded like a bomb had gone off. Everyone gave the man a venomous glare.

The noise, while occurring innocently, had been enough to send the howlers into a murderous frenzy. They leapt from the trees, attacking from all directions. Hugo popped off controlled bursts, conforming to what everyone else was doing. All the animals' eyes were red.

Just like the condors.

Miguel carefully lined up the nearest attackers and sent them flying back into the trees with the concussive force of his 12-gauge. Manuel had yet to open up with the M2, and for a good reason. Hugo and the others were too close for him to use it. The M2's report was deafening, and its projectiles were strong enough to tear a man in half. A smaller target—like a howler monkey—would turn into nothing more than a puff of red as it got hit.

"There's too many!" a soldier cried.

Hugo spun to help the man, but he was too late. The soldier was overwhelmed and dragged into the trees by a group of the creatures. His shrieks were cut off as he was killed.

"Mother of God," Hugo said, crossing his chest.

"Get down!"

Everyone dropped to the turf and covered their heads. Hugo went as far as plugging his ears with his fingers. Manuel pulled the trigger of his M2 and mowed down anything that moved. One of the monkeys was torn from Hugo's back, and he got coated in the beast's blood. Manuel swung the weapon back and forth, leaving no part of the rainforest undamaged. Trees fell in the distance, and when the belt ran dry, everyone raised their heads to observe the aftermath.

Manuel had clean-cut a section of the jungle around their camp. There was blood and red fur everywhere. No one was spared of the carnage. The left side of Hugo's face was slathered in the stuff. Miguel was the first to stand. He ran over to check on his brother. At some point during the devastation, Manuel had been injured. One of the animals had bitten him on the shoulder. The wound didn't look bad, but Hugo didn't think that's what the twins were worried about.

They were concerned that the sickness might be transmittable by a bite.

Let's hope not.

The group's morale was at an all-time low. At this rate, Hugo doubted that any of them would make it to El Dorado alive. Every time they met conflict—they lost a man. Hugo, Miguel, and Manuel were afraid they'd be on the menu. It would be only a matter of time before they were selected as dinner.

Miguel's radio came to life.

"Hello? Do you copy?"

He unclipped it from his belt, removed a chunk of fur from it, and answered. "Yes, we're here."

"We heard gunfire. Are you okay?" It was Matias. Aguilar was still offline.

Miguel eyed Hugo. Both men shared the same look. It was one of surprise.

"If that's true, then you must be close."

"Yes, that was what we were thinking too. There is a river nearby. We just discovered a deserted village on its bank. Meet us there if you can."

"Will do," Miguel replied, powering down his radio and returning it to his belt. He spoke softly so only his brother and Hugo could hear him.

"We need to ditch these guys before we are discovered and executed."

Hugo nodded. "Yes, but not yet. The men will be suspicious, and they still outnumber us three-to-one."

Manuel tested his shoulder and shrugged. He was okay with anything they decided. Miguel patted Hugo on the back.

"Okay. We'll head toward the river and hang back a bit."

"Then," Hugo added, "we make like ghosts and disappear."

With that decided, Miguel and Manuel took the lead, using Miguel's GPS device to guide them toward the nearest tributary. It wasn't far. Miguel calculated that it was less than half a mile to the northeast. Hugo brought up the rear and glanced back into the clearing. The empty M2 Browning reminded him of a monument in the middle of a bloodstained battlefield. It was an ominous sight.

Hugo turned around and quickly caught up with the others. They marched forward until Hugo heard water. They needed to get away before Matias and Aguilar spotted them. So far, their ruse had been a resounding success, but that was because none of the soldiers knew who they truly were. The act they had been putting on as Aguilar's men had worked well so far because they were all in the same, roundabout, type of work. Hugo and the Arroyos fit the bill better than most.

Okay, Hugo thought, *here we go.*

He pretended to trip and roll his ankle. He flopped to the ground and wailed in agony, grasping the "damaged" joint with both hands. The soldiers stopped and parted down the middle as Miguel and Manuel came rushing through. Hugo's act had been so good that Miguel was genuinely worried.

"You okay, my friend?" he asked, kneeling next to him.

Hugo shook his head and spoke under his breath. "Pick me up and tell the others to get moving."

Miguel grinned. He did just that. "Keep going. We'll help him and meet up with you at the river's edge."

The soldiers didn't look happy about splitting up, but they, nonetheless, did as they were told. Once they were out of sight, Hugo pushed out of Miguel's arms, and the three men made a right turn and continued further into the trees. They kept the river on their left as a guide. If their original timeline was accurate, they would reach their target destination by nightfall.

It had been nearly a day since Lorenzo Matias seized control of the expedition. Aguilar was in no shape to do so anymore. The guy hadn't fought him on it either. Matias wasn't sure if it was the stress of everything that had made the man nearly comatose or if he had begun testing his own experimental drugs. Aguilar had been clean for years, never once relapsing into his old ways. Regardless of the cause, Matias was now leading the small four-man team. He didn't want to, but he didn't want to die either.

He sat and waited for the other group to arrive. Matias estimated their position across the river from the direction of the gunfire and somewhere close. It seemed like they were finally having some luck. The current was gentle, and its depth was shallow. At most, it was waist deep. Matias imagined himself in a lawn chair with his feet in the water, sipping on an icy Pilsen.

Suddenly, there was movement across the river. A small column of fatigued soldiers appeared on the shore. Matias counted nine in all. It was a significantly smaller number than he thought he'd see. Something terrible must've befallen these men.

They waved to him and cautiously waded through the river. Even before the first soldier made it across, Matias began interrogating him.

"Is this it?" he asked.

The weary soldier nodded. "Yes, sir. We were attacked several times."

A commotion picked up behind the lead soldier. He turned and shouted across the river to the last man.

"What's wrong?" Matias asked, stepping forward.

"We seem to have lost three more men just now."

Matias was shocked. "*Three* more? Just now?"

The other man nodded. "Yes, sir."

"When did you last see them?"

"Not long ago—ten minutes, perhaps."

Matias was shocked that three well-armed military-types could just up and vanish in a matter of minutes. It didn't make any sense.

Unless...

Matias stared hard at the soldier. "What did these men look like?"

The soldier began describing men who Matias knew were clearly Miguel and Manuel Arroyo. Twins with shaved heads, well-built physiques, and heavily tattooed upper bodies. Their presence here made no sense at all, especially when the soldier started describing Hugo Nunez. Matias knew, for a fact, that the three men didn't get along with one another.

Hugo's presence wasn't a surprise since it was him who had been responsible for involving Jack. The smuggler was a softy and was loyal-to-a-fault to his friends. Technically, it was Matias who had gotten the ball rolling. Miguel and Manuel were two incredibly dangerous people. The only reason they would be working with Jack and Hugo was if they had been guaranteed a piece of what awaited them at El Dorado.

"The enemy of my enemy is my friend," Matias said, closing his eyes and breathing deep. It was better for Hugo to have the Arroyos working with him than against him. Plus, there was bad blood between all of them and Aguilar.

"Santiago!" Matias called. The drug lord turned away from one of the huts, rambling to himself. "It seems that your friend, Hugo Nunez, is here."

Just the mention of Valentina's brother seemed to refocus Aguilar. He quieted and squeezed his fists tightly. He spun and put his hand through the wall of the dilapidated hut. Slowly, he removed the bleeding appendage and looked over his wounds. He had a gash across his forearm, and his knuckles were equally injured. If he was in any pain, he didn't let on.

"Where is Nunez?" Aguilar asked. He stepped toward the soldier. The other man shrank away and pointed back across the river.

"I...I can show you where we last saw him."

"Good," Aguilar said, "and if we don't find him soon, it'll be your head."

The soldier swallowed and nodded hard. His eyes were wide with fright—as they should be. Matias had personally witnessed a handful of the atrocities that Aguilar was rumored to have perpetrated.

Like electrocuting a man for information. Jack had gone through that kind of inhumane treatment recently.

Matias was appalled by some of the things Aguilar had done, but he was too ingrained into the man's business to speak up or rebel against it. Matias was already skating on thin ice with him. The last thing he needed to do was give the psychopath a reason to turn his rage on him.

Aguilar crossed the river, pulling away from the others with every step he took. Matias and the soldiers had to pick up their pace to keep up with him. He practically flattened anything in his path while he searched for Hugo and the Arroyos. For a short while, Aguilar's mind had slipped into a strange area between real-life and fantasy. He daydreamed what it would be like to see El Dorado with his own eyes. He even fantasized about being its king and discovering what was birthing the guardians. Aguilar understood enough about mind-altering narcotics and hallucinogens to recognize that they were dealing with something hazardous.

He desired it as well as the wealth of the City of Gold.

"The King's Room," he muttered, seeing something up ahead.

He hurried forward and spotted a disturbance in the brush. A path had recently been cleared through the heart of a marshy area. His prey had barreled directly into it instead of going around it. Even from here, Aguilar thought he could hear someone shouting.

Unless it's a macaw mimicking someone?

"No," Aguilar said. He knew who it was. He smiled. "I've got you."

He planted his foot inside the taller undergrowth and found the earth to be firm. Aguilar continued forward, but he tested each footfall as if it were his last. The column of armed men mirrored his every move, snaking their way through the jungle until they heard, without a shadow of a doubt, multiple men yelling at one another.

Aguilar drew his pistol and stepped into a small opening in the trees. He nearly laughed at the sight. Hugo Nunez was up to his waist in mud and was struggling to free himself. Miguel and Manuel Arroyo were on either side of him. They both had thrown him vines and were attempting to pull him free.

"Well, isn't this an interesting sight?"

The three men froze and turned their attention on Aguilar. Soldiers spread out all around the mud pit, aiming their weapons at the trio. No one raised their hands. The Arroyos weren't about to let go of Hugo and let him *drown*.

And neither was Aguilar. He had something better in store for the man.

"Help them," he ordered.

Two soldiers aided each of the twins, and with their combined strength, they quickly plucked Hugo free. They dragged the filthy man further away from the pit before letting go. Miguel moved to help Hugo up but was told to stay back by one of the soldiers.

Aguilar holstered his pistol and smiled. "This is no time for a swim, Hugo."

The smuggler sat up and looked around. "I'm surprised you helped me at all."

Aguilar shrugged. "I require additional men, and the three of you are perfect for what I have planned."

Hugo glanced up at the twins. "And that is?"

"Well," Aguilar replied, "without Jack leading the way, my men and I are in terrible danger." He grinned. "I figured you three would be perfect candidates to be our shield if something were to attack us."

Aguilar shouted and was visibly pleased to watch his men strip Hugo, Miguel, and Manuel of all their gear—weapons included.

Hugo got to his feet. "What makes you think we'll help you?"

"Because," Aguilar said, getting into his face, "you don't have much of a choice."

No one argued with him. He was right. If they wanted to survive, they would have to do as Aguilar said.

Hugo tensed up as Matias walked up next to him. "Hello, my friend."

"You are not my friend—not anymore."

Matias frowned. "I did what I had to do. You don't have to like it, but you will understand it."

Hugo nodded. "You're right. I don't like it. You chose my sister's murderer over our friendship."

"Valentina chose her fate."

Hugo whirled around and punched Matias in the stomach. The treacherous TAC agent fell to the ground, holding his gut with both hands. A previous wound bled beneath his hand.

"So did you," Hugo growled, jaw locked.

"Enough!" Aguilar shouted. "Move or die!"

25

Gaspar led Jack through the trees. Six other men accompanied them. Each one was armed with a bow and arrow and a knife. They banked left and right, nearly doubling back twice. They moved in this manner for hours. Jack was lost and disoriented. He had no idea where he was or if he was even still in Colombia. He recalled that their destination was very close to the Brazilian border. And like with most countries that occupy the Amazon Basin, the further you got from the oceanic coasts, the more unexplored—the more *rural*—it became.

The path straightened out up ahead. The canopy grew inward, bending directly over Jack's head to form a tunnel of greens and browns. It was easy to see that the corridor was manmade. Things in nature didn't grow like this unless they had help. The path had been purposely cut into the, otherwise, wild terrain. Gaspar's people had been maintaining the area. They probably had been for generations.

Jack's heart fluttered.

"We're close," he whispered, getting a look from Gaspar. "Uh, never mind."

Jack didn't know for sure how close they were, but he could feel it in his gut. He had learned to trust that feeling over the last twenty-plus years of *aggressive living*. His intuition had served him well so far, and if he were lucky, he would see his fortieth birthday when it reared its achy, semi-greying head. Jack didn't feel old when it came to his age. The only time he felt like a relic was when he talked about his favorite movies and music and when he tried to get out of bed in the morning.

The sun bleeding through the leafy passage was surreal and calming. The sight was one of the most beautiful that Jack had ever seen. Some of his Yellowstone memories were similar, but this one really felt different. This was untamed. Yellowstone had its pockets of wilderness, but it couldn't shake a stick at the Amazon Rainforest. Only the Congo was as uncharted and unpillaged as the Amazon.

Well, maybe Antarctica too.

Gaspar said something and slowed. Jack, likewise, eased up. The two men closed in on the exit of the canopy tunnel, shielding their eyes from the blinding light. Before them was a clearing of immense size—Jack just knew it. Was this it? Had he finally found El Dorado?

The tribal chief stepped out of the passage and moved aside so Jack could see. It wasn't just a clearing. It was a narrow canyon that plummeted deep into the earth. Multiple waterfalls emptied into the space, covering the entire place in a misty wash. Looking up, Jack noticed that some of the trees had grown at angles, which had covered sections of the gorge. They acted as a form of camouflage and prevented the place from being seen from the air.

From Jack's high position, he couldn't see what was hidden below—but he knew it must be significant. Why else would Gaspar's tribe keep watch over it?

Jack swallowed, suddenly feeling very nervous. Long ago, steps had been precisely cut into the rock beneath Jack's feet. They led down the right-hand side of the cliff, following the natural curve of the canyon wall.

"Down there?" Jack asked, pointing over the edge.

Gaspar nodded. "Manoa."

Jack stepped toward the steps but stopped. "Wait, what did you say? Manoa?"

"*Sí*, Manoa," Gaspar repeated. The word meant nothing to anyone who hadn't done research into El Dorado, but Jack had.

Manoa was another name for the kingdom of El Dorado. It's what Sir Walter Raleigh had come looking for in 1594 over in Venezuela. Legends say that a gilded empire sat on the shores of Lake Parime, where the people—the Musica people—would ceremoniously cover their chief in gold dust and dip him into its waters. It was plain to see that the location of Manoa had never been in Venezuela. Raleigh's information, from whomever he had received it from, had been way off.

It had been here all along, Jack thought. *Right here.*

He rushed to the edge but couldn't see anything from here. He turned to ask the real-life Manoa chief—and that's what Gaspar was—but the man had not moved to join Jack. None of the natives had.

"You aren't coming?" he asked, motioning to the canyon before them.

Gaspar shook his head. "*Corazón de demonio.*"

That hit Jack hard. The Demon Heart frightened Gaspar and his people so much that they refused to attempt the climb. Jack knew he should've been worried, yet he still decided to go. He clutched the man's forearm and said his goodbyes.

"Thank you for everything."

Gaspar must've gotten the gist of what Jack had said because he nodded and clutched Jack's hands, placing them atop his chest—his heart. The gesture made Jack smile. Then, Gaspar and his men stepped back and let Jack enter the realm of... *Manoa? Really?* Jack had no idea what he was about to step into. It was a stupid thing to do on his own, but he did it anyway because, well, honestly, Jack had no idea why he was doing it. It felt like the right thing to do. At this point, with everything that he had been through so far, he needed to see it.

"I'm coming. Whatever you are..."

The staircase hugged the wall tight. The only constant was that it moved ever-so-slightly down. The steps themselves were only two feet wide, at most. It was as unnerving a trek as Jack had ever experienced.

And it took forever.

Matias looked down at the glowing green screen of Miguel's GPS device. On it was a single marked location. With Hugo and the Arroyos leading the way, Matias and Aguilar steered them in the correct direction from behind. The only thing the trio of hostages were allowed to possess were machetes to help them clear brush and vines. Aguilar had given the soldiers a single, explicit order to shoot them if they attempted to flee capture.

The group came to a magical tunnel of green. The canopy had been artificially bent into position. The display of resourcefulness was remarkable, bearing in mind that it was all done by a primitive culture. The Amazonian people were extraordinary in many ways, but Matias never expected to see anything like this.

The group entered the passage and followed it until they emptied onto a tall cliffside ledge. And they weren't the only ones there. Seven natives turned and drew back their bows. Hugo was the first to see them. He slowly raised his hands. Miguel and Manuel were stunned to see them too.

Matias was ready to gun them down but didn't give the order. None of the natives' eyes were red. These were normal men. He recognized one of them too. It was the man who had warned Jack about the guardians. Matias searched the small platform and saw that the American wasn't present. Had they pushed him over the edge?

No, Matias decided. He didn't think that Jack had been sacrificed. He was sure the locals had allowed him safe passage.

"Where is the American?" Matias asked in Spanish.

The tribal leader didn't reply right away. He carefully watched the rest of the group file in first. The natives took a collected step back. "He has entered Manoa."

Every single person in Aguilar's group turned toward the canyon. They all knew the legend of Manoa well. It had been ingrained into their history—into their DNA.

"Manoa?" Aguilar asked, shoving through Matias. "You're sure?"

The other man nodded. "Yes, and it's a terrible place."

"Is it?"

The native placed a hand over his chest. "It turns the hearts of men to darkness."

"What do you mean?" Matias asked.

But it wasn't the native who answered. It was Hugo.

"The toxin," he said, facing the tribal leader. "Something down there is making everything here sick, isn't it?"

The local nodded. "Yes."

"What is it?" Aguilar asked, sounding more intrigued than concerned.

The native, once more, put a hand on his chest. "The Demon Heart."

A smile crept onto Aguilar's face. Ordaz's map, the one he had hung on a wall inside his secret vault-like closest, had referenced it. "Show me."

The native shook his head. "I cannot. My people and I have taken an oath to never enter the cursed kingdom of Manoa."

Aguilar drew his pistol and leveled it at the leader's head. "You don't seem to understand. Either you show me this 'Demon Heart,' or you and your friends die."

The chief glanced at his men, getting nods all around. Aguilar smiled again, but he didn't get the answer he was expecting.

"So be it. We would rather die as men than be turned into monsters."

Twice did Jack stop to catch his breath. One time, he even sat and enjoyed the view. One section of the steps was a little wider than the rest. It was there that he decided to sit and take a load off. He nonchalantly dangled his sore feet over the edge of the drop. At this point, Jack wasn't bothered by the height. He marveled at it. It was hard for Jack to comprehend that places like this still existed in the world. Directly across from him, a pair of narrow waterfalls emptied into the gorge. In between the outlets was a species of cliff-dwelling bird. It had built an impressive nest inside a shallow alcove of rock. Jack saw movement inside of it but couldn't see what type it was.

His thoughts drifted. "And what about your eyes?"

Jack shook his head and climbed to his feet. He was close to passing out and needed to get moving to stay awake. It was mostly his body that was telling him to rest. Mentally, Jack was fine. He was dangerously overstimulated with the excitement of the next big thing, but fine.

The canyon's end was up ahead as Jack continued at a steady downward trajectory. He leaned left and looked down. He saw something promising. There was an opening at the base of the cliff where the left and right-hand walls converged. The sight spurred Jack into moving faster.

As did the homes dug directly into the rock.

There were dozens of them surrounding the single tunnel entry. Some looked to be two and three stories tall. Jack had seen similar things built by the Anasazi in the American Southwest. As far as he knew, that practice didn't reach this far.

And it wasn't a city made of gold.

"Damn," he said, feeling his excitement flatline. Still, he had a job to do. Plus, there was that cave at the center of it all.

Maybe the King's Room is inside the cave?

Before he could comprehend any possible answers, Jack noticed something on the ground just outside the cave. He produced his small binoculars and saw that the irregularity was covered in a fine layer of sand. It was a star-shaped pattern. The decoration perfectly matched the one on his dagger—the representation of the Demon Heart. Jack hoped it was more of a welcome mat reading "Congratulations on finding El Dorado!" than a sign screaming "Keep out!"

He moved on. Standing around wasn't going to give him any answers.

Two waterfalls emptied into a plunge pool. One flowed in from either side, beautifully cascading like a picturesque screensaver. The packaging that surrounded the fiendish Demon Heart was an attractive one.

As he got closer, he spied movement in the lake. It wasn't the Titanoboa, thank God, but it was something relatively large. There were a lot of them too. Jack was confused. He tried to recall everything he had learned about the rainforest before and during his mission, but the creatures Jack was seeing now didn't fit the description of anything he remembered. Their purplish-pink hide stuck out from the blue waters. Jack marveled at just how many were present.

Fifty feet above the pool entrance, Jack stopped and gawked, finally recognizing the animals for what they were. This species typically existed in Africa, not along the Colombia-Brazil border. They were one of the deadliest and most aggressive animals on the planet and something Jack had no way of defeating on his own if they decided to get rowdy.

He threw his hands into the air and laughed, letting them flop back to his sides. "Great... Hippos."

The infamous drug lord Pablo Escobar, the "King of Cocaine," had penned four hippopotamuses in a private zoo on his estate back in the eighties. After Escobar's death, the animals had been left to fend for themselves by the government. They'd been deemed "too difficult to seize." Now, they wildly roamed the Colombian waterways and could be found here and there, though it was a rare sight. It was said that only fifty or so of the animals existed.

But are they guardians? Jack couldn't see from here.

He stopped counting at twenty-five. He doubted that half of the hippo population lived solely in Lake Parime. This float had never been accounted for. If it had been, then Manoa would've been discovered long ago. Jack looked around, trying to figure out how the hippos had even gotten down here.

"There's another access point."

With that in his back pocket, Jack's comfort with the terrain and situation went from *none* to *some*. Aguilar was bound to show up sooner or later. When he did, Jack's usefulness would be at an all-time low.

Jack completed his descent but was still fifteen feet above the sandy shore. The bottommost section of the stairs had collapsed long ago. If Jack jumped, there would be no way of returning without someone's help. *Anyone have a six-foot folding ladder?* The journey was a one-way street for now.

Then, there was the float of hippos to worry about. Once Jack entered their domain, the biggest and nastiest of the animals would charge him—guaranteed. They were tremendously territorial and happily fought anything in nature not named an elephant. Hippos killed more people than any other wild animal in Africa. It was a fact that Jack had always found astonishing. Most people would think that honor belonged to a crocodile or a venomous snake. The Dark Continent's deadliest animal was the thick-bodied, somewhat comical, hippopotamus.

"Here we go."

Jack sat, turned around, and searched for whatever handholds he could find. He could've just as easily jumped down to the sandy beach but wanted to enter the hippo's domain with less gusto. And God forbid Jack rolled his ankle right before dealing with the float. He let go and dropped the last five feet, silently landing on one knee in a superhero-like pose. With one hand in the sand, he snapped his head up and was thankful to see that his existence had not yet been noticed.

But it will be, he thought, eyeing the lumps in the shallows. The shoreline wasn't all that wide, but it circled the entirety of the lake. Jack took a second to appreciate the landscape. There was hardly a ripple on the crystal-clear water's surface, and the air was cool and still. Lake Parime was picturesque. It belonged as a wallpaper on Jack's laptop.

But there were also signs of bloodshed. The water was so clean that Jack could see down to its sandy floor. There were piles of bones covering the area just outside the cave entrance. Jack couldn't see what species they belonged to, but he had a sneaking suspicion. If the Manoa were anything like the Aztec, then they had practiced the brutal ritual of human sacrifice. Jack slipped his hand over the ceremonial dagger in his belt. It had been designed to cut out the still-beating hearts of the kingdom's enemies.

Now, if Jack made it home in one piece, it would only cut open letters.

He reflexively swallowed and took a step away from the crumbling staircase. Nothing greeted him. The cave was still a few hundred yards away, and his footing wasn't the best. Years ago, Jack used to train on beaches much like this one—minus the undiscovered jungle paradise. He would even go as far as running through the shallows of the ocean too. But that was without the threat of being trampled by a 4,000-pound ornery hippopotamus.

Halfway there, Jack paused midstride and gazed back up to where he had begun his trek—back up to the ledge just outside the tunnel of green. Gunshots rang out, echoing throughout the long, slender canyon. Someone was shooting at someone else.

Or 'something' else...

It didn't matter to Jack at the moment. The disturbance riled the hippos. Four of them stirred, popping their thick heads out of the water. Each of them turned toward a petrified Jack Reilly. All he could do was stare back at them. He froze, hoping his benign presence would go unnoticed. The largest of the animals snorted a spray of water into the air. Then, it let out a guttural grunt.

Jack's shoulders fell. "Oh come on, man. Really?"

He took off at a full sprint. The enraged hippos let out a series of throaty calls and rapidly rose from the shallows. It didn't take long for Jack to see that he wasn't going to make it to the cave. He couldn't put on enough speed. He was tired, and the sand was much too loose. Plus, hippos ran really damn fast! On land, they could reach thirty miles per hour.

The largest of the four was nearly upon him. Jack allowed the bull to get closer, then darted right toward the rock dwellings. The sudden change in direction fooled the male—but not the other three. At the last possible moment, Jack dove forward, feeling something enormous connect with the bottom of both his feet. He was shoved, midair, through the narrow opening of the low-roofed cutout. He hit the ground and rolled into the rear wall with a thud and a moan.

He laughed out loud and was about to say something snarky but stopped when he saw something he dreaded. The bull stood fifty yards away from the dwelling, its red eyes glaring at Jack. But what could the beast do?

Wait, red eyes? Shit...

"I'm fine, right?" Jack, truthfully, had no idea if he was or not.

The hippo snorted and charged, lowering its colossal skull like a living, breathing wrecking ball. Jack wasn't sure if the animal could force its way inside, but it was sure as hell going to try.

Jack desperately tried to find a way out, but this particular dwelling was only one room and one story. His sanctuary was about to become his tomb. Jack flattened himself against the rear wall and shouldered his rifle. He didn't want to kill the bull, but he wasn't going to be given another choice. The hippo was twenty yards from the dwelling and closing in fast. Jack laid his finger atop the trigger and squeezed but didn't depress it enough to release its payload. He couldn't do it. Instead, he gritted his teeth and closed his eyes.

He took a deep breath. *This is it.*

26

Jack turned his head away just as stone exploded all around him. Miraculously, he wasn't seriously hurt. The only injury he sustained was from a tiny sliver of rocky shrapnel that had sliced through the top layers of skin on his chin. He opened his eyes, noticing that more sunlight was pouring into the dwelling now. Jack also spotted the bull hippo backing away, shaking its head. It didn't matter if this one had hurt itself. There were still three other purple death machines waiting for him to show himself. And if Jack didn't, he was confident that one of them would, eventually, make it inside and smash him into a gooey, slightly chunky paste.

A basketball-sized chunk of the ceiling fell and nearly crushed Jack's foot. He looked up in horror, expecting to see the entire dwelling collapse on top of him. Instead, what he saw made him smile. The hippo's assault had damaged the foundation of the floor above his head. Now, where there was once solid rock, there was an opening large enough for him to fit through. Using his six-foot-two height to his advantage, Jack jumped and reached up, gripping the edges for the new second-floor entryway. Luckily, the builders had been as short as Gaspar and his people, making this an easy task.

He pulled himself up as fast as he could. Jack heard the bull's heavy footfalls somewhere outside. The thunderous footfalls terrified him. The animal had recovered and was coming in for another round. Jack kicked and squirmed but got stuck. His rifle was caught on a rock. Panicked, Jack reached back down through the hole and felt around for the handgrip of his knife. He found it, yanked it free of its sheath, and swiftly sliced through the AK-47's strap. The precious weapon fell to earth. Jack slipped his feet through the hole, just as the rifle was pulverized beneath the bull's girth. On his hands and knees, he watched the rampaging animal frantically search for him. Realizing that Jack wasn't present, the behemoth backed out, taking pieces of the walls with him.

The floor beneath Jack rumbled.

"Oh no."

He got up and ran, happy to see narrow doorways interconnecting the dwellings. As soon as Jack entered the next room, the floor behind him fell apart. He kept moving, snaking through whatever opening he could find. A few were smaller, square cutouts—probably windows. Jack dove through one headfirst and rolled back onto his feet, charging onward without stopping. He couldn't. If the hippos didn't kill him, then the quickly deteriorating cave dwellings would.

The next home was a dead end. Jack had nowhere to go from here except out a lake-facing window. With no other choice, he reached outside and above the opening, digging his fingers into the first cleft he could find just as the extraordinarily constructed structure collapsed. For a moment, he dangled in the air by one hand, hearing the hippos noisily arrive below him. Jack was fortunate that his handhold didn't give out. The animals were stamping in place, waiting for him to lose his grip and fall.

Grunting like one of the hippos, Jack got his other hand up. He moved laterally and upward, heading toward the main cave entrance like a bug on a wall. It was slow going, but he was safe from attack. The cliff was chock-full of places to hold onto, but that didn't keep his hands from taking a beating.

Better than your bones, he thought, trying to ignore the snorting beasts. He could live with a few palm abrasions and blistered fingers. Living without a functioning spinal column was another thing altogether.

Jack paused directly above the cave mouth. He looked between his feet and spotted the half-buried star pattern beneath the sand. A breeze picked up around him, and amazingly, some of the sand got swept away to reveal more of what lay beneath it.

"Woah," Jack said, forgetting for a second that he was hanging from a wall.

The star pattern was, in actuality, an eight-foot-wide star-shaped mosaic of intricately-cut purple gems. The jewels had been precisely pieced together by some grand architect. Jack couldn't wait to see what was inside. With an entrance as grand as this one was, Jack could only imagine that the inside must be remarkable.

Jack reset his grip, releasing his hold on the wall one hand at a time. He shook each one hard, feeling the discomfort within subside with each subsequent shake.

The bull stepped onto the mosaic but stopped. Then, it lifted its foot and backed away. The other hippos didn't dare get as close to the male. Getting an idea, Jack took a breath and let go. He dropped and landed in a squat, using his legs like the suspension system of a car. Jack rolled out of the prone position and drew his pistol, aiming it at the red-eyed beast. It didn't attack. The hippo just lowered its head and glared at Jack, snorting a plume of sand in his direction.

Holstering his gun, Jack gave the animal a small salute and turned and hurried off. He wasn't going to test the bull's patience. If Jack was going to be given a gift and be allowed to enter the ten-by-ten cave entrance unmolested, then he was going to take the offering and run with it—literally. He clicked on his flashlight and booked it. His attention was drawn first to the corridor, which he could tell had been a natural opening at one point, but not any longer.

It had been chiseled and precisely altered into a beautiful collage of stars. Each one was slightly different than the other. The person responsible had either been innocently enthralled with the Demon Heart, or they had been possessed by its mind-altering influence and deranged like a zealous fanatic.

Whatever the hell that means.

Jack was still trying to put the final pieces together. He knew that seeing the Demon Heart in person would be the period at the end of the sentence. The language barrier between him and Gaspar had left Jack in a fog. He knew the *thing* was the cause of the red eyes and the exposed individuals' aggressive behaviors—man and beast.

What about me? he asked himself. Jack needed to take extra care. He had no idea what caused the disease. And if he became infected, was there even a cure? Jack had his doubts, but he had also seen what Gaspar's people could do. The tea they had brewed him had tasted so-so, at best, but it had given him a tremendous boost without the impending crash that followed a caffeine buzz. And the men back in Bogotá had also shown Jack what the drug lord could do with his creations. If a man like Aguilar got a hold of the Demon Heart's capabilities and turned them into some sort of synthesized super-drug, then the world, not just the Amazon, might be at stake.

The stone passage turned to stairs, and the starry ceiling continued for the entire length. The steps were short and well-worn. People had traversed this path many times, which made sense since people had lived just outside of it.

Whatever natural light there had been was now gone. Jack had moved far enough away, and deep enough inside, for it to be obscured from view. His steps were loud, and they resonated around him—so did his breaths.

His rhythmic footfalls lulled Jack into a trance-like state, and he finished the descent without thought. The floor leveled off, and when it did, Jack saw something odd up ahead.

Light.

"How?" he asked. His voice traveled on forever.

The illumination grew brighter as he drew nearer, but the source was still too far away to identify.

The route ended at the most magical sight. The chamber beyond was huge, covering at least one hundred square yards. But it wasn't the room that caught Jack's attention. It was the magnificent work of art built into the cavern's rear wall. A mammoth, fifty-foot-tall statue of a Manoa chief had been erected. And it was constructed entirely out of gold!

"El Dorado," Jack announced. "Well, I guess it's technically El *Rey* Dorado." He grinned. "The Golden King."

As some have theorized, El Dorado wasn't a city after all. It was a man—a golden one.

That didn't make the discovery any less significant. The Golden King must've been worth hundreds of millions of dollars, and it was the answer to one of the most argued riddles in history. Did El Dorado exist, and if so, what was it?

Jack forced himself out of his gawking stupor to examine the rest of the room. The light source was odd. A long, narrow pool of liquid gold stretched from one end of the cave to the other. It reminded Jack of a skinnier version of the Lincoln Memorial Reflecting Pool in Washington D.C. There must be some sort of hidden subterranean heat source that was keeping the collected gold from hardening. In turn, the molten material emitted enough light to see.

The floor around the pool was a grim sight. Bodies littered the area. Jack estimated that there were at least a hundred of them—maybe more. Some were reasonably fresh, but most looked like they had been here for a long time. Next, he gazed up at the left and righthand walls. They were decorated with an assortment of pictographs and ruins. The symbols reminded Jack of some kind of language—but one that he didn't recognize.

"Manoan?" he surmised. It was his best guess. It was most likely the language that Gasper and his people used to speak to one another.

And what of the true guardian of El Dorado, the feared Demon Heart?

Jack looked up and quickly backed away. "Oh, crap."

Vines grew along the stalactite-covered ceiling, slithering over nearly every square inch of it. But it wasn't the vines themselves that made Jack react the way he did. It was the purple, star-shaped flowers growing out of them. The *Demon Heart* was a flower, not a radioactive gemstone.

Their origin was a crack at the center of the ceiling. From there, the plant had spread like a fungus. The intrusive species had taken over what must've once been a pristine and sacred site to Gaspar's tribe. And its proximity to the floor had made it impossible to eradicate. Jack imagined that the current chief would've ordered his people to abandon the site and flee into the trees atop the crevasse. But some had returned. The human tribe of red-eyed guardians was proof enough.

And what about the animals who had been impacted by the Demon Heart? The answer must be that these vines are growing in the wilds of the Amazon too. Jack doubted that any of the creatures he had encountered thus far had come here to bask in the flower's presence.

How long has it been like this?

"But how have you hurt so many?" Jack asked, taking his eyes away from the craggy ceiling. He re-examined the floor and the dead, feeling like he was missing something significant. But besides being covered in a layer of dust, they...

Wait! That's not dust! Jack gazed back up to the ceiling, then back down to the corpses.

"It's pollen," he said, covering his nose and mouth with his shirt. He hurriedly inspected the ground around his feet and saw that it was clear of pollen. Either the flower's payload didn't reach this far back, or it had already been swept away by the gentle breeze buffeting his back. Regardless, Jack had been lucky. He had just walked right into the source of the red-eyed sickness and hadn't even known it.

He let out a relaxing breath. "I need to play the Powerball when I get home."

Jack thought back to the star-shaped patterns stretching from the big purple one in the sand to the smaller abstract ones in the tunnel passage. If the plant was so deadly, why had Gaspar's ancestors adorned the place in its image?

As he thought more about it, he began to put two and two together and suddenly figured it out. The stars weren't meant to be a celebration of what the chamber contained. They were a warning of what awaited anyone dumb enough to enter. The natives would've recognized the caution sign and steered clear. But a curious American adventurer would've charged right inside to happily have a look around.

"What are you?" Jack asked, seeing something between the statue's feet. It was too far away to tell what it was, but it kind of looked like a door.

Hmmm, he thought, pulling out his binoculars. *Bingo!* It was a door.

He pictured what would be hidden behind it and thought back to the script that had been written on Ordaz's map. It referenced the Demon Heart, but it also mentioned a place called the "King's Room." Jack, once more, gazed up at the Golden King. He had been a ruler of Manoa, maybe even the first. His room must be beyond the door at his edifice's feet. There was more to discover here.

Gunfire erupted back up the stairs.

Aguilar had, no doubt, found the steps leading down to the bottom of the canyon and was now waging a small war on the hippos that guarded the Manoa cave entrance. Deep bellows ensued as the automatic gunfire continued. After a few short minutes, the world returned to its previous, silent state. Jack didn't know how many on either side had died. The soldiers had done what Jack couldn't do. They had opened fire on the bull and his float—all in the name of treasure. It made Jack sick to his stomach.

And what about Gaspar and his people? Jack thought.

He went to draw his pistol but stopped. There was nothing he could do and nowhere for him to go. Firing upon the first person he saw would only get himself killed. So, he did the only thing he could. Jack sat on the bottommost step and waited. Soon, he would be back in the same predicament he had been in before. He'd find himself in the employment of the vile Colombian drug lord, Santiago Aguilar.

Jack pulled his thoughts away from Aguilar and returned his attention to the cavern. The gold pool bothered him. The legend says that the king had been covered in gold dust before bathing in Lake Parime. Unless that part of the story was as false as the lore surrounding a city made of gold, then historians had gotten yet another thing incorrect. Jack hoped he was wrong. The implications were too awful to think about. The king might not have gently patted pulverized pieces of gold onto his skin. He may have had something far worse than that done to him. And unfortunately, Jack was pretty sure he was going to find out precisely what once Aguilar arrived.

Or was he?

It was just as likely that Jack would get a gun put to his head.

Then, *boom.*

27

The remaining soldiers—nine in all—descended onto the beach and opened fire on the float. The bull immediately charged the armed men, forcing their hand. The brutish animal died with less than fifteen feet to spare. It was a sad sight. Hugo wanted the animals, guardians or not, to be left alone. To him, these hippos were sacred, *not* just an intrusive species.

Three more of the animals emerged from the water, but they did not charge—not right away. Aguilar urged everyone else to move out. Hugo, Miguel, Manuel, and now Gaspar, the tribal chief, didn't have a choice. They each scaled the broken section of steps and ended up on the sandy shoreline. Hugo's eyes darted from the other hippos to the dozens and dozens of cave dwellings. Suspiciously, a segment of the homes to the right of their destination had collapsed. The damage from the collapse looked fresh.

Jack.

The soldiers kept themselves between the water and everyone else. No additional shots were fired. The rest of the float had seen what had happened to their leader. The only way the hippos would get close enough now was when the soldiers ran out of ammunition. Hugo was confident he could bait the animals into attacking, but he didn't want any more of the animals to perish for no reason. Plus, the soldiers were effectively protecting him, too, not just Aguilar and Matias.

The three hippos were entirely out of the water now. Four more arose to join them. Hugo spotted another seven purple-ish lumps farther out, but closing in. The sight made Hugo's bladder squirm. Thinning out the soldiers' ranks might just come to fruition, regardless of what Hugo did or didn't do.

"Faster," Hugo whispered.

There were now seven very large, very angry hippopotamuses staring them down. So far, none had advanced any further than the shallows. It was evident that they were waiting to build up their numbers first. Soon, the red-eyed guardians would charge. A handful of the beasts would undoubtedly die, but so would a few of those in Aguilar's group.

"Hugo is right," Matias said. Seven hippos breached the surface, snorting a spray of water into the air. The sun caught the mist and formed a series of rainbows above the lake. "We need to go—now."

The animals charged.

Miguel and Manuel turned and ran, but Hugo didn't.

"Come with us!" he urged, holding out his hand to Gaspar. "We are friends of Jack."

The native didn't take any additional time to think it over. Hugo, Miguel, Manuel, and Gaspar all ran for the cave. Aguilar and Matias didn't follow—not right away. Two of the soldiers' rifles ran dry. Then another. Matias panicked and abandoned his post next to his boss.

"Lorenzo!" But Aguilar didn't stay angry for long. Matias was doing the smart thing. "Everyone! Fall back!"

Hugo looked over his shoulder just in time to see one of the men trip over another soldier's discarded rifle and fall. He attempted to get up but was temporarily blinded by a face full of sand. Before he could take a step, he was flattened by the float. His cries were cut short by the snapping of his bones.

Miguel and Manuel crossed the threshold first. Hugo was next, slowing for a moment to inspect the beautiful purple mosaic built into the earth. Gaspar skidded to a halt, mumbling something to himself.

"Come on!" Hugo shouted, waving him forward.

The native shook his head. He was terrified.

Hugo urged him onward. "Gaspar!" Still, the tribal leader didn't move.

Manuel simply stepped over and picked up the much smaller man. He threw him over his shoulder and carried him to the mouth of the cave. Gaspar yelled for Manuel to put him down, but the big man didn't oblige.

"Do it," Hugo said. "Put him down."

Manuel nodded and eased the chief to the ground.

Gaspar didn't bolt from the cave, though. The hippos were too close and had slowed and surrounded the entrance. It seemed that the beasts weren't going to follow them inside, but nor were they going to let them leave.

"Let's go. We need to find Jack," Hugo said.

Left with only their flashlights, Hugo, Miguel, and Manuel switched them on. The walls and ceiling of the tunnel were covered in stars. The sight caused Gaspar to shudder and take a step back.

"*Corazón de demonio.*" He reflexively put a hand on his chest—over his heart.

"We'll be fine," Hugo urged as Aguilar and Matias backed into the cave.

Matias laughed nervously. "Your assurance doesn't comfort me."

Hugo ignored Matias and moved off. He led the way with Miguel and Manuel ushering Gaspar along. The native seemed to calm down some as they moved. The initial shock of being inside a place he had sworn to avoid had nearly crippled the man. Hugo wondered how long it had been since any of his people had stepped foot here. So, he asked.

"Long ago," Gaspar replied. Not having a pinpointed timeframe from him made sense. Hugo suspected that the tribe didn't properly track the days and nights as modern man did, and if they did, he doubted they used a traditional, twelve-month calendar to do so.

"But some have," Miguel added. "The human guardians, yes?"

Gaspar nodded. "Some have decided to follow a darker path. Even their children are born into it."

"The eyes?" Miguel asked.

Gaspar swallowed hard and nodded. He covered his eyes with one hand. "They are born into the darkness."

That was a gut punch if there ever was one. The offspring of guardians were unwillingly made guardians themselves. The toxin could be passed down through a family's bloodline.

Hugo nearly broke out in a sprint when he saw the silhouette of a man sitting at the foot of the stairs. Jack stood and smiled at the sight of Hugo, the Arroyos, and Gaspar. He clasped the chief on the forearm, enjoying the reunion.

"Welcome to El Dorado!" he announced. But the joyful moment quickly ended as Aguilar and the others came into view.

"Oh," Jack said, "I was kinda hoping you guys had kicked the bucket by now."

Aguilar and Matias didn't pay him any attention. They were too absorbed with the room beyond him. Miguel took a step into the room, but Jack grabbed his arm and shook his head. He pointed at his own eyes and then the ceiling. Miguel looked up at the jaw-dropping discovery. The purple Demon Heart stood out against the earthen tones of the cave's ceiling.

"It's beautiful," Aguilar said, his voice trailing off.

"I can't believe we're actually here," Matias added.

Aguilar went to step out but stopped, sensing that something was wrong. The drug lord was as eager as anyone to explore the cave, but he was also a smart man. He pointed toward the five-story-tall golden idol and ordered his men to clear the grounds around it. One after the other, the soldiers slowly made their way out onto the floor. Gaspar muttered to himself the entire time, speaking in his people's native language.

The lead soldier crossed into the pollen-covered area and immediately dropped his weapon. His hands went to his head, and he screamed, falling to his knees. He scraped and clawed at his face as if it were covered in stinging insects. Everyone with half a brain knew what was happening. They were witnessing someone turning into a guardian.

It took thirty seconds for the soldier to climb to his feet. His legs were wobbly, and his words slurred and incomprehensible. Slowly, he turned and faced his former comrades. Everyone held their breath. With each inhalation, the soldier's irises transformed into a bright hue of red until they matched that of the Titanoboa and the hippos.

He stepped toward the others with his fingers hooked into talons and was promptly shot in the forehead by Aguilar. The gunshot rang out, reverberating around the chamber. Aguilar stepped forward, stopping within inches of the pollen's reach. He held out his hand and watched the yellow powdery substance attach itself to his flesh.

"Santiago—no!" Matias yelped.

Aguilar held up his other hand, quieting his subordinate. He was wholly enthralled with the toxic material. Satisfied with his experiment, he turned around. Aguilar presented his hand to the others.

"It only affects you if you breathe it in."

Jack snorted. "Yeah, well, unless you can hold your breath for an hour, that doesn't mean shit."

Aguilar grinned. "We have prepared for this possibility."

Everyone in his group dug into their packs. Jack was impressed when they all produced gas masks. Surprisingly, Aguilar ordered his men to give masks to Jack, Hugo, Miguel, Manuel, and even Gaspar.

One of the soldiers tried to force the native to put it on but was unsuccessful.

"Don't!" Jack shouted, stepping between the soldier and the chief. Jack looked around, noticing, for the first time, that he was alone. "Where's the rest of Gaspar's people?"

"He killed them," Hugo said, pointing at Aguilar with sadness in his voice. "The bastard ordered his men to shoot them where they stood."

It was the gunfire Jack had heard earlier before he had entered the starry tunnel.

"Watch your tongue, snake, or I will cut it out." Aguilar motioned for Jack to lead the way. "Go."

Jack growled but did as he was told. He still had his gun, oddly enough. If Jack wanted to, he could've drawn it and shot the asshole where he stood. Jack suspected that Aguilar knew that too. Aguilar also knew that Jack wouldn't take the chance if it meant getting other people killed in the process.

Manuel reached down and picked up Gaspar's fallen mask. He held it up and spoke softly to the native. The tribal chief nodded and allowed Manuel to slip it onto his head. Then, he gently adjusted it and patted the smaller man on the shoulder. Jack was impressed. Manuel had a surprisingly peaceful nature to him.

Jack breathed hard, testing his mask. The seal was solid, and it seemed to operate faultlessly. Jack took a tense step into the haze and relaxed. He didn't instantly change into a guardian, thank God. Jack took his time and knelt to inspect the first body. Like his buddies Bert and Ernie, this one was also wearing Nazi fatigues. He had belonged to the same submarine crew aboard *U-590*. He was the only one here too.

Jack stood and headed over to the next corpse. Based on the individual's clothes, Jack deduced that his arrival had predated the Nazis by a few decades. Matias agreed.

"Early twentieth-century British explorers?" he asked, kneeling beside Jack.

Jack shrugged. "Maybe, yeah." Curious, he carefully lifted the decomposed person's coat, spotting a lump within it. With his thumb and forefinger, Jack slid the object free.

"A journal?" Matias asked, leaning in close. Jack made it a point to remember that the guy was a Colombian and a TAC agent. Matias was very familiar with the El Dorado legend—more so than most.

"Looks like it," Jack said, standing. Everyone was still eyeing the deceased Nazi seaman.

Jack knew immediately who this man was as soon as he opened the cover.

"Holy shit."

The rest of the group gathered around him and Matias.

Jack silently read the first entry to confirm his finding. He closed his eyes and looked up toward the Demon Heart. It had claimed the life of one of the most famous British explorers in history.

He gazed back down at the body. “It’s Percy Fawcett.”

Fawcett had disappeared in Brazil back in 1925 while searching for what he had called the Lost City of Z. Was it possible that he had made it all the way here? His journal was proof enough for Jack. Who else would’ve had it?

Maybe his son, Jack thought. Only two men had accompanied Fawcett on his ill-fated expedition, his eldest son and his son’s close friend.

Silence fell over the group.

The implications hit Jack hard. If this place could claim the life of a man like Percy Fawcett, then what would Jack’s odds be? Fawcett was a pro and had survived countless perils within the Amazon Basin, and yet, even he had succumbed to the Demon Heart.

“What killed him?” Jack asked rhetorically. He slid the journal into his back pocket. “The pollen doesn’t kill people. It just poisons their minds.”

No one answered.

Jack didn’t like this. There had been a lot of death here, and he wasn’t seeing any evidence of what had caused it. Jack gave Fawcett one last look and moved on. For now, he would assume that it must’ve been the human guardians that were to blame. It made the most sense.

The deeper they moved into the chamber, the older the bodies got.

“Jack,” Matias said, pointing down at a particular body. “Looks like one of yours.”

“Mine?” Jack asked.

Matias nodded. “American.”

Jack confirmed as much. “Sure is.” He unholstered the deceased’s pistol and checked it over. “Colt M1911—standard-issue sidearm of the United States military for seventy years, including back in Teddy Roosevelt’s day. Did you know that Roosevelt personally explored the Amazon in late 1913 to early 1914?” Jack tucked the M1911 into the back of his pants. “He died shortly after returning to the States due to health complications stemming from him contracting malaria.”

“And that?” Matias asked, motioning to the handgun.

Jack winked. “Souvenir.”

Matias crossed his arms. “And the journal?”

Jack shrugged. “Light reading material for later.”

“Thank you for the history lesson, Jack,” Aguilar said, “but can we please move on?”

Jack held up a hand, silently telling the man to be patient.

He took a steadying breath and spoke. "All of this is relevant. Try taking a moment to appreciate the company you're in." He gazed at the drug lord. "You've already made it farther than men of Fawcett's ilk. Let that sink in before you rush off to your death."

"My death?" Aguilar asked.

Jack nodded. "Yep, 'cause chances are that none of us are making it out of here alive."

"What makes you say that?" Matias asked.

"What makes me say that?" Jack spun around in a circle with his arms out wide. "All of this does."

28

Reluctantly, Jack did as he was told, and he avoided examining the other bodies. He still gave them a quick glance, though. Their clothing helped him determine their origin and the possible timeframe of their arrivals.

As he passed, he thought he saw what might have been two men from the German state of Prussia. *Late 1800s?* Three others were French. Their heavily buttoned, blue coats were a dead giveaway. *Early nineteenth century? Napoleon's men?* Most of the deceased were from the time of the Spanish Conquistadors.

Ordaz, Orellana, and Pizarro.

Jack was truly in the presence of history.

"And death," he mumbled.

Hugo stepped up close to him. "Are we really helping this maniac?"

Jack didn't physically react to the question. "For now, yes. But if it makes you feel any better, I plan on ruining his day ASAP."

Hugo smiled wide. "That does make me feel better. So, what's the plan?"

Jack ticked off the steps. "Ditch Aguilar. Escape El Dorado. Don't die."

"Those are goals—*not* a plan."

"Shhh," Jack hissed, "someone is coming."

Matias caught up with them. "What are you two talking about?"

Jack thumbed back and forth between himself and Hugo. "Who, us? Oh, we were just talking about how much of a douchebag you are."

Hugo nodded. "It's true."

They were halfway to the idol when Aguilar rushed forward and left them in the dust. *Well, the pollen,* Jack thought, glancing down at his feet. They were caked in the stuff.

The closer they got to the Golden King, the clearer the door at its feet became. It now looked like more of a seal than a door. The round obstruction was twelve feet in diameter and a foot and a half thick. It had been constructed separately from the idol but perfectly matched the rest of it. The seal had then been placed into a track so it could roll out of the way.

"The King's Room?" Hugo asked.

"That's my guess."

"Treasure?"

Jack shrugged. "At this point, I have no idea what to expect."

Aguilar was already investigating the seal by the time Jack and the others arrived. He had come to the same conclusion as Jack.

"Help me," Aguilar said, grunting. He was trying to move it by himself.

"Look," Jack said, "there's a reason this thing is here, right? What happens if we move it, and we don't like what we find on the other side?"

Aguilar stopped and faced Jack. "Help me, or…" he shouted something in Spanish, "your friends die." The eight soldiers leveled their weapons at Hugo, Miguel, Manuel, and Gaspar.

"Fine," Jack replied, "but at least give me them." He pointed at the twins. "If you haven't noticed, they are freakishly strong."

"Let them come," Aguilar said, allowing the Arroyos safe passage to the seal.

With Aguilar's help, the three men dug their boots into the ground and shoved. The seal didn't budge an inch. Jack and Aguilar got lower.

"Again!" Aguilar ordered.

Nearly out of breath, Jack was happy when decades, possibly centuries, of dust and pollen cracked and fell away as the seal started to roll. They still couldn't see what lay beyond, but at least they got the ball rolling. They reassumed their positions and pushed. More grime fell away, equally caking each of the men below. Jack's sweat-soaked clothes were like a magnet for the stuff.

Finally, the seal was rolled away, coming to rest in front of the Golden King's left foot. The pathway beyond was shrouded in darkness except for the light that bled inside from the lower room. Naturally, Aguilar entered first. The corridor behind the seal was, at least, thirty feet long. Jack swung his light around and was appalled by what he saw. Unlike the pictographs depicting the Demon Heart in star form, the engravings here portrayed human sacrifice and torture.

The artistry was incredibly detailed and vivid. The message being sent was clear. Something that would haunt their dreams forever was about to greet them.

"It's…" Aguilar said, his voice catching. "It's beautiful!"

Jack entered behind him and saw what Aguilar was talking about. But it wasn't *beautiful* as the drug lord had pronounced it. Jack would describe it more like *revolting* or *abhorrent*. The next chamber was also about thirty feet wide, and its end was nowhere in sight. On either side of Jack, stretching as far as he could see, were statues of men in agony. They had been carved out of the same gold as the El Dorado idol and had been placed on gilded pedestals.

Gaspar took a shaky step inside and nearly fell into the wall. He rambled on and on about something. Hugo took his eyes off the horrible artwork and spoke to the tribal leader. After a quick back and forth, Hugo turned toward Jack. Even in the dim light, Jack saw the smuggler's skin go white with fear.

"He says that these are not carvings."

Jack glanced back and forth between Hugo and the dozens of statues. "What are they?"

Aguilar replied. "They are the kings of old."

"What?" Miguel asked, not understanding.

The kings of old? Jack asked himself. *What could that—oh.*

"The 'Kings' Room."

Everyone besides Aguilar turned to Jack for an explanation. "This isn't the king's treasure room. It's a mistranslation." He looked at Miguel, because it had been him and Jack that had infiltrated Aguilar's office and photographed Ordaz's map. "It's plural, not possessive. No apostrophe. The Manoa didn't dust their kings in gold and then dip them in Lake Parime, like the legends state." Jack pointed back through the entryway. "They dipped them in liquid gold—alive—and then put them on display like some sick art gallery. These men either died from their burns or suffocation." He took a breath. "How'd I do, Hugo?"

The smuggler silently nodded.

Maybe, in the past, the Manoa had dusted their kings in gold and bathed them in the lake. The number of people on display in the Kings Room told Jack that the practice had gone on for centuries. Sickness or war or, perhaps, starvation had driven the tribe to extreme measures. Then, the Demon Heart had moved in and chased them out. Gaspar and his ancestors then had taken it upon themselves to keep everyone away, but they weren't murderers. They had let Jack through without trouble. It seemed that they allowed mankind to direct their own fate. Gaspar had warned Jack about what lay beyond in the damned kingdom of Manoa, and it had been Jack's decision and curiosity that brought him here.

Gaspar was the only one that didn't want to be here.

And now Aguilar is the only one that 'wants' to be here.

"Um, Jack?"

Miguel pointed to something behind the ghastly effigies. Jack added his light to it and stepped between two of the figures. Jack responded by drawing his pistol. His sudden, aggressive response got a rise out of the soldiers. Matias held them back with a shout and a raised hand. He joined Jack and speedily drew his weapon.

"We need to leave," Jack said, stepping back toward the door.

"No."

Everyone turned and stared at Aguilar. He was still looking into the darkness beyond. His shoulders were slumped, but he was depressed. His body twitched, and he cackled to himself. Jack was watching the man come completely undone. His mind was fragmented and unable to piece itself back together.

"Santiago," Matias said, speaking softly, "we need to leave."

"No!" Aguilar spun and drew his gun.

He didn't pull the trigger, however. He just stood there glaring at everyone with his gun hand trembling. But Jack wasn't watching Aguilar anymore. He was looking past the drug lord as a shape emerged from the shadows. It lifted off the ground, showing off its large, red eyes. They already knew what *it* was because they had just found the shed skin of a colossal snake behind the gilded kings.

Jack aimed his pistol at the serpent, leading the way for the others to do the same. "Everyone out—slowly." Jack stepped back, keeping his eyes on the creature. Like the hippos in Lake Parime, the Titanoboa's presence hinted that there were alternate entrances to be found. While the Demon Heart had taken over El Dorado's chamber, the serpent had claimed the Kings Room for itself.

Aguilar happily faced the creature, dropping his gun as he did. He opened his arms out wide and spoke to it. Before the snake got any closer, Jack launched forward and grabbed Aguilar by the back of his shirt collar. This man deserved to die, but he also contained information that could cripple the world's narcotics ring. Plus, Jack needed more details on the Suarez guy—the black-market antiquities dealer who had sold Ordaz's map to Aguilar.

The Titanoboa landed and shot forward. Both Jack and Matias pulled Aguilar along, kicking and screaming.

"Close the seal!" Jack shouted. Miguel and Manuel nodded and moved to close it but were having trouble.

"We can't!" Miguel yelled. "It's jammed!"

Friggin' wonderful.

Matias shouted at the soldiers. They all disappeared. Seconds later, the seal began to roll back into place—with Jack, Matias, and Aguilar still on the inside.

"Wait for us!" Matias cried, releasing his hold on Aguilar.

"Lorenzo—stop!" Jack yelled.

Aguilar caught Jack in the facemask with an elbow. The blow nearly knocked the covering loose.

Jack didn't let go of the unhinged man. He spun Aguilar around and got behind him. Jack shoved him along, forcing him back into the main chamber. With inches to spare, Jack leapt through the opening. The grating hiss of the Titanoboa could be heard on the other side of the semi-sealed passage. It was nearly closed, and it would've been if three of the soldiers hadn't abandoned their duties to help Aguilar up.

"What are you—" Miguel was cut off by a *boom*.

Jack scrambled back and quickly got to his feet. He aimed his gun between the Golden King's feet as the seal was hit again. Jack could see the creature behind it doing whatever it could to roll the seal aside. In stunned awe, everyone witnessed the snake get its snout between the door and the idol's right leg. It dug in deep and pushed.

The seal slowly rolled back open. Jack was too dumbfounded by the Titanoboa's strength to do much else but watch. The barrel of his gun lowered. No one spoke. They were all spellbound by the animal's powerful display. With a clunk, the seal came to a rest. Slowly, the serpent slithered forward, keeping the majority of its length hidden behind it, inside the Kings Room.

Aguilar raised his hands and shouted, "Behold the god of the rainforest—the god of Manoa!" He turned and faced Jack, undisturbed by the monster coming up behind him. "We should all be so lucky to be in its presence."

"You're nuts!" Jack said, gripping his pistol tighter.

"No, Jack. I am not 'nuts.'" He grinned and ripped his gas mask off, inhaling deeply. "I am reborn!"

Aguilar dropped to his knees and roared. The show paused the Titanoboa's advance. It calmly reared up like a cobra and watched Aguilar with clear intent. The animal was curious. Its level of intelligence was clear. It was both amazing and terrifying to witness. They wouldn't be able to just spook the beast into retreating. Its scales were too tough, and the group's firepower was too meek. Half of the men, including Jack, were armed with nothing more than 9mm pistols.

One of the soldiers took a shaky step back and snapped one of the corpse's bones beneath his foot. The Titanoboa turned toward him just as Aguilar climbed back to his feet. His red irises grew brighter as the seconds passed, as did the breadth of his predatory smile. He blinked hard and removed his glasses, tossing them into the pool of liquid gold.

His eyesight improved.

"Scatter!" Jack shouted, pulling the trigger and running. The round hit Aguilar dead center in his chest but did nothing else to the *reborn* man.

The Demon Heart's pollen not only altered the guardians' violent tendencies, but it muted the infected's pain threshold, bringing it down to zero. It seemed to have the same reaction that the drug cocktail had on Aguilar's goons back at Abuelita's. Jack peered over his shoulder. The wound had already stopped bleeding. It seemed that the toxin also had the ability to heal its host rapidly.

"Not...good," Jack said, breathing hard, pumping his arms and legs as fast as he could. Everyone had followed his lead and ran for the stairway back to the surface.

"Santiago! No!"

Jack slid to a stop. He turned and watched Aguilar pick up Matias by the throat. He lifted the full-grown man off the ground with ease. Matias bludgeoned Aguilar's arms and face with closed fists but to no avail. Jack raised his gun with the intent to empty its magazine into the guardian's skull and torso.

"Lorenzo!" Hugo yelled, looking ready to charge back into the fight.

But it was too late.

With a bloodcurdling shriek, Aguilar squeezed and crushed Matias' windpipe. Jack was mortified. Matias clawed at the ground around him, panicking. He was dead in seconds, suffocating on dry land. Jack pulled Hugo along beside him until the smuggler was with it enough to move on his own.

As Jack neared the exit, he chanced a glance back. The Titanoboa wasn't following them. It had moved over to Matias' body. The creature unhinged its jaw and quickly began swallowing the six-foot-tall man's corpse. As much as Jack was sure that the serpent wanted to pursue its escaping prey, a guaranteed meal was something the animal wasn't going to pass up.

More like an appetizer, Jack thought. The Titanoboa wasn't going to stop with Matias either. It was much too big for a single human being to satiate its hunger. It was an awful thought to have, but it was true.

By the time Jack reached the exit, the only living beings inside El Dorado's chamber were him, Hugo, Aguilar, and the Titanoboa. The Arroyos and the remaining soldiers were long gone. Both of the guardians regarded the other. Jack ripped off his gas mask and dropped it at his feet. He watched intently, sure that the animal would strike down Aguilar.

But it didn't. The serpent and Aguilar both turned Jack's way.

"Son of a..." He pushed Hugo up the steps. "Go, go, go!"

29

Jack was halfway up the steps when gunfire erupted topside. No doubt, their noisy exit had gotten the attention of the remaining hippos. So far, he had yet to see anything coming up behind him. He had kept his light pointed backward for that reason. Hugo's beam was guiding them along up ahead.

Jack clicked off his flashlight and shielded his eyes with his hand. The sun wasn't all that strong, but being underground had seriously affected his eyes' light sensitivity. There was also subtle rainfall, making the humidity worse than any human should have to experience. The good news was that the precipitation rinsed the toxic pollen off their bodies.

He heard mayhem, and when his vision fully adjusted, he saw it too. The soldiers had freaked out and run headlong for the broken stairway, drawing the attention of the enraged hippos. It would be their doom. Luckily, Jack's people had smartly hung back. They knew that the hippos wouldn't cross the purple mosaic.

"Go right!" Jack shouted, leading the way.

No one argued with him. Hugo, Miguel, Manuel, and Gaspar all moved away from the fight between man and beast.

"Where are you?" Jack asked, looking for the other entry point.

Gaspar seemed to know what Jack was looking for. He shouted and pointed further down the beach. He pulled ahead of Jack, waving the others along. Jack didn't need an interpreter to know that the tribal chief was leading them to freedom. If anyone here knew where the backdoor was, it was Gaspar.

The battle quieted. Jack stumbled and stopped, witnessing the end of the Colombian Army's presence in Manoa. A large portion of the float had cornered the men below the unreachable exit. With no ammunition, they huddled together against the wall, hefting their rifles and pistols like clubs.

That's when the hippos advanced. Heads down, the living wrecking balls crushed their foes against the cavern wall. The screams of the men were short-lived. Jack turned away, unable to stomach the slaughter. He stepped away just as Aguilar exited the cave. The Titanoboa, however, was nowhere to be seen.

"Where's the snake?" Miguel asked, following close behind Gaspar.

Jack had fallen back but was quickly regaining ground on the team.

"No idea," Jack said. "Where...?"

Gaspar disappeared inside one of the dwellings. Jack wasn't expecting him to go there. He figured the secret passage to be behind a waterfall like the quarry had been. Jack didn't voice his concern. He trusted Gaspar to lead them to safety.

Jack ducked inside, confused to find the place empty.

"Up here!"

He looked up. Miguel and Manuel were reaching down to him through a hole in the ceiling. Jack clasped their hands and was yanked skyward.

"Look out!" Hugo shouted.

Jack withdrew his legs, feeling something pass beneath the bottom of his boots. He took a quick look. Aguilar had streaked below him in a blur, careening headfirst into the rear wall of the structure. The sound of him striking stone was sickening.

How the hell did he catch up so fast?

Jack let his query go and climbed to his feet. He followed close behind Manuel, scaling a narrow flight of steps up to the third level of the home. Cut into the right-hand wall was a hole the size of a manhole cover. Everyone slipped through as quickly as they could move. Jack got antsy, waiting for Aguilar to show his ugly, red-eyed mug. On any other day, Jack could've taken the drug lord in a fight, but not today. He was the type of enemy that Jack had never faced before.

An enhanced one. Even a typical steroid monster had nothing on Aguilar.

As before, Jack was the last one to make it through. Gaspar ordered the twins to pull down on a cut log. It took some effort, but the *lever* moved, activating the door above the exit. A slab of stone slid into place, crashing down to earth. Aguilar poked his head through the opening in the wall and glared at Jack, then vanished behind the curtain of stone.

Jack looked around at the jungle before him. *Where the hell are we?*

He went to sit but was pulled along. "Not yet, my friend," Hugo said. "Gaspar says that it might not hold Aguilar back for long."

Groaning, Jack fell in line behind the native and the others. "How do we stop this guy?"

Hugo translated the question. "He says that we cannot—not yet."

"Not yet?" Miguel asked, yelling over his shoulder. He sent a spurt of Spanish to the native. Gaspar's reply was short and sweet. "Oh," Miguel said. "I see."

"Come on, guys!" Jack yelled. "English!"

"He said the effects of the Demon Heart will wear off shortly unless he returns to the cavern for more."

That brightened Jack's mood. The toxin was potent, but its changes were brief unless you had constant exposure. If they could stay ahead of Aguilar, they would eventually be able to subdue him, or if need be, kill him. It gave Jack's hypothesis about the guardian tribe killing the explorers inside El Dorado water. It was proof that they habitually returned to Manoa.

"What about the human guardians?" Jack asked. "Can they be killed?"

Hugo asked Gaspar.

"Yes," Hugo replied, "they only use small doses—not enough to heal their wounds. He says that humans react differently to the poison than animals."

"What about Aguilar?" Jack asked. "What happens if he uses more than that?"

Hugo shook his head. "Gaspar doesn't know. No one has ever attempted such an awful thing."

They walked along a narrow footpath for some time. The trail was well-worn and clear of all grasses. It was clearly in steady use. Six inches to Jack's right was a severe decline. The terrain below was a mixture of rocks and horizontally growing shrubs. Gaspar's innate knowledge of the secret exit, the stone slab, and the path was beginning to bother Jack. If Gaspar and his people had taken an oath to stay away from Manoa, how did he know so much about it? If anything, he should've been more naïve than he had shown to be.

Or I'm overthinking this.

It would make sense that Gaspar's people had scouted ahead to understand the area. His ancestors could've left behind texts with instructions as a "break glass in case of emergency" kind of thing.

If you are forced to enter the canyon, here is a way to get out.

Jack wanted to get out of this Godforsaken jungle and get back to Wyoming and see his friends. He missed the cool, dry weather and the easygoing lifestyle. But he also enjoyed the adventure and action he was experiencing—just not the current death-defying circumstances.

A vast stone wall appeared on Jack's left. It had been there the entire time but was now clear of all obstructions. No trees grew here, revealing the cliff face. It rose into the sky, concealing what lay beyond. Manoa, the ancient kingdom of the Amazon Rainforest, which was, essentially, just a long bathtub, descending deep into the earth.

Gaspar stopped up ahead. Jack leaned around the others and spied him pulling a rope out of the bushes beneath his feet. It appeared as if they were going to descend the dangerous slope.

Sure, why not? Jack thought. *What else could possibly go wrong?*

Aguilar drove his fist into the stone slab for a third time, and still, nothing. It was too heavy for him to move. Jack and the others had gotten away. *For now,* he thought, growling. Aguilar retracted his bloodied hand from the stone, inspecting the broken bones with wonderment. Each time he struck the slab, the bones broke. And each time he retracted his mangled hand, they mended themselves back together without trouble.

But not now.

The healing properties of his body were fading. Aguilar was feeling exhausted too. Since inhaling the Demon Heart pollen, he had felt recharged—better than ever. His strength had multiplied too. It was strange, though. If the guardian tribe had access to the Demon Heart, why hadn't they used their gifts to wipe out Aguilar and his team when they had arrived at the river?

He flexed his injured hand. It didn't cause him any pain, but it wasn't healing either. In its current state, Aguilar knew it would eventually cause him a great deal of agony. He needed to do something—and do it quickly. Aguilar growled and lowered himself back down to the first level. Then, he headed outside. The hippos had returned to the water. They didn't pay him any attention now, and for that matter, they hadn't when he had made his way past the first time either. He wasn't sure why. But, the Titanoboa had left him alone too. They had sized one another up and concluded that they weren't one another's enemies.

Jack Reilly was.

We are the same, Aguilar thought, stumbling back to the cave entrance.

His hand was starting to hurt, as was his head. His previously improved vision was fading, and his eyeballs itched like crazy. The toxin was wearing off and returning his senses to normal. Aguilar needed more of it. He also needed to figure out a way for it to last longer. The natives here have had constant exposure for years. He needed to build up that kind of retention before returning to the jungle and finishing Jack off. After that...

Hmmm. Aguilar had no idea what he would do once the threat was gone.

He'd worry about that once they were all dead.

By the time he made it back down into the chamber of the Golden King, Aguilar's head was swimming. His equilibrium was gone, and he couldn't think straight. He could feel consciousness slipping away. He placed his hand on the wall just inside the tunnel exit. Unfortunately, it was his broken hand. He shouted and fell forward, landing inches away from the pollen's reach. Slowly, he edged into the haze and turned over, breathing in deeply.

As he had done before, he bellowed into the air. He felt his hand mend seconds later. His vision returned, as did his balance and strength. Aguilar shut his eyes and paid close attention to what was happening, using his experience as a narcotics manufacturer to his advantage. The Demon Heart's pollen was similar to drugs he was used to handling, but on a scale that he had never seen before. Even his facility's experimentations with pain blockers and steroids didn't work as effectively as this. He was used to his men crashing and returning to normal within a reasonable amount of time.

Aguilar took another deep breath and sat up. He climbed to his feet and closed his eyes again, feeling a comforting warmth course its way through his bloodstream. His thoughts cleared, but then a feeling of rage washed over him. He didn't fight it. Aguilar allowed the feeling to overtake him. Images of tearing Jack apart flooded his mind. He never thought one man could cause him so much trouble.

Hugo too.

The nearest body, the British explorer from before, had a shoulder bag looped around him. Aguilar gripped it and pulled. The bag came free, as did Fawcett's rib cage and spinal column. As the bones fell away, Aguilar opened its flap and dumped out its contents. There was very little inside, just a handful of trinkets, including a broken compass. It would be the perfect vessel for his prize. Looking up, Aguilar held open the bag and looked deep within himself, concentrating on the anger—the hate.

It's all he cared about now. Aguilar couldn't have cared less about returning to his old life—to his empire. Now, he just wanted to kill. He needed it.

Aguilar had no idea how much time had passed, but the bag now felt heavy. He examined it and found it to be two-thirds of the way full. He closed the flap, buckling it tight. Then, he slipped his head through the strap and draped the thick strip of leather across his left shoulder. It wasn't as secure as he would've liked but it'd have to do.

He looked for the Titanoboa but didn't see it anywhere. It must've returned through the opening at the base of El Dorado. It was the only option he had. Even with the Demon Heart's assistance, Aguilar knew he wouldn't be strong enough to move the cave dwelling's stone slab to go the other way.

The giant snake knew the land. Aguilar trusted it to have a path to the surface. He took his time and inhaled as much of the pollen as he could. Then, Aguilar took off in a sprint, passing by the gilded rulers in a blur. The further he moved into the room, the darker it became. For the first time, he realized that he had some kind of newfound night-sight. *Interesting...* The gloomier it got, the redder and brighter the world around him became.

He laughed and put on even more speed.

Aguilar skidded to a stop at a hole in the rear wall of the Kings Room. It was here that the Titanoboa had entered through. The breakage here had been a natural occurrence. The sub-thermal heat that powered the pool of gold was evidence of seismic activity. Long ago, there must've been an earthquake here. The event had caused part of the Kings Room's structural integrity to fail, as well as split the ceiling of the main chamber.

That's when the Demon Heart had made its move.

From then on, the Manoa were no longer able to safely enter the main chamber, except for the guardians that had happily experimented with it. Aguilar understood why they had done it because he felt incredible!

Aguilar stepped through the break in the wall and found himself in a space that reminded him of a Mexican cenote. The cavity held a pool at its center, and if Aguilar had to guess, the waterway connected to others in the area via underwater caves. The Titanoboa would've been able to effortlessly navigate it and pop out wherever it wanted.

But Aguilar couldn't. Not if he was going to keep the pollen dry.

He spotted several other, aboveground openings circumferencing the body of water and growled. The Demon Heart had given him many gifts, but a map of the area wasn't one of them. If Aguilar didn't pick the right passage, Jack and everyone else would escape. He walked the rocky shore and scrutinized each exit. The route directly across from the Kings Room was more worn than the others.

Taking that as a good sign, Aguilar entered the pathway and willed it to be the correct one.

30

Jack gripped onto the rope and walked backwards down the steep hill. This wasn't something he'd survive if he slipped and fell. There was nothing beneath his feet besides rocks, thick branches, and more rocks. The bottom was unseen, veiled from sight beneath the greenery. Luckily, the rope looked and felt like it was in good condition. Jack was happy it was in decent shape because quite a few people were using it simultaneously.

Twenty feet into the climb, Jack saw that the rope ended at a handmade anchor driven into the rockface. Then, a new one began. Gaspar's people had thought of everything, it seemed. By sectioning off the rope, it gave its user more leeway when it came to weight. It prevented too many people from being on one section of rope at a time. Once more, the tribe's ingenuity was impressing Jack.

They moved like this for four more sections of rope. The one-hundred-foot climb was a worrying one—even for Jack—mostly because he was tired, and his grip strength wasn't at its best. Frankly, his hands had taken a beating lately. Being at the back of the pack had its benefits sometimes too. If someone did fall, they wouldn't be taking Jack out. There was no one above him to do so.

As the leader of the pack, Gaspar was the first one to finish. Jack paused and watched the man reach out for a nearby tree limb. Like a man born for a life in the trees, he sprang onto the thick branch, climbing down to the ground as if it were nothing. Miguel was next. Then, his brother.

"He makes it look so easy," Miguel said, laughing anxiously.

The guy stepped onto the tree limb and swung his arms to catch his balance. The tree swayed in the breeze, and the branch bent beneath the heavier man. Gaspar was much lighter than all of them, including Hugo who outweighed the local by twenty or thirty pounds. The Arroyos were at least sixty pounds heavier. Jack was somewhere in between. Regardless, he wasn't looking forward to his turn.

Manuel performed the dismount like a practiced veteran, earning a smattering of applause from Miguel and Gaspar. Hugo gripped the rope hard and used every spare inch of his stocky wingspan to grab a hold of the limb. He made a daring leap into the tree, dropping and hugging the girthy branch. To Jack, he resembled a baby opossum clutching onto its mother's back.

"Well, that's one way to do it," Miguel joked.

"Shut up!" Hugo countered, breathing hard.

Jack moved further down the rope. He was now eye-level with Hugo. "Hey," he said. Hugo looked at him. "You're doing great. Just take it easy and finish this thing."

Hugo nodded his head, rubbing his stubbled cheek back and forth across the rough limb. If he wasn't covered in sweat, the friction might've started a fire. Blowing out a long breath, Hugo pushed himself upright, straddling the limb between his legs. He carefully scooted back toward the trunk and clambered to his feet. Then, like a three-toed sloth, he lowered himself down, clearing the way for Jack.

Jack climbed back up the wall a little and found a groove in the rock. He wedged the side of his left boot into it. Using his long reach, Jack fluently snagged one of the limbs and shoved off the wall. Holding the branch tight, he dangled in the air and felt around for the next one with his feet, finding it after a few tries. He reset his grip before letting go altogether and squatting down. Jack felt like a kid again as he bounded and swung down the tall tree, gracefully moving from one limb to the next. He dropped to the ground at the same time as Hugo, startling the slow-moving smuggler good.

"Gah!" Hugo yelped, getting a laugh out of everyone. "Show off!"

Branches snapped in the distance. Everyone quieted as Gaspar urged them onward. The man slipped through the foliage with little to no sound. He truly moved like a ghost at times. He would've made one hell of a Special Forces soldier with feet like that.

Jack hurried along. "Where are we going?"

Hugo asked. "He says we are going home."

"Home?"

"That's what he said, 'home.'"

The trees were less dense here, and the ground was packed tight. This area had seen its fair share of foot traffic. Gaspar's home was something Jack didn't ever expect to see.

Do they really live this close to Manoa?

If so, then Gaspar had some explaining to do.

Jack stepped through a thicket of shrubs and stopped dead in his tracks. Implanted in the middle of the rainforest was a village, not unlike the one the Ewoks had erected on the forest moon of Endor. Most of the homes weren't constructed on the ground. They were in the air, built as treehouses. Soundly erected bridges reached across the gaps between them, making traveling from one to the next a breeze.

The huts were of the same style as the human guardians' village, but these had been built up more and built better. Jack was struck by how many women and children there were too. A pair of boys ran right up to Gaspar and leapt into his outstretched arms. A very pregnant woman greeted him next.

Jack smiled at the sight of the happy family living in one of the harshest environments on earth. He didn't want to be here when Gaspar was forced to announce the deaths of his tribesmen at the hands of Aguilar. He faced away from the gleeful reunions and nearly fell over. Their village ended at the same cliff face that Jack had just scaled. There was a split in the rock out in the open for everyone to see. Jack had one guess where it led to.

"He lied to us."

Hugo joined Jack and spoke. Gaspar quieted his conversation with his family and gently patted his wife's belly before walking over. He spoke quickly. Hugo did his best to keep up.

"He says that they live at the base of the cliff to watch over the underworld. It has been foretold that, one day, a great spirit will emerge and lay waste to the rainforest—to his people's home." Gaspar faced the eerie split. It was large enough for a man to fit through, but not the creature. "They have vowed to protect this world from it, from their ancestors' mistake. They didn't destroy the Demon Heart when they had the chance. Instead, they embraced its gifts, and by doing so, almost wiped out their society." He turned to Jack and took a well-deserved breath. "War is not a creation of modern man. It is here in the trees as well."

The village was silent. Jack had underestimated the man several times, even, just now, by thinking he was a liar. Though he had technically lied, Jack decided to let it go. He held out his hand and clasped Gaspar's forearm.

"I'm sorry I doubted you."

A laugh broke out. It came from inside the split stone.

"Did someone say that a 'great spirit will emerge?'"

Santiago Aguilar emerged from the Manoa underworld like a demon possessed. He was missing most of his clothes except for his shredded pants. His shirt, shoes, and glasses were nowhere to be found. The only possession he carried with him was a ragged shoulder bag. He saw Jack's eyes flick to the accessory.

"A gift from Mr. Fawcett." He dug into the bag. "And this," he procured a handful of yellowish dust, "is a gift from El Dorado."

Everyone backed away quickly. Aguilar was enjoying the moment. He replaced the pollen inside the bag, sniffing the remnants off his skin. The jolt made his eyes grow brighter before fading back to their *natural* shade of crimson.

He's lost his freaking mind! Jack thought, unsure of what to do next.

Gaspar raised his hand, shouting an order in his native language. No one on Jack's team understood and neither did Aguilar because no one spoke the language. Tribal bowmen rushed forward, and they procured a single bow from their waist holsters. Strangely, the arrowheads were wrapped in animal hide. Each of the men untied the tips of their projectiles and readied them. Jack had no idea what they were and why they were being handled so cautiously.

Then, it hit him. Similar arrows had been used against them when they had been making their approach on the river. But would they work against a man like Aguilar—what he'd become?

Gaspar pointed forward, and all eight arrows were loosed simultaneously. They covered the short distance in no time, each one of them piercing Aguilar's flesh. Most punctured his abdomen, and a few struck him in the chest.

But he didn't go down.

Gaspar ordered his men back, leaving Aguilar alone with Jack and his team.

The Arroyos drew their pistols.

"It won't work," Jack warned. "Better save the ammo."

"What do we do?" Miguel asked.

Jack shook his head. "I don't know."

He glanced at Gaspar for answers and was stunned to see a small smile form on his face. The native knew something the outsiders didn't. Even Aguilar was confused. He glanced down at his pincushion-like body and stumbled backward. Each one of the entry sites instantly began to turn black.

"Poison dart frog?" Jack asked.

Hugo translated, and Gaspar nodded and replied.

"He says, yes, among other things. A secret family recipe."

"What recipe?" Jack asked.

Gaspar smiled. "To negate the effects of the Demon Heart."

Aguilar panicked and ripped the arrows from his body. He wasn't bleeding, but the wounds grew darker still. He locked eyes with Jack and snarled. Jack knew what he had to do. There were too many innocent people here for them to duke it out. He turned and fled, heading down a cleanly cut passage. Aguilar's wrath-filled cries made it easy to keep track of the deranged lunatic.

"Jack!" Hugo shouted, no doubt chasing after both men. The Arroyos were probably hot on Jack's trail too.

The pathway led in a single direction, making it an easy journey for Jack. But it also made it easy for Aguilar. Jack peered back and saw the man was closing in. The cocktail that Gaspar's tribe had come up with wasn't working fast enough. Or it meant that Aguilar already had *that much* of the toxin flowing through his system.

It didn't matter. Jack needed a plan. As of now, he was just trying to get the guy away from the families back at Gaspar's village. He tripped on a root and went face-first into the dirt, rolling down a sudden embankment. Out of nowhere, a drop came into view, as did the sound of rushing water. The thunderous noise was too loud to be a river. Jack had come to yet another waterfall.

He got to his feet just as Aguilar lowered his shoulder into Jack's gut. Both men fell to the ground and wrestled for position. The much stronger drug lord won that battle, but he was sweating worse than Jack had ever seen a man sweat. The antitoxin was doing its job, fighting off the Demon Heart's effects. Aguilar must've spiked a fever, causing the nearly naked man to perspire in excess. It also made it difficult for Jack to grip the man's flesh. He attempted to flip the guy over but couldn't get the correct grip on his arm. So, Jack covered his head with his hands and forearms and allowed Aguilar to wail on him until he found a better opportunity.

Each blow was like that from a title boxer. Jack winced, losing his breath multiple times. But Aguilar's strikes began to slow. Aguilar struck him in the ribs, but Jack countered the strike and flexed his core. He then launched a quick palm strike into Aguilar's face. The impact stunned the drug lord long enough for Jack to get his legs up and under him. He kicked Aguilar in the abdomen as hard as he could. It allowed Jack to roll onto his hands and knees. Aguilar stayed on top of Jack, though, riding him like a bucking bronco.

Snapping his head back, Jack caught Aguilar in the bridge of his nose with the back of his skull. The blow wobbled the drug lord enough for Jack to slip out from underneath him and get to his feet. The heat radiating off of Aguilar's body was incredible.

Jack lifted his fists. "You don't look so good."

Aguilar shouted and launched a series of jabs. Jack blocked them all, feeling confident in the likeliest outcome. Aguilar would burn himself out and collapse. Instead, he dug into his pouch and took a deep breath. The pollen seemed to rejuvenate Aguilar a little, but he still didn't look like himself.

Then, Aguilar did the worst thing imaginable. He blew the poisonous substance into Jack's face.

Jack hacked and coughed, reflexively inhaling. The narcotic entered his lungs and was quickly absorbed into his bloodstream. He instantly felt what Aguilar must've felt. Rage—an earsplitting call to violence. Jack had never felt anything like it before. He cried out into the sky as Aguilar pummeled his prone form.

"Jack!"

"Stay back!" Jack replied, still feeling a part of himself somewhere deep inside the growing mania. "Stay back! I—I'm compromised!"

Suddenly, Jack caught one of Aguilar's kicks, twisting his leg hard. Then, while still on his side, Jack lashed out with a quick kick of his own, sending Aguilar sailing through the air. Jack rolled onto his back and sprang to his feet like a ninja, holding his hands to his eyes.

"No, no, no... I can't... I need..." He dropped his hands and spotted Aguilar. "I must...kill!"

Jack stalked forward and unloaded a punch that broke three of Aguilar's ribs. Then, Jack kicked out the man's left knee, nearly dislocating it in the process. He ducked beneath a wild haymaker and delivered a rising elbow strike to his opponent's chin. Teeth and blood went flying. Jack had never felt so strong—so powerful. He knew it wasn't natural, but it felt good.

"No!" he yelled, stumbling away. "I—"

Aguilar charged Jack but was met with a stiff spinning sidekick. The impact sent Aguilar screaming over the edge of the waterfall. Jack fell back on his ass and clawed at his head.

"Get it out! Get it out! Get it out!"

Mercifully, the lights went out as he was clubbed from behind. Unconsciousness wasn't his savior either. His dreams were horrifying—

worse than the ones caused by his PTSD. Here, he dreamt of murder and mayhem, and he loved every single minute of it. Jack internally wailed. There was no end in sight.

Jack was groggy and disoriented, but he felt like he was back to normal as he opened his eyes. He found himself inside one of the huts in Gaspar's village. When he sat up, he noticed that he was missing his shirt. A young tribal woman silently sat in the corner of the hut. Her eyes locked onto Jack's chiseled upper body, and she smiled.

"Um, hi there," Jack said, raising his hand and waving.

She also raised her hand and softly waved back.

A voice spoke up somewhere outside, causing the young woman to scamper out the door. When she threw the flap back, sunlight poured inside, blinding Jack for a moment. As the covering fell back down, it was caught by a familiar face.

"Hugo... Hey, buddy." Jack gingerly got to his feet. "Woah." He shook his head and blinked. He was dizzy. "What—what happened?"

Hugo steadied him. "You don't remember?"

"Remember what?"

Hugo held Jack by both shoulders and looked him deep in the eyes. "You don't remember going crazy?"

Jack shook his head. He didn't recall anything of the sort.

Hugo recapped what had happened. Aguilar had blown a cloud of the pollen into Jack's face, infecting him for a time.

"I thought it was a dream," Jack said, recalling bits and pieces of it all.

"It was no dream," Hugo said. "Your eyes were red and everything. You were a guardian, Jack."

Hugo led him outside, keeping an arm under Jack's right armpit for support. The entire village was gathered around the center of the settlement. Somewhere, someone was making food, which was fine by Jack. He was starving.

"Jack!" Miguel shouted, hustling over. Manuel was right behind him.

Jack blinked against the light. It felt like he had a mild concussion. "My head," Jack said. "What happened to my head?"

Miguel looked shy.

"What did you do?" Jack asked.

"Me?" Miguel asked, holding up his hands. "Woah, Jack. You've got it all wrong." He pointed at Hugo. "It was him. He's the one who hit you with the rock!"

Jack turned to Hugo. "A rock, really?"

Hugo sheepishly shrank away. "You were freaking me out. Plus, you *did* say that you wanted someone to, and I quote, 'get it out.'"

Looking over the peaceful village, Jack decided what to do with his findings. He would report everything to Raegor and suggest destroying the Demon Heart. The Manoa deserved to have their sacred shrine back. They would also be the perfect people to keep a watch on the Golden King. They would be El Dorado's *guardians*.

Gaspar stepped over and clasped Jack's forearm again. He rambled on about how Jack had saved his people from the evil of the Manoa underworld. That wasn't true, but he could see how the villagers would think that was the case. As a reward, Jack was given the first cut of a delicious—

"Capybara?" Jack asked. Gaspar nodded, smiling wide. Jack clasped the elder's forearm once more. He released his grip and opened the leaf-wrapped offering. "Yay," he sniffed it, cringing, "my favorite..."

The roar of rushing water startled Aguilar awake. He was freezing cold, yet, still somehow warm. The antitoxin had caused a fever as his body fought to retake control of the contagion. In reality, Aguilar felt like he was going through withdrawals. He had experienced them before, and it was an awful thing to go through.

His head was killing him. Aguilar reached his hands up and inspected them, but he could barely see his palms. His improved eyesight was gone again, as were his glasses. He had tossed them into the pool of liquid gold while celebrating his newfound gifts.

And now those gifts were, likewise, gone.

Aguilar's hands flopped to his chest. Something felt off. There was nothing where the strap of his satchel was supposed to be. "Damn you, Jack." At least he knew where to get more.

He pushed past a wave of overwhelming nausea and tried to get up—but he couldn't. Aguilar willed his legs to move. They didn't. In fact, he couldn't feel anything from the waist down. Panicked, Aguilar forced himself to sit up, instinctively knowing that he had broken his back during the fall. He didn't remember hitting anything, but he must've struck a rock when he had landed.

His lower body was jostled to the side! In his current state, Aguilar couldn't feel it, but he knew something was there. Arms shaking, he pushed aside the pain and sat up onto his elbows. Shaking with fear, he tilted his chin down to his chest. There, wrapped around his knees, was the head of the mighty Titanoboa. Its devilish red eyes bore holes into him, causing the man's bladder to empty where he sat. The majority of the beast presently lay hidden, submerged beneath the murky water.

"No," Aguilar pleaded, "God, no." He held out his hands, trying to communicate with the serpent as he had before. "Please..." But he couldn't. They were no longer equals. With the effects of the Demon Heart gone, Santiago Aguilar was just another hard-to-pass-up meal.

The animal yanked its prey into the river. They both went under. The Titanoboa slipped its toothy jaws up to Aguilar's hips and locked them in. The dagger-like teeth pierced his flesh with ease. This time, he felt the intense, searing-hot pain.

The jolt forced the air from Aguilar's lungs.

But just as quickly as they had gone under, they burst back through the surface. In Aguilar's spotty vision, he saw that he was ten feet above the river. The trauma made him shiver wildly.

He looked down.

The Titanoboa *stood* directly beneath him. Its teeth suddenly pulled free, and its jaws opened wide. The drug lord fought and clawed for freedom but failed. With a twitch of its head, Aguilar was swallowed whole. He and the creature dove back beneath the surface. Water quickly rushed in, adding to the horror of the moment.

Aguilar gasped and tried to scream but instead inhaled water. His frenetic movements tapered off, and soon, he was gone. Gratefully, Santiago Aguilar drowned before the serpent began to digest him.

Printed in Great Britain
by Amazon